JUDAS THE HERO

THE BLACK MUSEUM

MARTIN DAVEY

This edition November 2021

Cover design by Jem Butcher Design
Published by The Black Museum

ISBN: 9781527237216

JUDAS THE HERO

FOR THE THREE ANGELS WHO
WATCH OVER ME

1 W⊛LVES IN THE WATER

7th May 1945.

The inky black water of the Golfe de Saint-Malo heaved gently under a night sky full of white, wispy clouds that were in a hurry to catch up with the escaping light disappearing over the horizon. The seas in these parts could be dangerously rough, but not tonight. Tonight, they were resting.

The floating gulls that peppered the surface of the water like spatters of white paint were resting too, gently rocking and rising with the rhythm of the sea, their beaks and chins tucked in tight, and wings pulled back to keep out the cold night air. Sleeping, peacefully. Dreaming of whatever it is that seagulls dream of.

Flying is tiring. Constantly scavenging for food makes for a stressful existence. Normally, the gulls would sleep for a few hours, recharging their batteries, but tonight it was not to be.

A sudden metallic clanking and muffled banging from deep down under the waves frightened them into the night sky, and then, with a cacophony of screeches, they flew swiftly away. The small waves they left behind forgot them instantly and like giant ripples they continued to roll south.

The noises from the deep grew louder and louder and then, with an angry whoosh of air that turned the water white and frothy, a German U-boat surfaced. Seventy-two hours ago, the Commander-in-Chief of the German Kriegsmarine had sent a telegram from the High Command's Berlin bunker to the Captain of the boat.

This was his last official order, and he made it as quickly as he could. The Russians and the British were just streets away.

The soft thump of their mortars could be heard everywhere as the Allies rained down their anger on the streets of the capital. Berlin was lost. For ever. Her streets were rubble-strewn tracks, and her buildings were flattened. She might rise again one day, but everyone knew that her soul had been ripped out. The Russians were exacting revenge on Germany's women in the most brutal fashion imaginable.

Berlin's next generation would not be pure of blood, that was for sure.

The walls of the bunker he was trying to shelter in shuddered under the barrage, and flakes of paint floated down onto the Commander's head like yellow snowflakes. All he wanted to do now was to get out of his uniform, into his disguise, and away from the bunker as soon as possible.

Damn the rest of them, he thought.

He had dictated this final last order to the young signals corporal and checked to make sure that it had been sent correctly. Twice. Then he disappeared into the sewer system underneath the bunker and was never seen again.

Moments later, a shell exploded in the doorway of the bunker killing the young signals corporal instantly. All that was left of him was a red smear on the wall and part of his headset. The radio he used to send the message had lost its voice now; it could only whine and crackle. The end had come.

It was all over in Berlin, that much was true, but many miles away and many metres under the sea, a message was being translated and deciphered on the last remaining Enigma machine. This one had been fitted with an extra wheel for added security, and as soon as the message was passed to the Captain and read by him, the screws of the boat began to turn, and it headed further out to sea and deeper under the waves.

Three days later, the submarine was precisely where it was supposed to be: 1,000 metres south of Jersey, the largest of the Channel Islands, with the small village of Les Creux off the port bow at 21.45hrs. Even though the Nazis had just lost the war, the boat was where it needed to be at exactly the right time. It had a very important passenger onboard. Even though the Reich had been crushed and brushed away like the dirt it was, some things could never be unlearned by the Teutonic brain. The Germans were, and always would be, slaves to their twin gods, 'Efficiency' and 'Discipline'.

Another deep whoosh of air from the starboard side ballast tanks stabilised the boat, and as the last of the seawater flowed down the sides of UX99's conning tower, the forward hatch popped open. A faint red disc of light appeared. The boat was still rigged for silent running. This was the last and the most secret mission in which UX99 would ever take part. Everyone on board knew it. Their war was over, and they had lost. They were still under orders, though, and still members of the elite Wolf–Kriegsmarine, so no passing British warship would be alerted to their position because of sloppy seamanship or a random light flare at sea. The red light dimmed as someone climbed up the ladder, then moments later the head of Obergefreiter Lindelhoff appeared.

Lindelhoff was a low-ranking yet battle-hardened sailor. He'd heard rather than seen more battles than most sailors or soldiers in the German military over the course of the war. He'd been torpedoed, depth-charged, rammed and bombed by the aircraft of four countries in six of the seven seas – and he was still alive. He sometimes felt this was more by luck than by chance. He sniffed the air and climbed the last few rungs of the ladder. If anyone had been looking at the submarine at that particular moment, through binoculars from the shore, or from the bridge of a ship, they would not have seen the head of a man peering out into the darkness. The head that looked around at the coastline of nearby Jersey was the head of a wolf – a Werewolf to be precise. The German U-boats were called the 'Sea Wolves', and most people thought that it was because they hunted the allied fleets and merchant shipping like a wolf pack. The truth was something far stranger, and even more sinister.

Lindelhoff sprang onto the deck. He wore a modified version of a sailor's uniform. It had been designed by the Fuhrer himself, they said. It had all the normal insignia and was made from the same material as a normal sailor's uniform, but there were differences to the cut. There were no arms to his shirt, and the dark blue trousers stopped at the knee.

The brown fur of his head and arms rippled as the wind blew in from the north. The deck was cold and wet, and the hard metal plates felt good against the coarse pads of his feet. His claws made a click-clack sound as he loped forward to inflate the little yellow dinghy that he carried under his arm. After he had filled it with air from a pump and the structure was rigid, he lowered it over the side, pulled it across the surface of the water, and positioned it close to the hatch. He had been ordered to prepare the dinghy and then wait. So, he waited.

It was good to be out in the open again, to see the sky and feel the wind. Every submariner loved and hated his boat in equal measure. The ship was their home and protector, but at times it felt more like a long black cell or a floating coffin. It had taken some getting used to, in the beginning; Lindelhoff had felt trapped during his first few months on board. He was restless and angry all of the time. The special urges he felt each day were harder and harder to suppress. At home it was easier; his nocturnal wanderings and servitude to the whims of the lunar calendar had been easier to control and anticipate when he had lived in his small village in the west of Bavaria. Of course, the other villagers knew that there was something a little odd about the Lindelhoff family. They were the strange, quiet folk that lived at the edge of the village. But they were also a family that kept itself to itself.

'Such good manners, and so clean and tidy,' said some of the villagers.

'Always willing to do extra work in the forest and the fields,' said the rest.

In truth, the village had a pretty good idea about what the Lindelhoff family actually were, and in a strange way they were happy to have them around – almost proud of them. Large predators never troubled the village, strangers and gypsies chose not to settle anywhere nearby, and the villagers' livestock grew plump and healthy. The village was protected.

Then one day a large black Mercedes drove into the village. A soldier wearing a strange silver badge on his lapels got out and started going from door to door asking questions.

It wasn't long before he was knocking on the door to the Lindelhoff farm. In a way the family had expected something like this, knowing that one day they might be forced to flee, running for their lives with an angry mob chasing them into the dark of the countryside. But today it transpired they weren't being chased anywhere. The Lindelhoff boys were being invited to go somewhere special.

An officer in a fine black and grey uniform sat at their kitchen table. He drank tea with them all and explained how men with certain special abilities were being asked to join a secret battalion. Men like the Lindelhoffs. His father had been very suspicious of the big car and the young soldier who knocked on the door at first. But as soon as the officer stepped into the farmhouse, he could smell him properly and knew instantly that the visitor was kin. The two older men talked at length, and Lindelhoff senior decided that his two sons would go with the officer in the car to a base on the other side of the great forest in the north. It was a huge honour, and the reward for service was great. They would never be hunted again. So, the boys went. They went gladly, and soon realised that there were many more like them. After three months of training the brothers were separated by their instructors; one went into the parachute regiment, the other to the submarine pens.

Standing on the deck of the boat at that moment, home seemed a long way away. Time had passed so quickly. He had

7

forgotten the smell of the pines, and the intense cold of the winter snow. Soon it would be all over, though. They would submerge beneath the waves and navigate the secret channels to the black docks underneath the island. Once there, they would refit the boat, wait, rest and feed, until they were called for again. He'd heard that the city under the island had grown bigger since their last visit. That there were many 'special troops' stationed down there now, guarding the secret weapons.

He looked up at the sky. It would be a long time before he saw it again. His uniform smelt rancid. He had spent far too many weeks in close confinement with the other wolves, and the smell from below made his nose and whiskers twitch. The scent-stories of one hundred of his fellow sailors made him feel nauseous. But at least the crew were still together. He had heard that lots of the 'wolves' from other boats had been taken away, to form special death squads. You could always send a werewolf where a tank could not go, and do at least twice as much damage, the generals said, over coffee and pastries in their warm, cosy Berlin offices.

This crew had earned a rest – a long one, thought Lindelhoff.

They'd fought in Greece, France, Turkey, Montenegro, and Russia. They always landed in secret coves and small inlets at the dead of night, then once ashore they loped inland to a predetermined location and butchered the troops stationed there. They'd ripped them apart and set their severed heads on spikes. Berlin had said that it was important that they always send a message to the Allies, so they had printed leaflets that were to be left with the decapitated heads and bodies of the fallen. The message on them read:

'Hello British Tommy and Russian Ivan. Look into the tormented faces of your friends and comrades. And understand that there are more deadly things to worry about than bullets, gas and bayonets.'

This hadn't scared the Allies that much though, because they just kept fighting, and ultimately, they had won.

The wind flicked some of the white foam from the tips of the waves onto Lindelhoff's paws. He looked at the dinghy and growled to himself. It had to be seaworthy, of course, and he'd been ordered by the Bosun to make sure that it was bone dry; his passenger didn't like the water apparently and now it was full of the stuff, so he tipped it over and shook it out. Now, it was mostly dry.

The special passenger would not be grateful for a wet run ashore, thought Lindelhoff, so he made the boat fast against the hatch and got in, placing the small oars in the rowlocks, and trying his hardest to keep the little yellow bag of compressed air in position against the side of the hull. The wind was getting up now, and the spray was falling horizontally. He was getting wet and angry, but thankfully he didn't have long to wait.

The little man in the fine clothes climbed up the hatch ladder, sauntered across the deck, and stepped down into the dinghy. He did it with an ease that surprised Lindelhoff; he'd been expecting to have to fish him out of the water at least once on the way over. The little man didn't wait to be asked or told how to cast off the ropes; he did it as if he had always done it, nonchalantly and casually, the way a seasoned sailor would do it. Then, he just sat back in the stern, and with a nod of his small head they were off.

Lindelhoff tried as hard as he could to row dry. Every time you rowed an officer ashore was an order from the bosun, and if that officer stepped ashore even slightly damp, Fuhrer forbid, you'd be in real trouble, so he tried to propel the dinghy forward as fast as he could without splashing any water into it. Normally it was a 50/50 scenario, and you had to take it on the chin, or snout, that you were going to get a bit wet. Incredibly, the water just seemed to bounce off him, as if he were surrounded by some sort of invisible field and, unnervingly, the little, odd smile never left his little, odd face. It took thirty minutes to get to the shore. The current and the wind hadn't made it an easy task, but werewolves are strong, and Lindelhoff was not panting too hard as he pulled the dinghy ashore. The man stepped out of the dinghy and onto the beach. His highly polished shoes gleamed in the night like smooth, dark, rounded stones. His cream trousers and blue blazer looked just as pristine and sharp as they had when he stepped out of the Gieves and Hawkes changing room twenty years ago. This strange little man, in his Sloane Street ensemble, seemed to be impervious to the elements.

Lindelhoff sniffed again at the wind, and immediately caught the smell of enemy soldiers on the breeze. It was the familiar leather tang of the Sam Brown belt, and the scratchy scent of scrubbed webbing and ammunition pouches that alerted him. He looked at the little man and motioned silently toward the cliff above with a hairy paw.

'Enemy,' he growled.

The man just smiled and waved his hand in the air dismissively. The waves continued to roll up the beach and depart with a subdued hiss, and he just carried on wandering around as if he hadn't a care in the world. Lindelhoff made the dinghy fast to a large rock. There was no pathway up from the beach, no steps cut into the cliff-face, or even a rusty ladder. They were in a cove with no visible exit, a suicidal place to land, but that didn't seem to bother his passenger. He continued walking casually across the sand, tapping at a stone here and probing at a strand of seaweed there with his walking cane. After a few minutes of exploration, it looked to Lindelhoff that the small man had grown bored and decided on a position at the base of the cliff to settle in and wait. It was as if he were expecting a set of lift doors, the kind you'd find in a swanky Berlin hotel, to open right there and then, and invite him in.

He wasn't exactly strange, thought Lindelhoff; there was just something about him that made his hackles twitch.

During the short voyage from Greece, the man had been eager to explore the boat. He'd looked in on engineering and asked questions about the propulsion system that had baffled the chief engineer. He'd wandered into missile loading and suggested targeting improvements that had actually improved the efficiency of the torpedoes. He'd even ventured into the mess room for the officers. The Captain had told the crew that their passenger was not to be addressed or bothered; he had the freedom of the ship, and if he wanted something then he was to be treated like the Captain himself.

After a couple of days at sea, it became obvious that he wasn't remotely bothered that the entire crew were werewolves or even that the combined fleets of the British Navy and the American Navy seemed to be after them. They endured night after night avoiding depth charges and hearing the whirl and hiss of torpedo screws passing overhead and underneath, but it didn't worry the strange little man in the slightest. Now, here they were. Their voyage together was over, and good riddance, thought Lindelhoff.

The man turned quickly and faced him. Lindelhoff got the uneasy feeling that the man could read his thoughts.

'You can go,' said the man.

He had the voice of a scalpel; very thin and cold, but it could slice you to pieces, easily and clinically. The hackles on

Lindelhoff's back and neck stood up again. He wasn't best pleased with his passenger's attitude, and war or no war, there still had to be respect, whichever rung of the ladder you had your paw on.

'Not even a thank you for rowing you across the sea in the dead of night under the guns and the eyes of the enemy, or a thank you for landing you here at the right time and dry?' snarled Lindelhoff.

'I am truly grateful for your assistance,' said the little dapper man. He didn't really mean it, of course, and he moved back towards the base of the cliff wall, bringing his walking stick up so that the metal cap at the end of it was pointing directly at the werewolf sailor.

Lindelhoff sensed the danger immediately. His sharp claws came out quickly and he crouched, ready to attack; he bared his teeth, and his powerful haunches tensed. The little man saw that his curt and abrupt manner had offended the werewolf, and he tried to reassure it that it was in no danger.

'Stand down, my friend. I mean you no harm. This walking stick is just a sort of key, it is not a weapon.'

The little man smiled at the werewolf, but Lindelhoff just snarled back. He wasn't convinced about the stick, and he'd prefer to be safe now and sorry for killing this man later. The man lowered his walking stick, however, and Lindelhoff relaxed.

'I'm leaving you now. Row back to the boat and tell your captain that the package has been delivered. Be well, Lindelhoff, and know this: deep inside this rock is a secret place where all of the occult power of the Nazis has been hidden. I won't say Heil Hitler! But I will say that this war is not over. We will have our miracle weapons, and our blessed victory, when the secrets of the Black Book are unlocked.'

The little man drew a pattern in the air with his walking stick, smiled, and then casually walked through the solid rock face of the cliff and disappeared.

Lindelhoff looked up at the sky; there was no moon. He untied the dinghy, waded out into the water and paddled back to the boat. He made good time because the tide was with him now, and it wasn't long before he clambered on to the deck, climbed down the ladder, and secured the hatch after him. UX99 slipped beneath the black, mirror-like surface of the water and was gone. Later, the birds returned, and went back to sleep on the surface of the water until the sun came up

2 NETS IN THE NIGHT

22nd June 2018, London.

The angel flew in low over the treetops; the downdraft of its powerful wings disturbed the older branches of the trees and made them creak and groan. High above the protesting trees, the landing lights of planes could be seen twinkling in the dark sky. The angel banked hard, stopped in the sky for a second, like a white smudge against the darkness, and dropped to the ground like a stone, spreading its wings widely to break its fall just in time and landing softly. It folded its wings back, ran its powerful hands through its hair, and checked that the new packet of condoms and the lube were still in the front pocket of its favourite jeans.

Everything was just where it should be, so the angel – all 6 feet and 9 inches of him – walked barefoot over the grass and into the quiet of the night. He was there for yet another tryst with yet another casual lover; arranged online, of course. It had been planned for weeks, and the angel didn't want to be late.

He walked along the pathway that led to the bridge that stretched over the railway tracks. The railway line could not go around this beautiful green space. London's geography would not allow it. So, in the spirit of blind progress, the common had been sliced in two, and tracks of cold iron were pinned into the earth. Years later a bridge was built over the tracks so that the people who walked there could be reunited with the other side of the common they had once known.

He walked across the bridge, and once he got to the other side, he stopped. He reached into his pocket for his mobile phone, tapped the screen to bring it to life, then again to select the correct App. The image of an attractive young man appeared. It was one of many. The first was a profile shot, the second a shirt-off shot, then an angry shot, and a kind shot, before the angel's favourite – the vulnerable shot. All of the images were arranged on a digital carousel and the angel swept the pictures of the young man first this way, and then the other. All the images showed off his handsome face, his lovely thick hair and a mouth full of perfect, white teeth. The angel smiled; he was eager, horny, and impatient to experience what he hoped was about to happen next. He walked down the path, making for the pond and the great oak trees where his date was waiting for him. As he approached the pond a small blue rectangle of light appeared in the darkness ahead. It was the screen of a mobile phone. The light disappeared, then reappeared again. This was the safe signal. Tonight's lover was there, ready and waiting.

The angel stepped off the path, moved under the branches of the tree and straight into a trap. His date was there, but so were his friends. Before the angel could unfurl his wings and escape into the sky, they threw a net over him. It was made from cold, hard ringlets of steel. It was heavy, forged with magic – and unbreakable. After a few attempts to throw the net off, the angel knew that he was going to have to try to fight his way out.

Angels are incredibly strong – even the smaller, lower-level ones – and his attackers knew this too, so rather than get close, they just smashed at the thrashing mass under the net with long iron bars. It was all over within seconds. The men dragged the angel and the net out from under the branches of the tree, then five of the strongest picked it up and carried it on their shoulders around the pond before disappearing into the night. Only the small white pockets of mist from their breath puffed into the air as they struggled with their load, marking their passing. They did not have far to go.

3 WINGS FOR THE WITCHES

The Dead Sea Shoals was one of Clapham's finest fast-food establishments. It was an institution to its residents, and far more than just a chip-shop. To them, the Shoals was a restaurant. It occupied an expensive piece of real estate next door to the Windmill Public House on the Common. The décor inside was tasteful, minimal and spare, but the welcome was always warm, and the food was always good.

There were brown, sun-bleached posters on the wall that told you where the fish you were about to eat had come from, and if you were really all that bothered, which rusty fishing vessel had caught them. There was the obligatory blue buzzing ring that flies are addicted to on the wall, and on the table's plastic condiment containers in the shape of red and brown tomatoes with green nozzles that looked like leaves. On the well-polished stainless-steel counter were wooden forks that had been cunningly whittled by a big, clever machine to resemble whales with open mouths. The seats were all comfortable and there was a fine selection of newspapers and barely out of date magazines to peruse as you waited for your skate, cod or plaice.

You could get practically any type of fish that you wanted here. It could be prepared in batter or breadcrumbs and with any number of garnishes and twists. You could, of course, add a saveloy or a pickled egg to your meal if the fancy took you.

The sign above the door outside showed a graphic depiction of a fish against a big black Helvetica number seven. It was arty and contemporary without being too gauche. All in all, it was a nice place. Clean. Tidy. Quiet, most of the time. But if you knew what went on there, behind closed doors and after hours, you'd give it a wide berth. Other things got served up at the Shoals you see; things like beatings, vengeance, violence of every description – and murder.

Tonight, is one of those nights. It's been at the Shoals; all the fish has been eaten, and thousands of potatoes have been chipped and fried. Every single chip fork in the box on the counter has gone, too. At the beginning of the evening there were enough to build a canoe. But now, all of them have been used to help those delicious little bits of potato heaven on their way down the throats of the punters. Everything is quiet. The counter has been scrubbed, and the kitchens are immaculate. Even the most zealous of health inspectors could eat his or her dinner off the floor, if he or she wanted to. Only the tick and tock of the clock can be heard. Everything is closed, locked up tight and all the lights are off. All of them apart from one, that is, in the private yard where the nasty things happen. Nasty things that no one ever walks away from.

A solitary, naked bulb illuminates something that was once beautiful, but is now broken and ugly. Deformed and smashed. It is the angel. The angel that thought it was going on a date. In its prime it would have done justice to any painting on the walls of any chapel. Now you'd be hard pressed to tell which bit was the top and which the bottom. It is hanging from a large iron spike that has been driven through both of its wings and into the brick wall. The spike has been driven with such great force that the bricks have been pushed backwards. Grout and red brick dust have fallen away from the wall and floated down onto the ground.

The angel has been beaten to within an inch of its life, and pools of black, sticky blood have formed on the floor beneath his feet. Every now and then it summons the strength from somewhere deep down inside to spit the blood it keeps coughing up onto the floor. The end is not far, not far at all. It looks up into the sky with eyes that are glazed and swollen, but there is nothing there. No escape, no rescue; only blackness and the familiar twinkle of planes coming and going. Death is coming. Coming fast. In between the sharp flashes of pain, the angel dreams of flight, soaring high in the sky on beating wings over a green patchwork of verdant fields. It remembers the taste of water as it flies through vast, wet, grey clouds. Its wings twitch as its muscles remember each bank and thrust.

A spasm of pain stops this memory of flight and brings it back to the yard with a crash. Blood drips from the tips of its toes into the ever-increasing puddle of blood on the floor. There are words cut into and scratched across its bloody chest, written in languages that have not been used or heard properly in well over a thousand years. Shapes and strange symbols crawl around the words like dripping spiders. These are binding spells and word locks that suck life away and cage the soul. These are dark words for midnight-dark deeds.

A man steps into the pool of light that surrounds the angel. He is a big man, very big. He is wearing dark jeans, heavy boots and a black jumper. Black curly hair falls to his broad shoulders and the handle of a large, wicked looking knife protrudes from his back pocket. Tattoos creep out from under the fabric of his sleeves, snaking onto his hands and around his fingers. He wears these strange symbols and shapes proudly; they are all well-drawn and intricate, the hand that drew them was skilful and well-practised. No prison needle or backstreet ink parlour were responsible for these. But they are more than just tattoos. This second skin works just like armour. The big man takes his blade out, feels the strength and weight of it in his hand and the cold evil of the steel… and casually thrusts it through the angel's wing.

The blade passes neatly between the radius and the ulna. There is a ripping sound, followed by a crunching sound. Then there is a pop, as the tendons pull away from the bones and the joints separate. The angel tries to scream, of course, but it has been given such a working over already that the scream sounds more like an old man wheezing on a bitterly cold morning than a cry for help. More blood fills its mouth and the dark red puddle on the ground grows arms and legs like a giant abstract spider.

'Soon there will be more of your blood on the outside than on the inside, freak. Soon you will be empty – soon you will just be a husk. All your history, your time, those experiences, and feelings will be gone, wiped away and forgotten. You look more like a flying colander than an angel at this moment in time. Will you tell me what I need to know now, angel?'

The big man pulls his knife out, wipes it on the angel's wing feathers and returns it to the sheath that lives in his back pocket. He grabs some of the angel's hair and yanks it upwards to look into the angel's eyes. Another bloody cough creeps out of the angel's throat. The angel takes a breath, opens his eyes and looks into the face of his torturer.

'I cannot tell you anything, Baptist. I cannot give you the map or the secret directions to the second gate. It must remain locked, Baptist. Always. Man is not ready for what lies beyond it. I cannot show you or tell you where the gate is.'

The man called the Baptist cocks his head to one side and smiles. It's the kind of smile that makes for wet bedsheets and recurring nightmares. He shrugs.

'You will give your secrets to me in the end; you know you will. You will tell me where I can find the hidden entrance, and how to unlock the gate when I get there.

'Come now, little bird, what does it serve you to withhold the truth from me? I have caught and killed many of your kind already. Each one was as brave as you are now at the beginning, but they told me everything I needed to know by the end. Step by step, death by death, I move along the path. I am nearing the end of that journey now; only a few small details remain. Soon it will be the end for you and your kind.'

The angel looks up and into his tormentor's face and it tries to force one last brave smile.

'The gate is closed to you and all those like you, Baptist. You belong back in the dry empty desert that spawned you and your brothers, but even that is too good a place for you. Your heart is a dry husk now. There is no love in it anymore, it has withered inside your chest, replaced with hatred and fear. The road you were placed upon long ago has come to a dead end, and here, in this time and in this place, you will meet your own end.

'Death comes for you too, Baptist! And it will come from a place that you do not expect. Those that stand at your shoulder now will give you up and send you into the darkness, and they will smile because they have been set free.

'Did you know that all angels can see into the future at the moment of their death, Baptist? Did you know that? As the energy of life and the glory of the light once given to us seeps out of our physical forms, even those of us that have fallen from the stars are granted one last look into the world around us. It is our choice whether we look back at our own deeds or look into the future of one that is close to us. I'm using mine to see into your future. And do you know what I see? I see a sad, lonely, grey rock in the middle of a great dark, angry sea. Birds screech high in the sky and you realise that they are laughing at you, Baptist. The waves are truly high there, so high that they block out the light; they crash on this dark, desolate rock as if they mean to destroy it and wipe it from the face of the earth. The white tips of these giant waves appear to have meaning. They rise like liquid mountains; they are relentless and precise. Their one true intention is to clean the rock of human sin. It is a grim place; lonely and absolute.

'An angel stands there; the one you fear the most, the one that haunts all of you. None of nature's force can sway him from his task. The rain and water move all around him, but not over him. He stands tall on the summit of the rock and smashes your body against the wet stone, again and again until the life seeps from your open mouth. Then he lifts your broken body up and takes you into the waves. He ties a great rock to you. It is so vast that even he struggles to lift it, and then he slips you into the water. You are still alive when you go in, Baptist; barely alive, but still conscious, your black, shrivelled little heart continues to beat. Into the darkness you go, Baptist. No grave for you, nothing to mark your pitiful existence; down you go, away from the light. But before you go, the angel whispers something to you, Baptist; it breaks your black heart and torments you for forever more. You will not die or age down there in the deep; you will live for ever, down there on the seabed with only a rock for company, for all the time that this world has. Heaven will never be yours. Peace will never be yours. You will be nothing and the deep, dark cold will be your home. Enjoy it!'

The man runs a tattooed hand through his hair and smiles again. He looks amused at the angel's prophesy of his impending doom and spits a large gobbet of phlegm onto the angel's head.

'A rock in the sea, killed by an angel and a prison cell made of water? I don't think so! Spin your yarns, angel. Many have tried to kill me before, but I'm still standing here. You should have looked into my future a little harder, my friend. Heaven means nothing to me. I have bigger plans than that. Plans and dreams that will unlock time and space and give me the dark power I need to establish a new force in this world.

'Heaven? No, you are mistaken, angel. Chaos and anarchy and the destruction of this country have been promised to me. I am the key in the door that will unlock the darkness, and all will perish, whether man, angel or anything else that gets in my way.'

The angel lifts its head one last time and looks into the man's eyes. For the briefest of moments there is confusion. But it passes. Gone. Its eyes glaze over.

'There is no place like the city in the sky, Baptist. There is nothing like it now, or ever will there be anything like it in the future. You will never experience it or know its majesty. Remember the rock and the sea, Baptist. You and The 10 will die down here on this world as you deserve.'

The big man sees the angel hanging and bleeding there and wants to finish it off, but the pain inside his head is coming again. He squeezes his eyes tightly shut as the voices begin to whisper and stir inside his skull. The unwelcome guest is coming to stay again, the one who holds the key to unlock his mind. It sounds like a faint rumble from far away that comes closer and closer until, with a shattering roar, it explodes inside his head and rages inside his mind like a frenzied beast. Then comes the whispering fire in his brain, painful and throbbing; he can hear sounds and words swarming all over him, beating him down. The words command him to do things; they hide little verbal triggers in his mind for use later on, and they give him power. Sharp lightning stabs of colour crash around inside his mind, causing him to lose balance and stumble. The moment passes. The present returns. The angel comes back into focus in front of him and he is back in the yard once again. He takes a deep breath and exhales. Calm. Centred. Blood everywhere. Angel blood.

He knows what he must do. Get on with it. Get it done. Get the answers.

He takes a moment. He breathes in and out deeply, and then he stands still and clears his mind. The headaches started many years ago, in Berlin. He remembers a meeting in a dark cellar. There was some violence and bloodshed, a blinding light, and then nothing. The headaches hurt him badly. Sometimes he vomits and passes out, but afterwards when the pain has gone the words in his mind begin to take form and grow; he knows what to do, and where to do it, and who to do it to. The words are messages and instructions. He knows they are, and he knows that he must obey them.

He opens his eyes again and sees the angel.

'You will fail,' says the angel once again, before it falls into the black abyss of death.

'We will see about that.'

The man called the Baptist steps forward and places the palms of his hands against the angel's temples. He murmurs softly, sending killing words and spells through skin that feels like cold running water inside glass.

There is something inside the angel that the Baptist wants. He tries to summon it, tries to suck it from the angel, but nothing comes; he resigns himself to the fact that he won't get what he wants from this one, it is too strong. His hands drop, and he opens his eyes and looks at the angel with something like respect. Then he takes a step backwards to give himself some room, and he kicks the angel as hard as he can in the stomach.

The blow is so ferocious that the angel's wings tear against the iron spike and rip apart. The angel falls to the ground with a wet slap. The big man reaches down and lifts it up easily like a broken doll. The knife comes out again and slashes downwards. One of the wings falls off and lands on the floor. It is a sad, poor end for something that has flown through the light of the heavens, seen strange distant worlds, and witnessed the history of mankind.

The man called the Baptist spits on the broken body.

He turns around and nods; a signal for the others to come. Moments later, more men step into the yard, and into the pool of light. There is Peter and his brother Andrew; James, son of Zebedee; Phillip and Bartholomew; Thomas and Matthew; James, son of Alpheus; Thaddeus and Simon, sometimes called the Zealot. They are The 10.

Once, long ago, they were brave, strong men; men who believed in something much greater. Good men, honest and true. They were the Disciples.

But now, they are just shadows of the men they once were. They have become criminals: thieves and thugs, pimps and terrorists, people-traffickers and mercenaries. The Baptist has done this to them. He has made them this way. They ran away from the Romans and hid in the deep desert. Under a cruel sun they began to die a slow death, first by thirst, and then by shame.

And day-by-day and year-by-year, they went from bad to the very worst that mankind had to offer. Soon the Middle East became too hot for them, as tales of their black deeds spread like wildfire. So they travelled further and further away. The Turks and the Magyars were disgusted by their barbarity and put a price on their heads. The Italians and the Spanish did the same.

Word travelled quickly around the Mediterranean. Soon, rival criminal gangs from across Europe were forced to band together to fight their common foe. Venice mobilised its pocket army and even the Borgias got involved.

But The 10 and the Baptist would not go quietly. They fought their enemies to a standstill each time because they could not be killed. They were immortal.

Someone had a plan for them. Someone was keeping them alive. Who that was, and why, is still a mystery. The Baptist says he knows, but he's not sharing that information with anyone else. Now, when they look in the mirror, they all know that the good deeds they have done in the past are outweighed by the bad, and they all know that it's the Baptist's fault. But they are too scared to tell him. So here they are, in a yard, in South London, with a dead angel to dispose of.

Each of them carries a weapon, and when the Baptist nods they know what they have to do. None of them wants to do what is expected of them but disobeying the Baptist can be fatal. So, they begin to hack the angel to pieces. The scene is an ugly one. Their blades lift and fall; blood and gore spatters onto the walls. Bartholomew wonders why he's doing this but remains quiet, as he always does, while Simon hacks away like a mad man. Simon the Zealot, who thinks he is second-in-command but is called 'chief weasel' behind his back. He likes the killing and does it like he does everything else, to extremes. The rest make an effort, but their hearts are not in it.

The big man watches from the back of the yard and smokes a cigarette amidst the carnage. The smoke rises gently in little wisps, and merges with the circle of light above his head, then disappears forever. He imagines that it is the angel's soul flying off into the night sky for a second.

Outside on the common, the wind stirs the trees and the branches crack and creak. The big man hears the noises and lifts his head like a hunting dog on point.

'Stop!'

The hackers stop hacking. The Baptist scans the night sky, searching, for any sign of motion up there. He strains his ears for the beating of strong muscular wings and the creak of leather armour but hears nothing. He turns his attention back to the men and the pulp that, not so long ago, was an angel.

'Collect the remains, bag them up and take them to the witches in Balham, they will find a use for them. The hair you can give to the Sirens of Battersea Bridge. Thomas and Matthew, take the wings to the Black Museum, wrap them carefully and mark them for "his" attention. They must be untraceable now. Do you hear me? No trace whatsoever. He mustn't know anything about us yet. There will be time enough for that.'

Thomas and Matthew carefully slip the wings into a plastic bag, and then seal the opening with melted wax.

The men scurry around, scraping and bagging. Soon they are finished and all that is left on the ground, under the small moon of artificial light, is a dark stain and several steaming plastic bags. The wings are bait for the man they have pursued all their long, long lives.

There is a rusty tap fixed to the wall in the small yard that is used to clean the raw fish and potatoes before they are taken into the kitchen to become fish and chips. The big man turns it on and begins to wash the angel's blood off himself.

He scrubs and scrubs at his muscular arms, even after the last spot has gone.

One of the other men approaches.

The big man stops washing and stares at him.

'If I may ask, John – if it's not too much trouble I mean – why are we killing all these angels? I don't have a problem with it of course – what you say goes, after all. Oh no, I'm happy to do my share, but I just wondered, you know, why?'

This man is a small man in every respect. He's thin and wiry, and stoops slightly. His hair is dark and parted on the side, and he has a face the colour of stale fish batter. A weak chin supports a hooked nose, and sharp, angular cheekbones keep them all in place. You wouldn't give him another glance if he bumped into you in the street, but he has clever, intelligent eyes that are always two blinks ahead.

His eyes are the eyes of a survivor. Shrewd and cunning. He takes his turn at the tap, adopting his well-practised servile persona. He washes the dark angel blood from his hands and forearms. The big man shakes his head and smiles.

'Because, James son of Alpheus, the angels know where the gate is and how to get inside. We don't. We need to crack one of them and then we can all escape, from all of this.' He waves one great arm around the yard.

'Yes, John. Of course, John,' says James, as he performs a well-practised bob of the head.

James looks around and the rest of the men, who have been listening, nod in passive agreement. They are not the Baptist's flock anymore, but they are definitely his sheep. James dries his hands on a teacloth that hangs from his belt, and whispers into the big man's ear.

'So, what do you want us to do then, John? Shall we stick another of those posts on that dating site and grab a new one that way?'

'Just find me another angel, James, that's all I need you and the others to do. Just set another trap on the Common and get me another angel. You can do that, can't you?'

The big man turns away and walks back inside without waiting for an answer.

James, son of Alpheus, watches as the leader of their small brotherhood walks away. He is worried. He's scared because he knows madness when he sees it. He's seen it before. He knows that there is something bad happening inside John's head. Big John isn't himself. He isn't balanced, he isn't right, and he's getting dangerous. Killing dangerous.

And if John's like that then it could spell really big trouble for the rest of them.

Maybe he should have a chat with Simon.

He turns away from the rest of them and heads inside. Simon is as slippery as an eel. Simon keeps his own counsel and it's clear to James that Simon would want to take control of the gang if anything unpleasant and terminal were to happen to the big man.

James goes up to his room and looks out of the window. This is where he does his best thinking. It's a small but comfortable room. Each of them has millions stashed away in their own private Swiss bank accounts. But they live modestly because drawing attention to their affairs has hurt them once too often in the past.

What were they doing here in London? Why this place, of all places? There were hundreds of better locations in which to live. Best not to contradict John right now, though; think about the bigger picture, and stay alive. Why not let him make the mistakes? Sooner or later, he was going to do something that even he couldn't fight his way out of. Then, James would be in charge. They could stop all of this and get back to doing what they did best. Make some money and go somewhere where the sun shone for more than two paltry months of the year. James looks down at his hands. They shake uncontrollably. John wants another angel to interrogate and mutilate, and James knows just where to find one. He sees the tree outside his window lean to one side as the wind blows across the Common. The Common is empty now – but it won't be for long.

James opens his laptop, taps in the passcode for the dating website he belongs to, and begins to write. Tall, muscular man would like to meet tall, male angel. Loves the outdoors and eating alfresco.

Angels love the Common. They are drawn by the openness of it. They like the peace and the quiet and the trees. James finishes his post, uploads a couple of pictures of a man, presses send and then lays down on his bed, turning the bedside light off.

The dark. Is that where we are heading? he thinks to himself.

4 THE SEC☉ND FALL

The night didn't so much pass as drag itself away, and then the dawn broke. The city stirred and came to life again like a human heart after CPR. Cold, harsh sunlight crawled across the concrete walkways and pulled itself up the walls of the buildings, brick by brick, before taking to the air and trying valiantly to take control of the skies. A stubby blue and grey office block sat uncomfortably amidst its newer and taller brethren. Midway up the north side of it was a window – the only one with any life in it. A man looked out from it and onto this grey and unforgiving landscape. High above the buildings, straggly rainclouds raced into the sky in order to take their positions like second-rate extras on a film set; the largest ones went to the back, and the smaller ones grouped together at the front. With perfect timing and positioning, they then formed a barrier that would keep the sun at bay for the rest of the day. The man in the window placed his palm against the windowpane. It felt like a slice of time. The glass was a wall between one moment and the next, almost. Today was his birthday, and he was celebrating it with a mug of weak tea in a chipped blue mug with a Metropolitan police force crest on it. He was busy reading a file about the disappearance of yet another angel. The number of the missing was growing.

This man's name was Judas Iscariot. He was once a disciple of Christ, then he was a traitor and a betrayer. Now, he was a policeman. It was hard to believe, but he was one of London's finest detectives, although not many knew of his existence. He had been a policeman in this city for the past two-hundred years. Fighting a secret war against the evil forces and creatures that never make the front pages of any newspaper, screen or blog. He had been hiding his existence from the wider world and working in a secret division inside Scotland Yard. His place of work was the Black Museum of Scotland Yard. And it was his job to keep Londoners safe from the dark forces of the occult.

He flicked through the report, sliding a smooth, manicured finger down the page, stopping every now and again to re-read something. He mumbled and hummed to himself in a mixture of many languages, then took a well-used and well-chewed pen from his jacket pocket and wrote in the margin, 'Angel Serial Killer.' But then he scribbled it out.

He closed the file and put it down on top of the ever-increasing pile of unsolved cases. This case was bothering him more than most. The subject matter was unusual. Angels in London were very common now. They were as much part of its fabric as red London buses, or black London cabs.

They worked in trendy bars and spit-and-sawdust boozers, they appeared on television, they lived upstairs, in the basement and next door; they held down normal jobs and tried to live normal lives. Angels were everywhere, just like artisan coffee shops and cycle-themed cafes where you could get a slice of carrot cake and a really expensive Italian windbreaker.

The man at the window remembered the day that they had first arrived. He had met many angels in the past but that was always in their city, or in places on earth where no human ever ventured. One day, as he was walking down Tottenham Court Road, he walked straight into an old lady who had dropped her shopping bag on the floor, his own mind on other things as usual. It was only after he had picked up everything from the pavement and repacked the old lady's bag for her that he noticed the world had come to a standstill.

There were lots of people watching strange scenes unfolding on the screens of televisions that were stacked like expensive carbon bricks in shop windows. And there was silence. There was a silence from the crowd and the city around them that was so loud it was deafening. There were no car horns or ding-dings from buses as passengers leapt on and off. There was no shouting from angry cycle couriers, or requests for spare change from the homeless. No snatches of conversation between mouth and screen. Nothing. Just a staggeringly loud nothing. The absence of sound reminded him of the hill and the three crosses at the top of it on that day, many, many years ago. All eyes were looking in the same direction. They were looking through the windows and there they were – angels. Real, living and breathing angels. Thousands of them, standing in the green fields of Surrey. Motionless. Waiting. The sun drifted across the sky and their shadows moved around them like the pointer of a sundial. Clouds passed overhead, and you got the impression that even they were slowing down to take a look at the small, ragged band of winged creatures below them. Rain fell and passed, and still, they didn't move. Not a muscle.

Later, after the talks between the Government of Man and the Council of Angels had finished, everyone learned that these angels had been cast down and out of heaven. They were homeless – celestial refugees from the land in the sky. They had nowhere to go. Lots of them were injured. All of them, sadly, were dejected and defeated. Some had blood red stains on their white feathers. Others had white bandages wound tightly around black wings. They all looked like they'd been in the wars, which, of course, they had. Every single one had fought: the children, the old, the sick, the men and the women, all of them. All wars end with the tears of the vanquished.

Stronger angels had cast them down. Bigger, more heavily armoured angels, the unforgiving type that followed orders blindly and gave no quarter. Most of the angels that had lost had come to Britain and decided to settle in London, and now they were part of the furniture.

Winged furniture.

Today, people referred to it as The Second Fall. The first one had been bad enough, and everyone knew what happened to the leader of that revolt.

Judas smiled to himself. He'd been around for so long now that he was on speaking terms with the original fallen angel, the one that had caused the first war in the sky and the First Fall. The Morning Star was one of his names. Judas knew most of the others and shivered uncomfortably when he recited them to himself.

Most of the angels had found homes for themselves in London, but some had flown up to the north of England, to the moors and the isolated places, and nothing much more had been heard about them. There were rumours of hidden cities, high up in the branches of the forests and under the rolling moors, guarded by hosts of fierce warrior angels. Most of it was true, but it made sense to keep that a secret from the humans. The angels in these quiet places kept themselves to themselves; they liked it that way, and their human neighbours liked it that way too. The angels wore their fate like they wore their wings. Out in the open and for all to see. Judas tapped his finger against the page and willed himself to concentrate on the file.

He turned the small, wafer-thin silver coin he always carried over and over in his left hand. It was really worn down. All the markings had been rubbed away. This piece of silver was his lucky charm, and also a constant and painful reminder of his past crime. The biggest crime ever committed, some said. Whenever he needed to think, he reached for his coin. He flicked it from finger to finger like some card sharp or magician. He turned away from the window, sat down and began to go through the photographs that had come with the report and the angel wings. Whoever had done it had enjoyed the task. It was plain enough to see that from the black and white photographs the Duty Sergeant had taken for him. He'd have to have another chat with all his angel contacts again. One of them must know something. Judas picked up the phone on his desk and dialled a number.

5 THE BUCKET OF BLOOD

Later that night Judas met up with an angel called Antenias in the Lamb & Flag public house in Covent Garden. Antenias was one of his informants. He worked in the props department of a famous West End theatre and wandered the streets of Soho by night. He was well placed to pick up all sorts of information. Antenias was one of the first angels to leave the city in the heavens voluntarily and make his home in London. He'd been here for hundreds of years, and he made no secret of his love and respect for the 'wingless ones'. He was also one of the good guys. Unfortunately, some of the angels had learned not to be so virtuous.

He arrived on time, as usual. He was always punctual, which was one of the things that Judas liked about him. They started the evening discussing the art of bare-knuckle boxing over a couple of very welcome but expensive pints. Antenias loved the Lamb & Flag, or the Bucket of Blood as it was known when Judas had first started drinking there. The small passageway that led from Floral Street to the side door of the pub was low and narrow. The Lamb had been the capital's best bare-knuckle boxing venue and it was still his favourite watering hole. But although Antenias was knowledgeable about gouging, killer punches, illegal throws and how many pints Charles Dickens could sink in an evening, he didn't know anything about the attacks and the disappearances of the other angels. There were rumours of course; the Council of Angels had been convened, and whispered warnings were circulating advising all remaining angels to be more alert. But there was nothing concrete.

Antenias apologised; he wished he could have been more helpful. The night wore on, and Judas tried to keep up with Antenias, round for round, but that was a mistake. Angels like beer, a lot, but they don't get really drunk like mortal men. They get happy and merry, their wings give small involuntary jerks, and they become a little forgetful, but that's it.

The following morning, Judas was back in the office with the mother of all hangovers and no new leads. He drank four big glasses of water and took a couple of aspirin. Then he ate a bacon sandwich and downed a bottle of grapefruit juice. He'd heard that apparently it disguised the smell of the breath so that you didn't hum of alcohol all day. Then he sat down at his desk, took out his notebook, read his notes for the fifth time, scribbled something down in his odd mix of English and Hebrew, and tucked the notebook away in the inside pocket of his jacket.

The screen of his computer whirred into life, slowly; the loading bar took longer and longer every day. There was a chance that he could get a new one, but it was a very, very small chance. He got up from his desk to give the aged computer a chance to wheeze into action and caught his reflection in the window. Judas had olive skin, light blue eyes and dark wavy shoulder-length hair. At 185cm, he was taller than average, but other than that he was very normal looking, really, nothing to write home about in fact. As a policeman, this was a good thing. He dressed well and spent a lot of money on shoes. Trickers of Jermyn Street were his favourites. They were so well made that you could use them in a fight as a deadly weapon.

He moved over to the window and stared out over London. The rain was still falling, and the wind tried its hardest to blow it out of town. Out of the corner of his eye he detected a flash of movement. An angel wearing the uniform of one of the bigger parcel delivery companies flew past, carrying a big white cardboard box covered in colourful stickers and those see-through plastic squares that held important shipping documents. The package looked heavy, but it could have been twice the size and still not bothered the angel. They didn't seem to mind working zero-hour contracts. They just liked to be of service. Judas tracked the angel as it flew around the building again; it was obviously having some difficulty in locating an address, and he watched as it flapped its powerful wings once before coming to a complete stop and hovering in the air. It reached into one of its pockets and took out a digital tracking device, checked to make sure of the address for the delivery, then swooped down and out of sight.

Air Mail had really taken off again, thought Judas.

A filthy-looking cloud ambled over the skyline. It was another of those wet and windy Mondays that help you to start the week badly. Judas turned around and forced himself to think about work. He needed to forget the hangover and the headache and concentrate; to do his job, start joining the dots and making some sense of all of these crimes.

The noise level down below started to rise as the station came to life. Last night's drunks were being asked to politely vacate their warm but now smelly cells with the enthusiastic nudge of a size nine boot. They all exited their cells, collecting their valuables in their very own MET issued brown envelopes, and walked down the steps that they had fallen up the night before. On their way down, they passed the freshly scrubbed new Constables in their immaculate uniforms on their way up.

It was the half-cut replacing the hungover.

Judas picked up a pile of dog-eared manila files, stuffed with scraps of different coloured paper, from the centre of the desk. A few post-it notes fluttered out and down on to the floor. He read the title on the front of the file: Witchcraft and crimes of an occult nature in Surrey. It was a little outside his jurisdiction, but witchcraft was witchcraft, and the normal police did not touch crimes like these. They got passed up to the Black Museum department. His department.

A casual skim of the incident report told him that some hikers had gone missing on the Downs. There were witness statements from a few local pub landlords. They'd reported seeing the hikers arrive in their expensive, water repellent anoraks and rucksacks, have a few pints and then wobble off into the night to look for a hedge to throw up behind and somewhere to pitch their tents and camp for the night. They had arrived in good spirits and left a little worse for wear.

'Just a few campers out and about, enjoying the countryside and doing a bit of walking,' one said. The landlords had nothing bad at all to say about them.

Then, a dead body had been discovered by another party of hikers, with strange markings scrawled all over it. At first, they thought the markings were just prison tattoos. A sharp needle and a bottle of writing ink in the hands of a dyslexic inmate, or one without a steady hand, often made for embarrassing skin pictures. But on closer inspection it was obvious that these were definitely not that sort. These intricate symbols and shapes seemed to move and twitch. The local police force was called in, and calmed the nerves of the hikers by explaining that the moving ink was in fact a combination of heat-haze and sporadic muscle movement. In reality, the local boys in blue had guessed that it was a Code 16 and used the Black Museum hotline.

The case had been marked 'urgent' and bumped up to him. Judas put it to one side of the pile on his desk with all the other urgent case files.

The computer on his desk clicked and buzzed as the hard drive valiantly tried to prove fit for service. He was about to sit down when another file caught his eye. This one had been silver-flagged. Judas flicked it open and started to read the top sheet. A Black Priest from the East that the department had been monitoring for the past two-hundred years had re-surfaced in London – and needed looking after.

Didn't they all, he muttered to himself.

He closed that file and began to thumb through the rest of the files one by one; there were more practitioners of the dark arts bent on global destruction, malevolent spirits, zombies, ghosts, murderers, and magical sects that needed investigating.

It's never going to end, is it? thought Judas.

He looked heavenward.

But that's the idea, isn't it?

He placed the last file back on top of the pile and picked up his tea again.

It was cold and even more disgusting than usual, but he drained the mug regardless.

Lots to do, and all the time in the world to do it, he said to the empty room.

He went back through all of the files, making notes in the margins and occasionally breaking off to put differently coloured pins in the giant map of Greater London on the wall opposite. His mobile phone beeped and chirped, as useless messages and alerts used up his data and memory. There were hundreds of little blue-headed pins in the map already and the addition of some new ones meant that he was going to be a busy boy for the foreseeable future. His laptop pinged. The number of messages in his already overflowing mailbox increased by one.

6 FIRES IN THE MIND

Judas perched on the edge of his desk and looked at the map on the wall to see if there were any patterns forming on it. He traced imaginary lines from point to point in his mind and tried to remember if there was anything unusual about that church or that statue, or whether anything unusual had happened in that graveyard, or near that river. But nothing sprang to mind. No patterns. There was something, though, and it felt like trouble brewing. His headache made itself known again, and he was forced to admit defeat and sit down properly. The tea here was always bad. It came in faded blue mugs, and gave you rumbles in the stomach that had defeated every pharmaceutical company on the planet. Maybe it was the bromide that was rumoured to have been added to the water, or the tea, or the soap in the lavatories? The tea on top of the hangover would have toppled even the strongest of men, so he really needed the pills to kick in and start working. That, or put in for a head transplant.

He needed to clear his mind. He rubbed at his temples and focused on a crack in the wall by the filing cabinet. He relaxed and allowed time to pass over him. Meditation and deep breathing techniques, gleaned from one of the many instant calm manuals that populated the sagging shelves of the 'Master your Mind' section at the bookshop, had helped him learn to put the present on hold and turn the life noise down. The crack in the wall got bigger and bigger in his mind's eye, and he started to drift down into the dark space that the crack was becoming, away into the past and his memories. His was a much longer journey than that of most people; full of horror, regret, some good times of course, and lots of routine and pain.

You can't kill time, and if you have too much of it, eventually it kills you.

He needed to reduce the amount of noise. In order to do that, all he had to do was float away down one of those silent channels of the past, to subdue the slamming of the cell doors down below and the squeak of rubber soles torturing the linoleum; just float into the past and send the present into the future. The sun took a turn around the walls of the office as he calmed his mind, and he was able to put some much-needed energy back in the tank.

When he opened his eyes again the light in the room was saying its farewells. He looked at the big white clock on the wall above the door, and realised that he had been meditating, or something like it, for a couple of hours. His mind was now clear, and the hangover was gone, thankfully. He was back in the office. The computer on the desk in front of him had died and needed rebooting – or just booting out of the window. The red light on the desk phone blinked impatiently back at him. He'd missed a few calls, it seemed. He'd cleared the answerphone messages from last week so that he had some room for this week's deluge. Judas took out his silver coin and rubbed at it.

His meditation had unlocked the memory of a brief visit to the Reichstag in 1939. He'd had a conversation there with a girl that he may have loved, or killed; he wasn't sure – '39 was a difficult time for everyone. She had introduced him to many of the more colourful characters that called Berlin home at that time. They had had a good time together. Some of the people he had met with her were just visiting from different planes of existence and other magical realms. They were interesting and knowledgeable. Judas learned much later on that a few of them had been arrested and taken to some secret schloss, never to be seen again. Himmler had developed an insatiable appetite for dark magic by now, and he was always hungry. Word travels fast amongst people that move in these sorts of circles, so warnings went out; all that heard them acted on them quickly and disappeared, taking their light and their brilliance with them as they fled to safer shores.

There were a few, however, that liked what they were seeing, and decided to remain. They stayed in Germany and pitched their banner alongside the red and the black. There were lots of other things that he had remembered from this terrible time, but everything was cloudy, juddering in and out of synch like a film being forwarded and then reversed at 30 frames per-second, leap after leap, chunking back and forth before pausing. He knew that she was beautiful, dangerous and mysterious, and for some strange reason he thought she may have something to do with the angel slaying case he was working on today, but he wasn't sure of that either. The only thing that he could remember clearly was a shower of silver paperclips that fell like sharp rain and bounced up off the stone streets in slow motion. Then there was a storm of paper with scientific drawings scrawled all over the pages that blew in from the east. There had also been some space rockets, angry red missiles, green fires, magical symbols and something else in there – it might have been crashing waves and black cliffs – but it wasn't clear. It would come to him though, eventually. Best not to chase it. Let it arrive in its own good time. He rubbed absently at his silver coin and tried to make sense of what he was feeling.

His mind was a mess today and he couldn't keep anything straight. His memory was acting like one of those plastic bags that gets trapped in a circular breeze, spinning around and around, never able to fly away, or crash to earth with a muffled rustle. He was troubled. Something wasn't right. Something bad was coming – he could feel it.

7 BLACK GLASS IN A BLACK SKY

When Judas was troubled, his scar ached. He reached inside his shirt and traced the puckered ridge of scar tissue that ran all the way up his stomach with his thumb, from the third belt loop at his waist to its grisly terminus just below the knot of his tie. He shivered. And well he might, because this was his beginning. He remembered that night, the night of the great betrayal, and as usual it made him feel sick. His knees went weak, and acid raced up into his mouth. A quick kiss on the cheek and the damage had been done. The one man that could have saved them all gone, all for a few measly little silver coins and his own worthless freedom. Why hadn't God just let him die that night? Why hadn't HE just let Judas swing from the branch of his suicide tree, and let the crows pick him clean? There was an easy answer, of course.

God didn't want anyone taking the easy way out. God had other plans. Judas got his thirty pieces of silver and his moment in the limelight, with a pat on the back from the Brotherhood of Barabbas and their Roman muscle. Then came the crushing waves of guilt, the black fits of despair and the sickness of mind and body. It was then that he realised that the only way out was the easy route – suicide.

He ran away to hide in the olive groves, crying until his eyes turned the colour of spilt wine in the dirt. Then, during a quiet moment in the emotional storm in which he was cast adrift, he chose a time, and he chose a tree. He stole some rope. He tied the strongest knot he could muster and threw the pulling end over a stout branch. He was so frightened that night that he couldn't open his eyes. His muscles rebelled and froze solid, refusing to do the deed, but the pain spoke loudest, making him brave for a moment. Judas had tied the loose end of the rope to a nearby rock. He remembered testing it by swinging on it a few times. It held fast. So, he put the noose that he had made with his own hands over his cursed head, and he hung himself.

But he didn't die. He hadn't been allowed to.

It was then that God appeared, and things got really, really uncomfortable.

He remembered that moment clearly. It was impossible not to. The crash of the lightning that cleaved the sky into a million pieces of black glass. The rain pelting down onto his upturned face through sparse branches overhead. The black olives falling with a pitter-patter all around him, and the burning of the rope around his neck.

Then Judas saw HIM. At first, HE appeared as a dark silhouette, backlit against the flash of the white bolts of his lightning anger. When the light died, there he was, huge and monstrous in the blackness of a broken sky. Wherever his giant form stepped, shards of light crackled all around him like electric snow. Every single bird, insect and animal held its breath, as if not daring to breathe in the presence of their maker. Then Judas heard a noise. It wasn't a word, or any sort of language that he had heard before. The rope around his neck snapped, and he fell to the ground. The earth he fell onto felt like warm ice, and the mud and decaying leaves he was laying in crackled and oozed at his touch. He felt his dead body lifting from the orchard floor, and energy flooded back into him. His broken neck was straightened with a touch, and the gaping hole in his torso where his stomach had burst was sealed with another.

He heard strange words that seemed to come from everywhere. They boomed and smashed into him, filling him up and burning him from the inside out. Then – silence. He was alone in the olive grove again. He was standing under the tree that he'd hung himself from only moments before. The rope lay on the ground next to him. Snapped and singed like a careless snake in a forest fire. He felt a gentle pull on his mind and body from far away, and he started to walk. He put one foot in front of the other; further and further away they took him, the force of the pull irresistible. He left the olive grove far behind in no time at all. Each step was a giant one, and each carried him many leagues at a time.

The sun came up and went down again and again, and he found himself near the sea. He heard the crashing of the waves onto the golden sand of the beaches long before he saw them. He realised that his senses had become more acute. He could see long distances and over mountains, and he could hear everything more clearly now. Even the termites and the birds were too noisy at first. Judas walked along that coast for days, hiding in the dunes from the Romans, sleeping in ditches and bushes with only the scorpions for company, until finally he found an abandoned boat that would take him across the sea and far away.

Two nights later the boat docked at a small fishing village. Judas felt the now familiar pull to leave it and start walking again. Along the way he found that he only had to ask for water, or bread, and someone would give it to him for nothing. He tried to offer something in return, but they would not take it.

Here, have it, it is our pleasure, these people would say.

Complete strangers and fellow travellers alike could not stop themselves from doing all they could to help him. They fell over each other to be of assistance and would take no payment for it.

Oh no, sir, please, let us help you, they insisted.

They gave whatever they had, gladly and willingly. He had only to ask for passage on a baggage train or a camel, and a place would be found for him. Often paying guests or passengers would be asked to leave the caravan to make space for him. He found that his voice could open any door, and he could charm or persuade anyone to do anything he wanted.

Soon, he stopped being surprised by what was happening to him. He stopped wondering why people did whatever he asked. He realised quickly that he was being manipulated, directed; there was a job he needed to fulfil, a purpose for him as yet undefined, but he felt that the day was fast approaching when he would find out why he had been saved and to what end. If he'd known just how fast it would come, he would have hidden himself away and eaten the key.

Everything was going well. Life was good – until he reached Joppa. It was the biggest town that he had been to so far. He was healthy, he had been fed and watered and carried most of the way, he had money in his pocket, a fine beard, and even finer clothes. He had been drinking heavily all day and was urinating against the wall of a house in one of the darker backstreets when he was taken for a traveller by a gang of street robbers and given a beating that should have killed him. It didn't. The thieves tried punching, kicking, stamping and then moved on to slashing and gouging – but nothing worked. No blow could bring Judas down and no weapon could pierce his skin. The thieves became so exhausted they gave up and fled.

'He should be dead, it isn't natural!' the ringleader shouted as the group ran for their lives.

Judas got back to his feet, dusted himself off, chased them down and knocked them all to the ground. He could sense their fear and see it in their eyes. All the guilt and all the shame he felt exploded in a tidal wave of prolonged, vicious anger. He turned on his assailants and beat them to death. He smashed their heads to pieces and ripped their ears off. Afterwards he calmly took their purses and rolled their bodies into the nearest ditch for the rats.

In that very moment he realised that he was immortal, and it made him feel very, very different. He went looking for trouble in all the right places. He was speared, stabbed, burnt and strangled, but nothing marked him or caused him any pain. He was invulnerable to everything, and that included the passing of time.

He started to forget the great betrayal and enjoy this new life. The black moods and the heavy sickness of guilt disappeared. He stopped hiding and wandering, using the money he robbed from the crooked merchants, the thieves and the money-grabbing bureaucrats, to pay for mistresses and a suite of rooms where he held parties. Lots of parties. They got wilder and wilder, and the guests got more and more unusual. Bad attracts bad, and soon there were all the worst kind in his home. Charlatans, backstreet chemists who brewed poisons, dancers who stole secrets to sell, assassins that could teach you one-hundred ways to kill, and mages that purported to be able to summon demons and evil spirits.

Judas welcomed them all, learning new skills and attaining knowledge that could not be found in any library.

The drink flowed, the drugs were imbibed, and the nights merged into one big black heaving mass of perversion. He was searching for something. He was looking for a way out. But the door was still firmly closed to him, and it was moving even farther away. He had no idea when it would open or if it would open. So, he just lived. Badly.

8 A CAPTAIN OF THE HOST

One night, one-hundred years after Judas had left the orchard, a man appeared at one of his legendary soirées and introduced himself. Judas knew straight away that this man was different. He felt different. He moved unlike any normal man, almost gliding. It was hard to believe he had legs under his robes, in fact. He had something that Judas wanted badly. He had dangerous knowledge. He'd been to far-off lands and had experienced things that few others had. Judas liked him immediately and welcomed him to his home. Judas wasn't naturally so open, yet he felt compelled to befriend this man. It was as if they were both magnetised, and inevitably they connected.

Judas enjoyed the man's company immensely, and it was only a short time before Judas discovered he was not actually a man at all. He wasn't even human. He was something else entirely. This entity was one of the lower demons – the first, but by no means the last that Judas would meet. These dark beings seemed to be drawn to him like moths to the flickering flames of a torch in the night. Demons are intrigued by anything that God has touched or marked. Such blessed things or people are a curiosity to them; something to spy on, inform on, stare at. Judas realised that these entities saw him as a rare sort of animal in a human zoo, a magical creature in a cage. Later, he found that he had become big news in the demon world.

Could he be used, abused or tormented? Many of the others wondered if he could grant them a favour or tell them dark secrets. So, they sent envoys to ask and solicit for an audience. But the answer was always a resounding no – to all of them. Judas couldn't help himself, let alone anyone else.

The following decade passed in the blink of an eye, and everyone and everything changed. Everyone and everything, that is, except him. The dark partners of his first life drifted away. Judas had learned all he could from them, whilst they had failed to break down his defences or discover his true purpose. His many lovers despised his eternal youth; they grew old, bitter and resentful. One after another they left, informing on him to the nearest holy men before they went. They spat out their venom and hatred on the floors of as many temples as they could buy their way into. They told their truths about Judas and his ways, careful not to incriminate themselves, of course. But the holy men couldn't, and wouldn't, believe what they were hearing. It was all too fantastic. They were the powerful men in this town, they would know of any dark dealings, and they would deal with anything sinister swiftly, if it appeared. Secretly, they accepted huge sums of gold from Judas for their silence.

From then on Judas decided to stop taking new lovers. He liked the peace and the quiet that came with their absence. He couldn't take any more of the silly moods, the pathetic fights, or the constant questioning. Why didn't he get any older? Why couldn't he share his secret? Or was it that he wouldn't share his secrets with them? He chose to be alone for a century or two, and all went well. He was master of his own destiny. His wealth grew and grew. Instead of finding excitement in the darkness, he found light within the light. He abandoned the drinking dens and the late nights in low places. Instead, he invited scholars from all over the east to visit him. His great wealth paid for an education that was second to none. His new friends patiently instructed him in the new magic of physics, languages, science, the stars, engineering and more.

Judas built a library, and soon it was filled to the rafters with books, charts, poetry, spells and secrets. He spent all his time there, taking his meals and sleeping under a ceiling painted to look like the heavens. For the first time in years there was a light, a small pinprick at the end of the long dark tunnel that was his life.

He came to know each manuscript well and the library started to feel smaller and smaller. Judas had consumed every last scrap of knowledge that it possessed. His mind was full of questions that the books and pages that surrounded him could not answer. Then, one night, a messenger arrived. It was the Archangel Michael. He arrived in the dead of night. He could go anywhere he wanted and not be seen, of course. He had just decided that night was the best time to make an entrance.

Judas did not hear him arrive and woke to find him sitting on the end of his bed. The angel was immense. His giant wings were impossibly white in the moonlight. They seemed to catch the light, absorb it, and fold it into their fibres. He was beautiful, of course, and wore a great silver blade in a black leather scabbard at his waist, embellished with magical symbols. The angel was silent at first. He sat and observed Judas for what seemed like ages. His gaze was frightening. He rarely blinked; it was as if he could see inside Judas' mind and read his thoughts.

Like a giant bird, his head tilted from one side to the other as he examined Judas. A wry smile was followed by a quizzical scrunch of the eyebrows. There was a conversation happening between the archangel and someone else that Judas was not privy to. Then the angel nodded and sniffed the air. His mind was calculating and calibrating. Then he spoke.

'Do you know me, mortal?'

Judas sat up in bed, puffed up his pillow, and shook his head.

Michael began to explain why he was there. His voice hit Judas like a lightning bolt wearing boxing gloves; he felt pressure all over his body, pushing at him from all directions at once.

'I am the Archangel known as Michael. Some call me the Captain of the Host; others just call me the Lord's vengeance. It is my great honour to be Heaven's sword and shield; mostly its sword, I'm afraid. It is also my honour to keep watch over all angels. Some of them need more attention than others – but that is another story. If you live long enough, I shall tell you of them. I was chosen for this task because it is of the utmost importance to the city of Heaven. It is a heavy burden for me. You should know that I am incredibly powerful. More powerful than any entity you have met so far. I do not have the capacity for pity. You shall know that in time, too. I cannot help that; I was created this way. I have spent many of your mortal years looking into your affairs, and I have not liked what I have seen.

'But there is still time for you to change, Judas. I'm not sure what manner of creature you are, or why Heaven keeps you alive. And that makes me suspicious. It also means that I must spend more time with you, down here, among men, and that does not fill me with cheer. So, listen carefully to what I have to say, and for your own good, do as I say when I say it. Listen well, because this is your task, Judas. From now on, you are a servant once more. Your life is His, and mine, to some extent, and today is the first day of your long, long journey back to grace.'

Michael then stood up, and Judas saw that a great light shone from inside him. It was painful to look at him, yet it was impossible to look away. Michael reached down and placed one enormous, perfectly formed hand on the top of Judas' head, and he delivered his message. Thoughts flowed down through his body, along his great arms and into Judas' mind. Words and plans were planted like seeds, way down deep inside his consciousness. There they would wait to be watered, waiting to come to life at some other time, yet to be disclosed.

Moments passed that felt like hours, then Michael removed his hand. Judas fell over and immediately vomited. The evening's vast dinner and the copious amounts of wine he'd consumed splashed across the cool stone floor, spattering onto the rugs and the pillows. His ears bled, and his eyes watered. Once the nausea passed, Judas sat up on the bed and covered himself with a sheet. He hadn't realised that he was naked, and Michael hadn't mentioned it either. Judas wiped his mouth and drank water from a clay urn beside the bed with a thirst like a camel emerging from the desert. He almost vomited again when he saw the mess he had made.

'And what if I just decide to do nothing, angel? What if I just keep living the way I want to? I'm invulnerable and immortal, so why should I do as you say? This long, long journey you speak of, and these hard tasks, sounds like something that should be handed over to someone else, someone that actually gives a damn! Take a look at me! I'm not a good person. You know what I did back there. I can be bought for a purse of silver. Find someone else. Find someone worthy. The streets are full of them.'

Michael smiled a truly terrifying smile. He removed his belt and scabbard, placing it carefully on the dining table. It was so big that the pommel hung over one end of the table and the killing point over the other. He had to make sure that Judas understood the gravity of his situation. So, he dragged him from his bed by the hair and beat him unconscious.

Judas felt physical pain for the first time in over a hundred years, and he did not like it. He was still immortal, and no matter how many blows were rained down on him he still lived. But he found out that night that this angel packed a punch the size of a small planet and could really, really hurt him if it chose to.

After Judas had prised himself off the floor and stopped vomiting, he sat on the bed and listened to Michael – with both ears. If he'd had more than two he would have listened with them as well.

'Judas, you have been cursed, or blessed – depending on which way you choose to look at the situation – with immortality and other gifts. Your mission is simple. You are to use this gift to right wrongs, wherever you encounter them. It is a simple and straightforward task, Judas. On one side there is the good, and on the other, the bad. Use your judgement, learn how to tell the difference. Punish severely, only when the crime is severe. You do not need to lay waste to an entire region if you catch someone stealing a loaf of bread. I will be by your side in battle should you need me, Judas, and I will also watch over you. Go where the evil is greatest. Root it out. Make this place a better one.'

He picked up his sword from the table, fastened it to the great leather belt he wore around his waist, then flexed his beautiful wings. He said no more. There was nothing more to say. Judas just nodded and watched as the Archangel Michael, Heaven's biggest bruiser and most lethal enforcer, jumped through the open window and up into the stars.

9 THE BLACK MUSEUM

Judas would never forget the events of that night. It was the beginning.

But that beginning was an awfully long time ago and Judas wondered just how much longer he'd have to fight the good fight for. It had been so long now that Judas wondered if he'd just been forgotten. It was highly unlikely. God didn't forget, and you had to work damned hard before he forgave. Judas had struggled with the idea of being forgiven, because his crime was so heinous. And what was forgiveness, really? It was stuff that was peddled from the pulpits on Sunday mornings by snake oil salesmen and quacks. Then again, he needed to hope for something. He had betrayed God's only son, and then the rabble had carried him up to the top of the hill and crucified the poor chap, placing a crown of thorns on his head and stabbing him with a big spear. But forgiveness for that? Judas just shook his head and tried to think nice thoughts.

While he was doing this, the phone on the table in the office started to ring. It had one of those annoying ringtones that made you want to throw something really hard and watch it shatter into a million pieces. Peace and tranquillity won the day, though, and Judas decided to just ignore it instead.

He was back at home sweet home – Scotland Yard, also known as the Yard or just HQ. It was 2020, it was lunchtime and his stomach needed feeding, but he had something that he had to do before he could savour the delights of the canteen.

Judas stood up and checked his appearance in the mirror. Still no grey hair, no lines around the eyes and no yellowing of the teeth. Well over one-thousand years old and not a scratch on him. Well, hardly a scratch. He gave his hair a quick run through with a comb; it was still thick and glossy, and he wouldn't have looked out of place on a poster on the window of Tommy Guns or another one of Soho's cool hair-chopping parlours. He straightened his tie and left the quiet of his office on the 7th floor, heading down the corridor towards the door of his real office – the Black Museum.

The Black Museum, or the Funny Floor as it was better known to the rest of Scotland Yard, was the Metropolitan Police Force's best kept secret.

His scar twitched again. It always did when he had to go into the Museum to speak to one of his sources. He had hated talking to them in the beginning, but now he didn't mind it at all. The Black Museum was a malice magnet. All of London's bad energy and evil was pulled there and stayed there for ever. The Black Museum was a sponge, but it was also a very unique sort of prison.

This morning, Judas had to speak with Jack the Ripper regarding a string of nasty murders with an occult twist that were happening in present day Whitechapel. If you needed to know the time, you asked a policeman. If you needed to know who was responsible for a series of grisly attacks, you asked the blackest murderer who ever lived. Judas arrived at the door, removed his wallet from his trouser pocket and swiped a black credit card sized key over the flashing keypad to door number 24. The door gave a spiteful little click before it opened, almost begrudgingly; he stepped across the physical boundary, and into the Black Museum.

'Anybody home?' he said to the empty room.

What he heard in reply was the sound of thousands of evil whispers, and the scratching of dead nails on history's blackboard.

The Black Museum had started life as The Central Prisoners Property Store on the 29th of April 1874; it was located at No.1 Scotland Yard, just off Whitehall. Five years earlier, the passing of the Prisoners Property Act had enabled the Police to start collecting evidence to display for teaching purposes. The first exhibits were the grisly weapons and death masks of the murderers who were hanged at Tyburn. The blacker side of human nature being as it was, meant that the storeroom was filled from floor to ceiling before the first year was out. Soon enough, the Chief of Police decided to put the storeroom to better use. And thus, he created the Black Museum of Scotland Yard.

The then Chief hoped that by showcasing the evidence collected for some of the most heinous and dastardly crimes ever committed, detectives could learn from the criminals and new members of the force would see that, however foul and terrifying the act, justice and light would always prevail.

For a while he succeeded, and the Museum was busy. But, as time duly marched on, hand in hand with science, the Museum was forgotten, and eventually closed. People could find all they needed to know about crime in paper files and metal cabinets, and interest in the world's darkest Museum died.

But the collection started to live a life of its own.

You can't put that much evil in one place without something unpleasant happening. Strange rumours started to fly around the Yard, and soon the Museum was moved. And then moved again. Wherever it was housed, things were seen – unexplainable things. Late at night, in the shadows and the dark, cold things moved and murmured. People started to feel the evil seeping through the walls, peering out at them from the dark recesses of the corridors and cupboards. It wasn't long before a night in the cells at the Yard became a genuine deterrent for even the hardest criminal. The Chief of Police didn't need to be a detective to work out a possible hypothesis for the strange occurrences. He locked the Museum up and threw away the key.

Years passed, and the Chief of Police passed away with them. No one bothered with the Black Museum again. The cleaners were happy to neglect it too, and office furniture was stacked up against the door to hide it.

Almost one-hundred years to the day after its creation, the Black Museum received a visitor. A young police officer had asked permission to see it. He visited it each day for six months. It was rumoured that he was making an inventory prior to yet another change of address. That was as far from the truth as was humanly possible.

P.C. Neame was the great-grandson of one of the Black Museum's first custodians, Inspector Jared Neame. He was also rumoured to be an occultist, and a Freemason. He was a quiet man, a solitary man; someone not to cross. But a couple of the station bullies had decided that he needed bringing down to earth. Neame listened carefully to their jibes and threats, then threw them both inside the smallest cupboard he could find in the Museum. Strangely, neither man was missed for three days. They emerged, white-faced and urine-soaked, and both immediately applied for a transfer. One went to the Orkney Islands, while the other decided that manning the Land's End police box was a definite career progression for him.

P.C. Neame was never bothered again, and he rose through the ranks quickly. One day he was a lowly P.C. and the next he was an Inspector. He held special meetings with high-level cabinet ministers in Downing Street and was said to be on first name terms with the Prime Minister. It did not surprise the officers at the Yard, then, when the Black Museum and the floor it was housed on were reopened, restricted to all but a select few. No one went to the 7th floor. No one stopped the lift there. The 7th floor was just the 7th floor. Best left alone.

Inspector Neame started to recruit. He was looking for constables that were special, open-minded, and intelligent. He didn't care where they came from, just that they were brave and loyal.

That's how the first Black Museum Policemen came into being. There were very few of them, and those that joined stayed for life. It was often a short life.

Then in 1985 Neame recruited a detective from an obscure division that no one had ever heard of. The new man arrived, settled into his lodgings and started to work. He was seen often at regular functions or wandering through the corridors of the station houses. He was tall, dark haired and not much of a talker. On the odd occasion where formal uniform was required, he would attend in the uniform of a London Constable, wearing the letter J and the number 30 made from silver on his shoulder epaulettes.

Judas Iscariot had joined the Met.

Do good for God and fight evil wherever you find it, had been Michael's message. So that's just what Judas had done. His long journey from the Holy Land had taken him to many places, and now it had brought him to London.

Shortly after Judas joined the Black Museum department, Inspector Neame was promoted once again. This time he didn't just move upstairs, he disappeared entirely. It was as if he had grown wings and flown away. Which wasn't far from the truth. Neame vanished, and Judas took his place. He was now in charge of a small, special and very secret police force. Ideally placed to fight evil and make a difference.

Judas took his place at the head of the newly formed Black Museum Force. It was a natural fit. He inherited the few detectives that worked there already and began to work through the heavy caseload left by his predecessor. These cases were the ones that the normal Police did not, and could not, investigate. He had made lots of friends and enemies since he'd arrived in London. There were gangs of ghouls in West Ham that held some ancient grudge against the police, sprites in Dulwich and magical beasts in the sewers under Camden... the list went on and on. It seemed that as soon as one case had been solved, another would become a priority for investigation.

London was a big place and it never got boring, unfortunately.

Judas used his curse well. Soon it became known in the underworld, underneath the London Underground, that there was something more frightening in town than any monster. Now, there was a monster killer.

And this monster killer was on a clean-up mission.

Judas liked the work. He liked the investigating, the chasing and the fighting, and he didn't really mind the paperwork either. What played upon his mind, though, was the eternal question: how long must he do this for? How many lives did he have to save before he was permitted to stop, and what would he get as a reward for all of the hard work?

Alone at night, he asked the darkness that question many times, but was never answered.

Once inside, he looked around the Black Museum. It took a couple of minutes for his eyes to become accustomed to the gloom. There was no natural light inside because the exhibits didn't like it. They grumbled and whispered if even a small desk lamp was lit.

He took a seat at the large leather-topped writing desk in the centre of the room. On it was a telephone, an antique black model, with a flex and a numbered dial. Beside it were small 'in' and 'out' letter trays. The drawers were empty and had been nailed shut. There were scratches around the key holes on each drawer, giving the impression that something valuable was inside. Or perhaps the keyholder just had terrible eyesight.

'Can I come into the Key Room please?' Judas asked.

The silence was shattered by the sound of giant wings beating, and something heavy landing nearby.

'I have to come in to speak with one of the sources,' he said, more softly this time.

Silence filled the room again.

'Please may I come into the Key Room?'

Judas was getting bored with playing games now, and his voice was beginning to reflect that.

He sat as still as he could and waited. He could feel the Custodian moving all around him. There was something angry in the way it moved and talked, a restrained ferocity, malice that was cold and heavy. It liked quiet, and it didn't like to be disturbed. Judas sat there and wondered just how powerful it was; it did keep all the evil locked up tight within the Black Museum boundaries after all, and some of the inmates locked up inside were very dangerous indeed. When things were quiet, Judas intended to map the Black Museum, plotting its pathways, its secret rooms, and doorways that opened out on to who knew where. It would be quite an adventure. He'd been to many places in London's past already, but the Black Museum was vast, and new places were added every day.

'Pretty please?' Judas asked as nicely as he could.

There was a ripple in the air, and the door behind him opened with a loud click.

'Thank you,' said Judas, and he walked over to the door. But just before he could reach for the handle, Detective Sergeant Williams came in.

He looked his usual good-natured self. He was tall and broad-shouldered, and with the arrival of middle age, he was also getting broader around the middle. He was wearing his familiar one-size-too-small brown jacket, and the happy-go-lucky grin that he wore everywhere.

'Judas,' he said, with a slight nod of the head.

'Say hello to Williams please, Custodian; be nice now.'

Somewhere, far off inside the Black Museum, something heavy fell, with a loud bang.

'A bit more touchy than usual today, Custodian?'

Williams had a soft, sarcastic tone that he used to full effect when interrogating suspects. Unfortunately, it didn't work on the Custodian of the Black Museum.

Williams was Judas' partner and his day-to-day human contact with the Met. He was on the official payroll, whereas Judas received his pay in other ways, and from other sources.

'Jack?' said Williams.

'Jack,' said Judas.

He opened the door to the Key Room and Williams followed him inside. They walked past more rows of glass cabinets. Each of them was full of faded black and white photographs of mutilated bodies, and grim-faced police officers.

Judas and Williams walked towards a large green door at the far end of the room.

'We talk to Jack and to Jack only, okay?'

'How about you talk to Jack, and I stand directly behind you?'

'Coward,' said Judas.

'You're so right,' said Williams.

The room shuddered again as the next door opened.

In the centre of this room was a table. On it sat a collection of random objects. There was a shoe, a curtain hook, a piece of felt from the rim of a hat, a crumpled betting slip, a nightmare in a jar, a vicious lie and a pool of child's blood, amongst other things. Judas approached the table and picked up a white gentleman's opera glove.

He held it tightly. 'Don't let him rile you, Williams.'

There was a loud cracking sound, followed by a rush of air that smelt of the sea, coal dust and horse sweat. It smelt of a London from a long time ago. Judas and Williams could hear snatches of conversation, and the rhythmic thump of a hammer on wood. A ship's horn sounded, and waves rippled and clapped against a tar-coated jetty down on the Thames. The year was 1888.

'What do you want?'

The voice that lifted up through the smells and sounds of the city was sharp and clipped. It felt cold, and Judas gripped the glove tighter in his hand.

'Hello, Jack.'

'We're not going to get very far if you use that name, Judas.'

'I'll use whichever name I feel like, Mr Ripper. I can let the Custodian deal with you if you like, you know how cruel and spiteful it can be. It could pack you and your story up, and hide you away somewhere dark, somewhere quiet, away from the other inmates. You'd be all alone and lonely. Would that work for you, Jack?'

"Jack it is then, Prince of Betrayers. What is it that you want?"

'Angels are being murdered. At least one a month. Know anything about it? Heard anything about it from any of your lovely friends?'

'A killer of angels. A serial killer of angels. How lovely; how very modern. What does he do to them? Don't spare the details my friend, it will help me to help you. Leave no detail out now.'

Jack's voice was a vomit of treacle.

Judas looked at Williams. They both knew what Jack the Ripper wanted. He fed off the grisliest of details; it energised him and satisfied his lust for blood and gore.

'I'll be back in twenty-four hours, Jack. Have something for me or I let the Custodian have you for twenty-four hours.'

'Just give me a little taste please, Judas? A mere morsel, a little hint of madness and white skin sliced in the night? Go on, it gets so boring here. Just a little something to give one a glow?'

Judas and Williams could hear the wanton lust in Jack's voice. It nauseated them both. There was a soft clinking noise in the background. Judas guessed instantly that Jack was playing with his knives. In the distance he could hear the sound of oil lamps fizzing into brightness as the lamplighters ascended their ladders to give London some much-needed illumination. Sash windows closed with a muffled bump, and copper hoops slid along curtain poles in parlours as the night was once again barred from the homes of the Whitechapel fearful.

London must have been a truly amazing place back then, thought Judas.

It was a shame that an animal like Jack the Ripper, and many others, had turned it into their own bloody stage, and fodder for the pages of the next Penny Dreadful.

Judas replaced the glove on the table. The sounds of the great city and its magnificent river softened, then disappeared entirely.

'Why is Jack's key a glove, Judas?'

'I'll tell you another time, Williams. Let's leave that monumental piece of work to do some detective work on our behalf, while we go speak to some people that know an awful lot more about angels than we do.'

They walked out of the Key Room, carefully shutting the door behind them.

10 THE SAINTS ☻F CLAPHAM

They left the Museum and the 7th floor, taking the private stairwell down to the car park behind the Yard. Judas pointed at the driver's side of their car. Williams opened the door and jumped in. He was revving the engine before Judas had a chance to open the passenger door. The gates to the yard opened automatically and Williams put his foot down. The bottom of the number plate scraped loudly on the concrete ramp that led up to the gates, earning him one of those 'what a dick' looks from two young CID officers who were just clocking off.

Moments later, they were through the gates and heading south. Judas checked the rear-view mirror, just to make sure the number plate wasn't skidding across the road behind them.

'Vauxhall or Battersea?' asked Judas.

Williams was driving badly, as usual. Judas gripped the edge of his seat and wondered how Williams had passed his advanced drivers' course in the first place. He had a tendency to judge the position of the car on the road by how well the driver's side front wheel covered the white lines in the middle of the road. It made oncoming traffic nervous and passengers fear for their lives.

'Battersea I think. I do like to see something green every day if possible.'

Judas looked across at his partner. If he kept driving like this, they'd be lucky to see tomorrow.

Williams turned left onto the bridge. They drove over the brown waters of the Thames and into South London. Joggers and professional dog walkers jockeyed for position on the pavements either side. Judas wondered how much money the average dog walker made. As far as he was concerned, no amount of money was enough compensation for picking up that much crap. Williams drove on, continuing to cause heart-attacks at every turn.

The Black Museum division of the Met had a fleet of dark blue Ford Mondeos. They had the regulation race-tuned engines and rock-hard suspension, and each carried a small arsenal of weapons in the steel-plated boot. The car that Judas and Williams were driving also had the regulation six-inch carpet of discarded coffee cups, sweet wrappers, and seven-day-old sausage roll flakes on the floor. CID and the other departments had their fleet of cars cleaned regularly. But standing orders stipulated that any car with a registration beginning with BM was left alone, not to be touched on any account; they were pretty much exempt from any parking restrictions, too. There weren't many perks of being a Black Museum copper, but this was one of the better ones. It didn't go down well with a lot of people, but if they knew the nature of crime the Black Museum was fighting, they wouldn't be so quick to grumble.

'Judas?' The heavy machinery of Williams' mind had been working hard over the weekend, it seemed.

'Yes?'

'Why are Jack the Ripper and the rest of them stuck in the Museum? Why can't they escape? I mean, what holds them there, they're just memories now aren't they? And how does the Custodian keep them all confined to their own little slices of time?'

Judas nearly ripped the edge of the passenger seat clean off as a large white Audi took evasive action ahead. Williams calmly dropped the steering wheel down a centimetre and coasted through the gap the other car had left. The sound of horns blaring and expensive tyres depositing their tread on the tarmac faded into the background behind them.

Judas checked the rear-view mirror. No damage, and thankfully no casualties.

'I'm not sure I can give you all the answers to your questions regarding the Custodian of the Black Museum, to be honest. But I know that it's incredibly powerful; it would have to be to keep evil characters like Jack locked down tightly. You saw how Jack reacted when I told him that I would let the Custodian have him for twenty-four hours didn't you?

'The Custodian seems to be able to move through time, too, and it only lets people inside the Black Museum that it wants to let in. It's certainly old, and it has a nasty temper. It hasn't changed in all the years I've been here, either. And before you ask how long that is, it's a long time. It's funny though, because I got a similar feeling when I met something else many years ago. It has the same sort of signature, if you like.'

Williams stopped at a red light by Stockwell tube station. Cycle couriers and commuters on Boris bikes weaved through the traffic, jockeying for position on the grid painted on the road in front of the cars and buses, like F1 cars waiting to roar off on the green light.

'I think the Custodian has been given a job to do, Williams, a job that it doesn't like very much. It could be some kind of punishment, or possibly a test of some sort. If it's a punishment then it must have done something truly epic, and if it's a test, then the end reward has to be something really worth having.'

Williams was checking his mirrors and glaring at a painfully thin yet dangerously fit-looking cyclist who was nonchalantly leaning on the bonnet of their Mondeo so that he didn't have to remove his Italian racing shoes from his Japanese pedals.

Williams waited before the last rank of cyclists had stuttered away and the road ahead was clear before gunning the Mondeo in the direction of Clapham Common.

'Where are we headed?'

'St Paul's please, Williams.'

Williams weaved through the traffic. Road works had slowed everyone on four wheels down; those on two wheels were doing slightly better, it seemed.

'When we get there, can you hang back a bit and let me have a chat with them first? The Saints are a good bunch, but a little shy.'

Williams laughed out loud, and nearly ran over a cyclist on a Brompton.

'The Saints aren't shy! Look at the way they dress.'

'You might sneer at the way they dress, Williams, but they're a very old group. They settled here when Clapham was just a small Surrey village. They did a lot of campaigning against "blood sports" and fought slavery whenever and wherever they encountered it. They look timid and quiet, but they can handle themselves. Nothing gets by them down here either. Their enemies call them the Saints because they've always fought against anything evil, and the name stuck. Their old enemies are no longer with us. So you get an idea of what type of people they are."

Williams pulled up at the kerb outside the church. It looked like all churches do: calm, tranquil and serene.

'I'll be back in half an hour. If I'm not out by then, head back to the Museum and wait for me there.'

Judas gave the door a good slam. He knew it annoyed the hell out of Williams, and he was rewarded for this small act of defiance with a spiteful parp of the horn. They were small victories, but they all counted.

St Paul's church in Clapham was a solid-looking building; some might even have called it severe. It was hemmed in on three sides by similar looking buildings of red brick and defended from the road by stout black railings. Judas pushed the gate open and stepped into the grounds. The air shimmered for a second and blurred like a heat haze. Judas stopped, spread his arms out wide and turned slowly around, showing himself to the four corners of the churchyard.

He waited for a second and then turned around once again.

'I come to ask for the help of the Saints.'

Seconds later there was a sound like metal scraping on stone, and a man appeared from behind one of the gravestones. He looked about forty, was of average height, and wore a suit similar to Judas' own. He had grey, shoulder-length hair that reached down to his shirt collar, and his face was lined and weather-beaten. A vicious-looking scar ran diagonally across it.

'What can the Saints do for you today, Judas? We are bound to help you whenever we can, what do you need?'

The voice was deep and strong. Here was a man that you crossed at your peril.

'Good morning, Thornton my friend, how is your son Henry? That last scrape with the Wandle River gypsies was a fierce one.'

The man called Thornton walked across the grass towards Judas and stopped a few yards from him.

'We will not tolerate the baiting of dogs, bears or mythical creatures here, regardless of whatever ancient rites of passage the river folk think they have. We will do battle with them if they hold any of their fights on our land, and we will win, of course. Henry is well; I think he grows to like the combat more and more. It will pass, of course – in time. He was savaged by something the river people were hiding down by marshes, in one of those painted wagons they use for taking rides out to the country. He will walk with a limp for a while, but it should heal. The foul beast is destroyed, of course, as well as the three folk who fed and cared for it. There will no doubt be a blood feud – with these people there always is. Come, we can talk inside.'

Thornton walked back to the gravestone he had appeared from and casually vanished behind it. Judas followed. Old stones in graveyards are not just markers that tell the name of the interred; they are doors, if you know how to open them. Judas scraped the stone with a pound coin from his pocket and waited. The air blurred once again, and he momentarily lost sight of Thornton. The shimmer cleared quickly, though, and he began to make out the form of Thornton walking away from him down a long wooden-panelled hallway.

Judas followed, and the graveyard disappeared.

The sound of singing could be heard faintly from behind one of the doors as they passed. Occasionally, a door in the distance opened and then slammed quickly. They kept walking side by side and the hallway stretched on. Thornton stopped, plucked a key from his pocket, opened a door on the right and stepped inside. Judas followed. The room they entered was warm; a small table sat against one wall, and two large red leather chairs occupied its centre. A square mat lay on the floor between them like a colourful ravine that both chairs were condemned to stare into for all eternity. Thornton took one and offered the other to Judas.

'Tea, coffee, or something else?' Thornton waved his hand around in the air.

'Tea is fine, thank you.'

A pot of tea and two cups with saucers appeared on the table. Thornton poured.

'I've been having some trouble with the angels, Thornton. Someone or something has taken a dislike to them and is butchering them, I've had twenty-one disappearances in the last six months. Before that, we had the occasional accident when one would fly into a passenger plane's engine or take a wrong turn over a military no-fly zone and get taken out by a surface-to-air battery, but these disappearances and murders are different. First, the angels go missing. Then I presume they're beaten, badly, then their wings are chopped off and sent over to the Black Museum, marked for my attention. We spoke to the usual crowd and got nothing. And I can't get a lead on their identities because the body parts turn up in plastic bags.'

'The wings. Are they an offering, perhaps?'

Judas placed his teacup down and sat up. He was never comfortable down here, and Thornton had a habit of never quite saying exactly what he meant or knew.

'I don't think so.'

Thornton stirred his tea and shifted in his chair.

'The Fallen are not really angels anymore, Judas. They gave up that right long ago, you know that as well as I do. We tolerate them, and do our business with them, because they dream of going back, especially the ones in the north. One day they might – who knows?

'We have heard nothing of angel killers here, but I will try to find out what I can. But whilst you are here, there is something troubling us that you might be able to help us with.'

Judas wanted to take his notebook out but quickly realised that here probably wasn't the right place to do it.

'What kind of trouble, Thornton?'

'We're not altogether sure. Some of the others will go out this evening to find out more. We have felt something growing these last years, something sinister. The other dark things that live here in the south have started to get braver; they move about more freely and cross the ancient boundaries more than they once did. We caught a slaver heading across the Common carrying this.'

He reached into one of his pockets and produced a piece of dark, crumpled paper with a crude rendering of the number 10 on it.

'It's all the slaver had on its person, and it fought like the demon it is to stop us taking it. Once we'd prised the paper from its hands, it started moaning, trembling and clutching at itself, then it broke free and before we could catch it, it threw itself under a car. Died instantly. To fight so hard to keep a number on a piece of paper secret is a mystery to us, and to kill itself rather than return without it? It is strange.'

Thornton sipped at his tea. Judas knew there was more coming. Thornton looked troubled. A good policeman knew how to wait. Long silences were powerful conversation magnets.

'A few nights ago, we heard that there was a big slave market operating down by the Colliers Wood, so we sent a few of our people down there. There is a lot of new building going on and the secret Church Roads are disrupted. We have noticed a sign that has started to appear on the old staging posts, the tavern walls and the fighting pits: "The 10". We don't know who they are. We are heading to the Wood tonight. We have heard that the slavers are intending to hold an auction of both children and adults, but we will stop them.'

Judas finished his tea and set the cup down gently on the table. Thornton was one of those strong, silent types; he was sparing with his words, on the whole, and once he'd finished talking, he usually stared at the tips of his fingers, awaiting a reply. Today was no different. Judas straightened his tie and brushed a fleck of lint from his jacket.

'I know that you do not often need my help, Thornton, but do you think I could come with you tonight, strictly to observe? I won't get in the way. I need some help with this case, and I might get some answers at this market.'

Thornton rubbed his palms together, then began to trace the line of the scar on his face downwards with his fingertips.

'Of course. You may come and go as you please. I will take you back outside now. Tonight, we will travel by the Trinity, and come up by the Oasis.'

They walked back along the long corridor in silence, climbing the wooden stairs that led up to the graveyard and stepping out into the daylight. Thornton shook hands with Judas; there was the familiar scrape of metal on stone, and then he disappeared again.

Judas looked for the Mondeo, but it was gone. It was not a hardship. Far from it.

Judas smiled because he was going to be spared Williams' driving. He walked through the iron gate. Rain clouds were forming overhead, and umbrellas were beginning to bloom like black flowers.

Judas took one of the new buses back across the river. He missed the old vehicles, and the clippers who clung to the poles at the back to help you on, whether you needed it or not. But the new buses were at least a common sense nod to the past. London needed them and Judas was learning to love them. The trip back to the office should have provided the perfect time for him to get his thoughts in order, but instead, he daydreamed. He watched London passing by from ten feet in the air and before he knew it, he was back.

11 THE WINGED WATCHER

The Yard was incredibly busy, as usual. The rotating wedge was being used as a backdrop for yet another interview, and banks of cameramen and reporters were jostling for position in front of another harassed-looking Police Inspector. The crowd of reporters seemed to grow bigger and bigger by the day, while the size of their cameras got smaller and smaller. An interview used to be a three-man job, but now all that was needed was a phone and a pair of sharp elbows to get to the front. Judas ran up the steps and took the lift to the 7th floor. As he entered the office, Williams tried to look like he was ensconced in some of the files.

'How do you spell "lycanthropy", Judas?'

'Like it's written in my report, sergeant.'

Williams held up the report he was pretending to read and pointed at some of Judas' scrawl.

'That's not English, is it?'

'No, it's Aramaic. And that's the right way to spell lycanthropy in Aramaic.'

Judas sat down to eat a sandwich and had another cup of bad tea. Williams continued to try to look busy. It didn't feel like any time at all had passed before the light sensor in the office was triggered and the evening lights came on. Judas rubbed at his eyes. He'd been reading non-stop for hours. He stood up, stretched, placed his paper plate and half-eaten sandwich into the bin and took his overcoat from the stand.

'Do you need me tonight?' asked Williams.

'Not tonight. Why don't you get off early and spend some quality time with Jemma and the family?'

Williams smiled and raised his eyebrows. It was his favourite look.

'It's Jane, remember? You bought her a nice vase for Christmas. The one with the post-modern three kings following a satellite on it.'

'Sorry Williams, of course it's Jane. I'm taking a trip down the Church Roads tonight, so I won't be back until tomorrow morning at the earliest. The Saints are taking me to a slave market near the Colliers Woods.'

'Sounds like fun. Give my best to old man Thornton and his new model army.'

'You're a funny man, you know that Williams. When I see Thornton later, I'll be sure to tell him you like the way he dresses his crew.'

Williams just smiled. He picked up his copy of the Guardian from his untidy desk and left for the night with a spring in his step.

Judas watched him leave the building from the window above. It was getting dark, and he was soon rubbing shoulders with the army of commuters across the street. Judas was just about to get back to the files on his desk when he caught a slight movement in the shadows behind his partner. Was there something there? Instinct told him that there was. Was it just the flap of another coat? Williams crossed the street, and the shape detached itself from the wall and started to follow him. Judas was out of the office and running for the stairs before the office door hit the frame. He ran down the stairs avoiding the lifts – they would be full of the homeward bound at this time of night – across the street, on to the Broadway, and up to St James's Park underground station. It was rush-hour, and the fact that the streets were six-deep with commuters was hopefully going to save Williams' life.

His sergeant wasn't in very good shape, but he was handy in a fight. Most of the time. Williams' problem was that he was too trusting; anyone with a hard luck story could get close to him and then hurt him. Many times, in the past, Judas had needed to intervene to save his life, or stop him from making a major blunder. He was a nice man, a good soul, not much use in this line of work, unfortunately.

Judas ran hard. Ahead of him he could see Williams' familiar grey coat with its black collar tuned up against the cold. The pavement was crowded with commuters on their way to the underground station, so Judas stepped out into the road and straight into the path of an oncoming black cab.

There was a squeal of braking tyres, then the sudden impact of a Hackney Carriage driving at 30mph in a 20mph zone. It shuddered through him, starting in his right knee and passing all the way up his spine to the base of his neck. He heard a snap as another vertebrae gave way. Then he felt the tarmac trying to exfoliate his cheek to the bone. The black cab skidded to a halt and the driver leapt out. He was shaken and couldn't decide whether to call for an ambulance or shout to the passers-by that it wasn't his fault. He needn't have bothered, because the man he had just creamed at 30mph got up, and calmly ran off.

'Stay right there, you, I'm calling the Police!'

The cab driver fumbled for his phone, but the shock of the accident made him tremble and he dropped it in the road, where it was promptly destroyed by another black cab heading in the other direction. The thirty or so pedestrians who had witnessed the accident couldn't believe their eyes; nor could they believe their own stupidity afterwards, as none of them had had the good sense to film the crash and post it on their social media accounts. They had all missed an opportunity to earn hundreds of likes and 'shocked and stunned' emojis. They'd have to tell everybody what happened the old-fashioned way, using the spoken word in a real-life conversation, face to face. How terrible for them.

'I AM the Police!' shouted Judas, flashing him his warrant card as he ran past.

Judas looked back at the driver's surprised face, and the stunned crowd, and was relieved that there was not a mobile phone in sight. He ran on and barged through the crowds, using his elbows to good effect and earning a few reproachful looks from people who absolutely knew that the pavement was their own private kingdom. Once he was clear of the ugly knot of humanity that had gathered by the traffic lights, he could look up the road properly. Williams was nowhere in sight. Judas cursed his bad luck and set off again.

Thoughts were racing through his head. Williams was not lost – Judas was immensely strong and incredibly fast, and when he finally reached St James's Park tube station the crowds were already massing around the main entrance, like sheep heading for the dip. Judas smiled. Big crowds normally stopped nasty things happening.

The man that had been following Williams watched Judas run off up the street towards the tube station. He had not been seen, which was good, and quickly stepped back into the safety of the crowd.

Judas had just been hit really hard by that taxi, thought the man.

The impact should have killed him, or at the very least earned him a ride to the nearest hospital with some tubes sticking out of his throat. But he had just got up and run off. The man turned his collar up against the cold and headed south. He shook his head and imagined the conversation he would have to have later.

John would have to be told that the one he was after would be hard to kill, thought the man known as Simon the Zealot. He hurried away into the night, turning to look over his shoulder to make sure he wasn't being followed. He found a dark, quiet corner, took out his mobile phone and dialled the Shoals to report in.

St James's Park tube station was a brute of a building; grey, cold, squat and heavy. The doors that led to the barriers and then down to platforms were on the corner of the building, so naturally, crowds were often bottle-necked at the entrance. Judas exhaled a breath of relief when he saw Williams disappear inside. He hung back and watched the crowd shuffling along; if Williams was being followed, the pursuer would have to make their move now in order to stay close to him, or risk losing their quarry below.

It's practically impossible to do anyone any harm in a tube station these days, on account of all the cameras. He watched and waited, but nothing happened. No shadowy figure, no sinister presence – whoever had followed him from the Yard was long gone now.

Judas turned and began to head back to the station. He had only gone a couple of paces when one of the statues high up on the walls of the tube station moved. Judas tried not to react. He didn't want whatever it was up there to run for it, so he casually walked on and stepped into the nearest darkened doorway to hide. He counted to twenty, then looked back towards the station. There, on the wall, about thirty feet above the pavement, was a stone statue of a man holding an infant. In the recess behind it was a black shape. Was this the shape that had followed Williams from the station? Williams had gone, and it had not followed him, so what was it doing?

Only one way to find out.

He calmly left the cover of the doorway and walked back to the station. He tried to look like any other commuter – hunched over, brow-beaten, worn out by timesheets and profit margins. He was getting closer to the shadow, but it hadn't moved. The crowd thinned and he walked faster; he could definitely get up there quickly enough to get his hands on whatever it was, as long as he could get just a little closer. He was almost directly underneath it when the dark shape casually leapt up onto the roof and disappeared. Judas jumped up, caught the ledge and levered himself up. The shadow stopped to look down on him from the roof edge. Judas breezed up the fire ladder, hand over hand, at an explosive rate. When he reached the top of the ladder he vaulted over the edge of the roof and landed on the gravel. He stood up, took a step back and instinctively clenched his fists, making ready to fight. The shadow he was chasing had stopped running. It didn't need to, because it was attached to the last person or thing that you ever wanted to square up to and argue the time of day with.

12 INVISIBLE ROADS

'Hello, Judas,' said Michael.

The Archangel Michael – he of the big, flaming sword and the snow-white wings of steel – was leaning against the base of a telecommunications mast with his arms folded across his chest. Unfortunately for Judas, he was also smiling, and that meant that there was trouble headed his way. Michael was either wearing his holiday clothes or trying to look inconspicuous; Judas hadn't the heart to tell him that he had failed to pull off either look very well.

The Archangel's long white hair flowed down over his shoulders. Its condition would have made any shampoo manufacturer go weak at the knees. It was the cool, urban, hipster-angel look.

'Hello, Michael. If you'd wanted to see me you could have just called; I just scuffed one of my monk-straps on the last rung. My cobbler's going to go mad; he only put new soles on them last week.'

The Archangel Michael was standing twenty feet away; he flexed his mighty wings, and the next thing Judas knew he was by his side. Judas was fast, but compared to Michael, he was moving in slow-motion with the handbrake on and wearing a ball and chain around both ankles.

Michael reached out with a large white hand and caressed the side of Judas' face. It was like being stroked by an articulated lorry.

'I needed to get you away from the Museum for a quiet word, Judas, there are too many ears there. You are taking the Church Roads tonight, I believe?'

'What's it to you?' asked Judas, trying to appear brave and failing fantastically.

Michael put his arm around Judas' shoulders and squeezed. His arm was incredibly heavy, and the sheer weight of it made Judas wince. The threat was implicit, and Judas knew that he would have a bruise the size of a dinner plate in the morning.

'You are taking the Church Roads tonight?' Michael repeated.

Judas tried to shrug the angel off, but it was impossible.

'Yes, I am. I don't know where you're getting your information from, but I am tagging along with the Saints from Clapham, down the Trinity to the Oasis. They are having some trouble with the child slavers down there, and they want to find out more about an organisation that goes by the name of The 10. It may have something to do with the angel slayings that we're looking into. It may be something, or it may be nothing, not sure. Anyway, what brings El Capitano to London?'

Michael did not reply; silence was one of his more effective weapons. It was also infuriating. He removed his arm from Judas' shoulders and stepped over to the edge of the building to look down. The roof was covered in gravel that crunched and crackled under the feet of even the smallest of pigeons, yet the angel made no sound.

Judas approached the edge and stood next to him. The rush-hour was in full flow below, thousands of people rushing home to loved ones, to their recorded soaps and pointless football matches against teams in Europe with names like cheap washing machines. He could see a man in a fluorescent orange bib frantically handing out free newspapers with both hands. He would probably have used his feet too if he could.

Michael turned, suddenly. He picked Judas up as if he weighed nothing, and then launched himself into the air.

'South?'

'South it is,' replied Judas.

Judas looked down on London. It was a hungry, growing city. One lazy baker, one big fire, a plague and two world wars had been unable to dampen its spirits or slow its growth. Judas had come to love the place.

'Now that's a city!' he shouted as loudly as he could into the rushing wind.

Michael beat his mighty wings once and then rolled over, so they were both looking up into the night sky. The stars seemed brighter and clearer from up here. Michael pointed to a particularly bright star, surrounded by a halo of lesser ones. Judas knew immediately what he was pointing at. It was the City of Heaven.

'No, Judas! That is a city! All other cities created by man are nothing compared to it. You should visit it once you have finished your work down here, whenever that is; in a thousand years, perhaps?'

Michael knew just how to push Judas' buttons; he had become quite good at it over the years, or so he thought. He casually angled his wings and they rolled back over again, so they were looking downwards.

'You're a funny angel, you know that Michael? Really funny in a kind of rubbish funny kind of way.'

Michael looked down into Judas' eyes. For a split-second Judas thought he saw some warmth or love there, and that the angel was about to say something profound, but the moment passed, and he just beat his wings once again. They flew up, and into the clouds. Emerging from the white banks of floating water, they flew straight into the path of a helicopter that was on its way to the helipad in Battersea. Michael calmly angled his body and pushed the helicopter to one side. The action was done so smoothly that the helicopter simply twitched a bit, before flying on, unscathed.

Judas always felt tiny, weak and insignificant alongside Michael. Of course, anyone would, with the exception of Lucifer the Morningstar – the rumour was that even Michael thought twice when Lucifer was involved. Lucifer drove Michael to perform well in everything he did. If he gave Michael a task to complete, Michael was like a puppy desperate for attention. A very muscular, rip-your-head-off-without-thinking-twice sort of puppy. Me. Me. Me. Look at me!

Judas wondered what life was really like for him, if life was the right word. What did he do when he wasn't flying around issuing corrections to those who had fallen from favour? Where did he sleep? Did he sleep? What did he eat? Any other questions were quickly saved for another day as the angel started to swoop downwards in a series of graceful arcs, reducing speed and altitude with each turn; he could have dropped out of the sky like a hawk, but he was carrying a human being, so he made his descent a little more slowly this time. They were over Battersea one second, then Stockwell the next, flying lower and lower. Judas pointed down towards a fragmented car snake made of white headlights and red taillights.

'We should follow the Wandsworth Road until it hits the railway line; make for the space behind the church after that.'

Michael nodded and angled his powerful wings once again; the sharp change in direction took Judas' breath away.

He saw the Wandsworth Road railway station ahead and pointed downwards. St Paul's Church was near. Michael landed right outside the church doors, carefully placed Judas down onto the ground, then flexed his wings; they folded backwards and tucked themselves in. He only looked mildly terrifying now.

'The Saints should be here any minute now, Michael. They're a quiet bunch, but very handy in a scrap.'

Judas stretched and turned the collar of his coat up – the flight from the Yard had given him a bit of a chill. He put his hands inside his coat pockets, and while they waited, he read a few of the names on the stones nearby. He felt Michael stiffen even before he heard the sound of their arrival. The leader of the Clapham Saints stepped out of the darkness.

'Thornton, may I present the Archangel Michael. Michael, may I present the leader of the Saints; he calls himself Thornton.'

Thornton stepped out of the shadows. He was on familiar ground, but for the first time in the two-hundred or more years since Judas had known him he did not look his normal, composed self. From where Judas was standing, he looked a tad scared. Meeting Michael for the first time did that to you.

'Why do you call yourself the Saints? A strange, presumptive name to choose, is it not?'

Michael took a step closer and looked down at Thornton.

'We came to this place a long time ago, angel. We came from far away over the sea, and finally we made a new home for ourselves here. A great evil forced us from our homeland. We fought against it, and when we were betrayed, we were forced to flee for our lives.

'So, when we saw that the same evil that had destroyed our homeland was beginning to grow here, we decided to make a stand and fight it once again. The people who lived here already appreciated our actions and it was these people that started to call us the Saints of Clapham. We did not choose the name ourselves, angel. There is nothing holy or divine about us, although strangely we do live long lives, and we are not easily harmed. We are who we are, no more and no less. We fight for what we think is right. We have done so for a long time and will continue to do so until such time as evil has been defeated or until we are able to return to our lands across the sea. In time, we hope to see it rise once again. What do people who have no home dream of more than that?'

Thornton was a natural leader. He was nowhere near as imposing as the angel standing in front of him, but he was not about to show weakness, especially not with the others looking on. Michael listened and just smiled. Judas hadn't seen him do that for a long time.

'We are both a long way from home, Thornton, leader of the Clapham Saints,' said Michael.

The angel placed a hand on Thornton's shoulder, and something powerful and binding seemed to pass between them. Thornton bowed his head, and when he raised it again there was a fire in his eyes that had not been there before.

'Come forward!'

Thornton waved a hand in the air, and the rest of the Saints stepped into the light. There were twenty of them in total – ten men and ten women, all dressed in sharp, well-cut dark suits and crisp white shirts. Williams would have nodded at the sight and made his new model army joke again. None of them carried any weapons, and having seen them in action before, Judas knew that they didn't need them. He would also have to ask them how they managed to stay so damn clean regardless of where they went. Whether deep underground in the sewers, or out in the wide-open spaces of the marshes in the east, they always stayed absolutely pristine. It was bloody annoying.

Thornton walked over to the old rusty church gates and locked them with a large, ornate key that had just appeared in his hand from nowhere, then disappeared just as quickly after. He stood for a second, took a deep breath and then closed his eyes. They all waited quietly then, after a few minutes had passed, Thornton pointed at an old lichen-covered gravestone in the far corner of the churchyard.

'We travel along the Church Roads tonight, through the Trinity and down to the Oasis.' Thornton walked towards the gravestone that he had just identified, and the rest of the Saints followed him towards it in near silence. There was a faint swish-swish-swishing sound as their feet moved gently over the well-tended grass of the graveyard. That was the only sound they made. Judas felt like coughing or making some sort of sound, just to prove to himself that they were really there. Michael looked down at Judas. One of his eyebrows was tilted upwards, and Judas realised that Michael was perplexed.

'What are these Church Roads that they speak of?'

'You don't know? Well, that's a first – something the all-powerful Michael doesn't know. I shall be dining out on this for years. You know they'll be printing that one on those slips of paper that they put inside Christmas crackers. "You won't get this one," they'll say. It could even be a cheese question in a game of Trivial Pursuit.'

Judas smiled. Then he decided that keeping his teeth in his mouth and his head on his shoulders was a good idea, so he stopped crowing, and started explaining.

'The Church Roads are ancient pathways. No one knows exactly when they were created, to be honest. We call them the Church Roads because they run from church to church, all the way from the very north of the British Isles to the south, and from the east to the west. I used to think that they were secret paths for the Church and its soldiers, a way they could travel across the country without being seen, like a sort of persecution-free highway. But after a bit of digging, I found out that the roads were here long before the churches were even built. They run through, over and under the whole country, and are really handy if you need to get somewhere quickly and quietly. They draw their power from the Ley lines. Normal people can't see them, and they can't walk on them or follow them, either. We are travelling along one such road tonight. It runs down from the Oasis, and ends near the Trinity, at the location of one of the slaver's pits.'

'Why don't your enemies use them too, if they are so useful?' said Michael.

'I don't think that they open to just anyone. The Saints can use them, and I can use them. I've heard that there are some others that are often seen travelling along them. We call them the Wandering Folk. Occasionally someone from the normal world happens to stumble onto one of the roads by accident. It's very rare, but it does happen. They find themselves on here by chance and travel along one for a while, then they start feeling dizzy. Unless one of these guys or one of the Wandering Folk helps them to get off and back to civilisation, they die.'

Michael's eyebrow dropped back into its rightful position. The last of the Saints disappeared behind the gravestone, and Judas and Michael followed. It was their first journey along these roads together, but something told Judas it wouldn't be their last. They were going to be travelling along roads that were older than the stones of Stonehenge, to find out more about the mysterious 10 and whether they were linked to the angel murders. If they were lucky, they'd get to destroy a child slavery market at the same time. Judas looked at Michael's sword and knew that if they found the camp then it was going to be a warm night's work, and there would be far fewer slavers with heads still attached to their bodies tomorrow. He wasn't about to shed a tear.

13 SLAVES IN THE WOOD

They stepped past the gravestone, and the view changed immediately. Clapham was still there but it had faded; it had lost its hard edges and become softer. The buildings were still there and so were the people and the cars, but they had become translucent. They had become ghosts of themselves. The noise of the real world was still there too, but only just. It was a distant echo of itself, like the real world heard through the spout of a teapot. After the noise of everyday London, the quiet hum of the road was unsettling, but they soon got used to it.

Ahead of them stretched a cobbled-stone pathway that led out from the church boundaries, across the common and southwards. The Saints walked in two lines on opposite sides of the road. Occasionally they would turn and look out onto the faded other London outside, watching and looking for something. Judas and the angel walked on behind.

'What are you doing here, Michael?' Judas looked up at the angel.

Michael just walked on; he was taking everything in, watching, listening and storing every movement and moment away.

'I have been tasked with keeping you safe, Judas.'

The phantom image of a car passed directly across the pathway in front of them, distracting the angel momentarily. Judas smiled.

'It happens when the new roads that are built cut across the Church Roads, nothing to worry about. Anyway, keep me safe from what? I've been down here for a long time, and I'm very hard to kill. Impossible, in fact. I haven't had much use for you have I?

'Why did He make me like this and then send you down to look after me? Bit of overkill, isn't it? You are the Captain of the Host, after all.'

Judas looked up at the angel again and saw that he was smiling.

'We should test that theory, Judas. Which methods have your enemies tried on you so far? I can remove them from my list so as to save time.

'Have any of them tried to throw you into the heart of a sun, or tied you to a boulder and rolled you into an active volcano in the deepest pit of the underworld? What about placing you under a really heavy rock at the bottom of the ocean; anyone give that a go?'

Judas put some distance between himself and the angel.

Michael reached out and put his hand on Judas' shoulder. Judas was about to try and pull away, when he noticed that the Saints had stopped moving; all of them were looking outwards, through the shimmering walls that enclosed the Church Road. Something had drawn their attention, and their hackles were up.

Judas decided that being closer to the angel was actually safer for him than being further away and moved under the protection of Michael's outstretched wing. Thornton moved silently down the line of his team towards them. Every now and then he would stop and whisper something to one of them, and they would disappear through the wall. Once he had given his orders he came forward and spoke in a hushed tone to Judas and Michael.

'We are nearing the Bec. The road drops down from here towards the Colliers Wood. We heard that some slavers camped here a few nights ago. We are going to step off the road now and take a look; there may be some sign of their passing. Be good enough to wait here; my people know these places and work better on their own; we will be back shortly. Hopefully with some news of them.'

Thornton waved a hand, and all of the remaining Saints stepped off the path, through the faint blurred wall that separated the Church Road from the real world and disappeared.

'Do you want to follow them, Judas?'

Michael moved over to the edge of the road and touched the wall. He seemed intrigued with it and held his hand there for a few seconds, enjoying the sensation of something new.

'I think they'll be fine; they normally are.'

'How many times have you worked with them?'

The angel turned away from the wall; it had learned all it could about the Church Road's boundaries with that single touch.

'A few. We found ourselves on the same side back in the 1800s, when the slavers were a bit more adventurous than they are now. We've joined forces quite a few times since. Whenever I've needed some extra help they've always been there. And if they need my help, I do my best to provide it. Sometimes they just need information, and if I can't help then I take them to the Museum; Thornton seems to get on well with the Custodian. They spend hours waffling away to each other in there. The Museum always seems more friendly, after one of their chats, funnily enough. It must be on account of Thornton being pure of heart and all that, whereas yours truly isn't quite so virtuous or whiter than white.'

Michael looked at Judas and cocked his head to one side again. His eyes widened and a small smile formed on his lips.

'What do you know of the Museum then, Judas? You spend a lot of time there; how do you get on with him? Do you speak? Do you pass the time with him like Thornton?'

Judas felt a chill and fastened another button on his coat before returning the angel's smile.

'Why do you say "him"? It sounds like you know more about my Museum than I do.'

The angel smiled even more broadly.

'Your Museum, Judas? Why has it suddenly become yours?'

Judas was about to answer when the Saints returned. They had brought something with them and this thing didn't look too happy about it.

'This thing was trying to steal another child for the market this evening; the child is safe now, but he is not.'

The angry, thrashing little thing that the Saints had brought with them looked around at his new captors and started to shiver and flinch. They shoved it into the middle of the path where it cowered and whimpered. It looked like a small man; just a small man in normal clothing, until you looked a little more closely. It had dead eyes; eyes without any white in them. There was a yellow tinge to them where the white should have been, like mashed, bruised bananas, and there was something not right about its hands and feet either. They curved the wrong way – outwards instead of inwards – while the fingers were broken backwards from the joints and moved like a wonky gate.

'So, this is a slaver, then?' Michael yanked it up by the hair in order to get a better look at its face.

The slaver's eyes opened so wide that Judas could see a dirty red rim of flesh around the black and yellow pits, and when the thing looked into the angel's face it clearly knew that it was in the sort of trouble that you don't get to crawl away from.

'What do you wish to know, Thornton?' Michael lifted the small figure off the ground and held it high in the air. The slaver wet itself, and the urine formed a small yellow puddle on the floor underneath his swinging body.

'Ask it where the market is to be held, and what the password is to get in.'

Michael casually placed one of his huge hands around the slaver's neck. The slaver knew what was coming next and started to babble and squeal like a piglet. Its voice was sheer and high-pitched, and looking past the glamour it wore like a disguise, it was just a stunted, twisted little creature. These creatures were as horrible on the inside as they were on the outside. This one had limbs like overgrown twiglets with extra nobbles. It was particularly ugly, and the more Michael squeezed its throat, the quicker its outer form fell away. Within a few seconds the little man had disappeared and had been replaced by a shrivelled, foul-smelling thing. It was grey-skinned and stunted, with a shaved head and squashed features that looked as if they had been pushed into the centre of its face. Yellow nails protruded from twig-like hands that scratched at the air in jerky, spasmodic movements. Its mouth was a dark slash, and its eyelids were clamped together tightly to keep out the poisonous light that emanated from Michael's wings.

Michael squeezed a little harder, and the slaver's eyes blinked open. He looked into them and asked the questions. They were delivered with such menace that the slaver didn't bother to try and hold out. It started to talk immediately.

'The entrance words are "I am a helper from the south", and the market is in the old Council Office.' Thornton took a pen and pad from his jacket and wrote everything down. He then gave it to one of his team, and she ran off down the path the way they had come. Judas wondered what Thornton had been feeding his team, because she was out of sight in a few seconds.

The slaver squirmed and shook as it spoke. Michael had taken all of its secrets now, and casually dropped the little beast onto the ground; it immediately rolled itself up into a ball and began to rock, gibbering and murmuring, dribbling and spitting.

'The old Council Office is a building site at the moment; the old buildings are being turned into flats. The whole area is fenced off; I think the slavers will hold their market in the foundations below, where it is dark and warm.'

Thornton walked over to the slaver and gave it a vicious kick.

'How many of your kind will be there tonight?'

The slaver shook its head, then spat on the ground at Thornton's feet.

'I can ask the winged one to touch you again if you want?'

The slaver lifted its head, giving Thornton and the angel its best angry glare. It tried hard to look confident and unafraid, but it knew that it was not long for this world. Within seconds, all the fire and fight went out of its eyes, and it started to babble.

'A hundred. Most of the southern clan. Very nasty, armed and dangerous; you will not get out alive. Maybe they sell you along with the baby humans? It's deep down there now; very deep, no light, no way out. You go in, you not come out.'

Thornton reached down and lifted the slaver up. He looked at it for a short time and then placed his fingertip against the forehead of the creature.

'I send you on now to the darkness and the cold. Your path was ever thus. Go now and be nothing. Take your pain and hold it to your heart for ever.'

The slaver began to tremble and shake. Judas looked on. He had seen this before, and there was no escape. It was a death, and a kind of death that was not in any way kind. Being turned into nothing and being forced to experience the pain that you had caused and inflicted on others for what remained of time was horrific. The slaver started to fade. First its hands and feet blurred and then disappeared, then its limbs followed suit. It was trying to cry, but couldn't, because its organs weren't there anymore. Within seconds, the slaver was no more. All that was left of it was a small puddle of urine on the cobbles of the Church Roads. It was a nasty way to die, but then again it had been a nasty way to live. Some might call it an execution. The Saints preferred to call it a release.

Thornton rubbed his thorny hands together as if to wipe away the memory of the slaver, then he and the rest of the Saints walked on, followed by Judas and the angel.

The distance between the churches of St Paul's, Oasis and Trinity when walking the Church Roads was a short one, and Judas, the Saints and the Archangel Michael arrived at the Colliers Wood just in time for the slave market to begin.

14 CHILDREN FOR SALE

South West London was the new place to be. All the smart property people were snapping up the big houses in the area and turning them into flats, so that they could rent them to kids and stop them from ever getting their grubby little feet on the property ladder. It was at the end of the Northern Line in more ways than one and used to be the end of the line for property hunters. No one wanted to live there by choice. These days it was in demand, and gastro pubs and coffee shops were popping up where corner shops and betting shops used to be. There were more and more women with bumps and new prams that were marketed as ergonomic infant transportation modular systems than ever before. Once you saw a shop selling imported Italian bibs and Swedish feeding mats then you knew that the area had arrived. In order to make way for more of this madness the local Council Offices had been sold off and were on the way to being turned into very stylish shoeboxes with an en-suite. At the moment the building was just a skeleton of concrete with giant, white, Germanic-style numbers sprayed onto its façade, surrounded by squat, yellow digging machines and metal fencing that wore sandbags for shoes.

Judas, Michael and the Saints stepped through the shimmering wall of the Church Road and entered the building site. Their sudden appearance, as if by magic, frightened the dozing pigeons and sent a cat that was just about to wake the pigeons himself running for its life. Thornton pointed at the building site office. All of the Saints acknowledged it with a barely discernible nod of the head and drifted inside. Judas was about to follow when Michael grabbed him by the arm, which really hurt; he'd have to ask Michael very nicely to go easy with him. Michael pointed at his wings, and then at the office where the Saints were now hiding. There was no way that Michael was fitting in there, so they hid themselves inside the main building instead. Moments later Thornton appeared and padded across the building site on silent feet to their hiding place. He whispered something to the nearest black suit and one by one they drifted off into the darkness.

'They will find the market and slip inside and await my orders; no one will escape unless we want them to.'

Thornton stood to one side as soon as he had delivered his message and kept his own council. All of the lamps and yellow security lighting dotted around the site went out one by one, as if a giant mouth had crept up on them and gently huffed them to death.

The darkness was complete now.

'You know what or who the Museum is, don't you?' Judas had been thinking about what the angel had said earlier.

'Why did you say "him" like that? What's he done to earn your displeasure?'

Michael smiled the smile that Judas hated. The smile that said he wasn't saying anything right now, and that he knew frustrated the hell out of Judas.

Before Judas could make one of his nearly legendary wisecracks, one of the Saints returned and whispered to Thornton.

'We have found the entrance. There has been a lot of traffic in and out; some of my people are watching the other exits. There is a pipe, a big concrete pipe that leads away from the building; a man could stand up in it. If anything wants to escape it has to go deeper, or out through that. We shall go in, break up the market and take the slavers now.'

'I need to find out what "The 10" means, or what it signifies, so don't kill everything – please?'

'As you wish, Judas.'

Thornton smiled his grim smile and his scar twitched as he did so, giving him a roguish appearance in the night. Then he was gone along with the rest of the Saints.

Judas and Michael followed the Saints across the building site. They reached the concrete foundations and stopped; one of the Saints pointed at some steps that led down under the building. One by one they filed in. Michael folded his wings in tightly and by some strange magic shrank down his size too, so that he could move freely in the tunnels. The Saints didn't seem to need any artificial light to see where they were going. Judas had remarked upon on it once before and been told by Thornton's son John many years ago that the Saints could see equally well in light or dark. They went down and down. Water dripped from cracked pipes above their heads and flattened on the concrete flooring with a sad excuse of a plop. Ahead, they could make out a hum of voices below in the earth; harsh, sharp, squeaking little voices like giant rats singing. Judas could see a faint glow in the tunnel ahead. He was about to say something when one of the Saints nearest to him placed a warning finger to his lips.

'Gate Keeper.'

The Saint pointed, and just ahead was a large fat thing sitting on a collection of upturned milk crates. Bottles and empty beer cans were piled up all around him. The Gate Keeper swished a rather nasty looking club – fashioned from two cricket bats bound together with gaffer tape – back and forth. At the end of it, a huge round stone-cutting saw blade was nailed into the wood. It was useless for fighting in a tunnel, so Judas knew that there was a bigger space to fight in up ahead. Good news for them – bad news for the bad guys.

The Gate Keeper wore cargo shorts that were ripped and frayed and showed far too much bum-crease. A dirty black t-shirt was tied around his neck like a muffler; putting clothes on in the morning obviously wasn't high on his list of things to do. His head, if you could call it that, was ash white, in the shape of a giant rugby ball that had been kicked into submission. It was obvious that he hadn't spent much time above ground in a long while. He was the muscle on the door, but he'd picked the wrong night to work. One of the Saints approached. He made no attempt to disguise himself, and calmly tapped the Gate Keeper on the shoulder. The Gate Keeper spun around faster than a blob of his size should have been able to and raised his club defensively. The Saint just put a calming hand on his shoulder, then punched him on the side of his rugby-ball head, just above the temple. The Gate Keeper looked confused for a second, then his eyes went blank, and he sat down again in a heap. The Saint looked back down the tunnel and motioned for them all to come forward. The Gate Keeper was sitting there in body, but in his head, he was very, very far away.

A slave market by definition was not a nice place, especially if you were the one standing on the block and looking out on a sea of people that may want to buy you and torture you. The slavers stole little children to order, and if they could guide a drunk or a tramp down into a tunnel then they'd do that, too. The promise of a drink or something to eat or a warm bed for the night did for the adults, while the children just got bundled off and were seen no more. There must have been over a hundred slavers down there in the concrete foundations at the drainage junction where all of the tunnels met; they were all armed, and pushing small groups of children, dirty and dishevelled, forward onto a large square of flattened cardboard boxes. This was obviously the viewing stage. Above them, sitting on top of a tennis umpire's chair, was an odious looking little creature wearing a white lab coat and a top hat. He was the auction master. Fires in oil drums made the space hot and sticky, and the smell of the children's fear and the slavers' excitement was nauseating. Michael pointed at an opening on the far side of the tunnel and Judas stiffened as a group of well-dressed men and women entered. Each one passed a small scrap of paper to the auctioneer as they passed his chair.

Judas pointed at them.

'Thornton. The humans, they're the buyers. I want them all alive.'

Thornton nodded and gave a signal. The Saints slipped into the tunnels around them and disappeared. The auction began when a little blonde girl wearing a blazer and straw hat from one of the private schools that lined the Common was pushed forward. A bidding war started between two of the men. Their interest in her was obviously not healthy and it made Judas sick to his stomach. The bidding continued. The girl cried, and the slavers hooted and yelped as the bidding went higher. They were so excited that they didn't notice the figures in dark suits leave the tunnels behind them and take up position all around the auction.

Fighting in a small space was not pretty. In fact, fighting in any space was not pretty, but when you had a group of two-hundred-year-old warriors dressed in dark suits up against a nasty clan of vicious little slavers it could get very messy. Throw in an angel and an immortal traitor and things could get bad quickly.

The Saints waded in and ripped the slavers to pieces. Michael leapt over the bloody scrum and stopped the smart set from escaping, while Judas rounded up the children. Not a single slaver was left alive. Thornton signalled to his team, and one by one they placed a fingertip to the heads of the dead bodies. Each one faded, and then disappeared completely. In the end there was no evidence of their existence at all; only the flattened cardboard boxes and the smoking oil drums remained. Judas hurried the children to the surface. He had moved quickly to extricate them from the battlefield; they were still crying and snuffling but they sensed that they had been saved and moved accordingly. They tumbled up the stone steps and into the fresh air. Judas looked down at their weeping faces. It had been a near thing. Thornton emerged from the foundations of the buildings; behind him came the buyers, and behind them came a very angry angel.

'Let's get them on the Church Roads quick; we can question them there.'

Thornton nodded. 'I will deal with the children first.'

He took each child gently to one side and then looked deeply into their eyes. He was wearing his kind face, and the children relaxed and calmed down instantly, as if under a spell. He took each child by the hand and just said 'Forget'

It was a simple, solitary word, but it was delivered in such a way that each child flinched at first, as if something had been taken away from them, which it had. But then their eyes grew wide again, like children's eyes are supposed to be, and they all started to chatter amongst themselves as if they were in the playground. Thornton spoke to one of his men and they led the children away.

'There is a Police station near here, the children will be safe, and they will be returned to their families.'

Judas turned around and looked at the things that were trying to pass as men and women. What was a human being doing down there with those creatures, trying to buy children? He could see that they were rich and rotten. Their deviant appetites had fast exceeded their humanity. The sight of them repulsed him and he didn't try and hide his feelings. He'd seen some disgusting things in his time – this wasn't the worst – but he still had trouble believing that the human heart could turn so black and poisoned.

'Michael, if you would be so kind as to escort these ladies and gentlemen onto the pathway for me, we can begin.'

15 THE TEN

Michael casually herded them onto the Church Road. One of the women snapped a heel, and a couple of the men tried to protest, but there was absolutely no chance that their voices were going to be heard now. They all reacted in the same way as they stepped out of the reality that they knew and were comfortable with and stepped onto the Church Roads. First, their faces registered surprise, and then the fear kicked in: unchartered territory, strange surroundings and hostile guides will do that for you. It was pure unadulterated fear, accompanied by a low moaning sound that really irritated Judas, so he grabbed one of the men roughly by the lapels of his expensive and now tattered dinner jacket. The man looked like he should have been buying champagne for an eastern European pole-dancer in one of the city's exclusive clubs, where all you needed to be a member was a brain the size of a peanut and a bank balance bigger than an African warlord, instead of attending a child auction in Colliers Wood; he had that easy, money-can-buy-me-your-love look about him. Judas detested him the moment he smelt his £500 aftershave (or 'scent' as he probably called it whilst gazing at his reflection in his clinically white bathroom).

'You gave the slave auctioneer this?'

The man looked down at the piece of paper in Judas' hand. 'Not mine,' he said.

Judas smiled. He was hoping that this was the way that the man was going to play it.

'Have you ever seen an angel pull a man's arm off?'

The man just smiled the bravest smile his weak chin could offer and shrugged his shoulders. It was one of those 'I've seen it all before, my friend' smiles. Michael heard what he said and quickly stepped forward, and with one muscular flick he extended his great wings out to their fullest span. It was an impressive sight. The fire in his eyes and the giant silver sword swinging at his waist helped a bit too. The man's eyes opened so widely that his eyebrows were almost at the base of his neck. Michael unceremoniously picked him up and started twisting his arm off. The sound of the arm meeting a shoulder socket squelching through a 100% wool jacket was one that Judas hadn't heard before, but it made him smile, nonetheless.

'I think he wants to say something,' said Judas. Michael continued to pull and twist, and with a pop the man's arm came away in his hand.

'I said, I think he wants to tell us something.'

Michael tossed the arm away just like an uneaten chicken drumstick and dropped the now harmless and armless dead body to the ground. He wouldn't be missed.

Michael casually singled out another of the men and picked him up.

'I don't care; there are eighteen more of them. They all had the paper on them, they're all as guilty as each other, I am vengeance, so let's see who talks fastest.'

An angel in arm-tearing-off mood is not a pleasant sight, and Michael's actions had the desired effect. More than one puddle of urine formed between the legs of the pathetic group as fear took over and moved in permanently.

The men and women clambered over each other to tell all that they knew; they couldn't confess quickly enough. But Judas wasn't interested in their petty little crimes, their low-grade perversions, or their second division sexual escapades, he wanted to know more about The 10.

An hour of pitiful wailing later and the men and women sat in a huddle on one side of the path. They were spent and empty. Make-up ran down the women's faces in black splashes, and red eyes full of tears gazed out from under heavy brows; their clothes were ripped, and their hair was on end. Judas had finished questioning them, but Michael and the Saints had not. Not by a long chalk. Judas walked up the road with Thornton by his side. Occasionally they would hear a scream or a groan, so they walked more quickly, and the further up the Church Road they went, the less they heard. A short while later, the rest of the Saints and Michael caught up with them.

Judas was always surprised at how normal the Saints looked after a battle. There were no bloodstains to be seen, or rips in clothing, they looked just like they had done at the beginning of the evening. He'd have to ask Thornton at some point just how they managed to do that. As for Michael, he didn't even have a hair out of place. Everyone looked fresh and dynamic. Judas felt far from it. He had a quick smell of his armpits when he thought no one was looking and was relieved to find that he was okay. It had been a long night, and he just wanted to close his eyes and get some sleep, so he was happy when they stepped out from behind the gravestone that masqueraded as a doorway in the churchyard. Morning had broken already; dew was laying on the grass and spider webs spun by incredibly industrious spiders in the night held droplets of water that looked far too heavy for their delicate strands. Seeing the London, he loved like this made Judas smile. It mattered, what he'd seen during the night, of course it did, the children's faces full of fear and then happiness and the blood and the fury of the battle underground; but sometimes, just sometimes, he loved the beginning of a new day. Right at the beginning he'd feared the dawn of a new day. The guilt, and the cold stabbing of shame at what he'd done, made him depressed and he'd want to kill himself over and over again. Maybe he was changing. Was he learning to love life, instead of just going through the motions of it?

Judas said thank you and goodbye to Thornton and the Saints and watched them disappear inside. One second they were there and the next they were gone.

Judas started thinking about the Museum. Heaven knew what Williams would be doing there on his own. He was about to set off when Michael approached and asked to walk with him a while. This didn't normally happen – when Michael asked rather than commanded Judas to do something Judas started to worry. They walked for a few minutes in silence and then Michael spoke.

'Judas, how do you feel?'

Judas wasn't expecting pleasantries, so his words caught in his throat.

'Why do you ask?'

Michael stopped and turned to face him. Then he carefully brushed a lock of Judas' hair to one side. Judas thought he should flinch but didn't, which was an odd sensation.

'Feel? Feel after last night?'

Michael raised one of his perfect hands to stop the rest of the words tumbling out.

'How do you feel inside, Judas?'

Michael was looking at him strangely and Judas was compelled to open his heart to him.

'I feel different, Michael. I have been feeling, actually feeling, moments and times lately. It has been a long time since I cared about anyone or anything.'

Michael dropped his hand and turned away.

'I will return, Judas – soon,' he said and then he jumped into the air and flew off. Judas watched him cleave a cloud in two and then disappear into a morning sky criss-crossed with the vapour trails of airliners. What was that all about? he wondered. Then, right on cue, the rain started to fall.

16 THE RIPPER OPENS UP

Judas watched London slide past in the upside down world of raindrops on glass windows. The cab he had hailed was taking the scenic, tourist route back to the Yard. Judas wondered if he should flash his warrant card and speed things up a bit but decided against it, settling back into his seat and closing his eyes instead. He waited for the driver to start telling him about the famous person he'd had in the back of the cab last week but the driver, seeing Judas close his eyes, just turned on talkSPORT on the radio instead.

Judas' brain started to whirr and click and rumble. He heard the words of the men and women who attended the auction ping-ponging back and forth inside his head. The 10 were the muscle, The 10 were faceless and nameless, The 10 just were, they knew people, they had fingers in every pie, they had political clout, they had an army, they had been around since the dark times, they were new but they were old, they were brutal and unforgiving, there were 10 of them.

Everything and nothing, thought Judas. Lots to go through, and nothing to go on. The black cab swerved in and out of traffic. The roads were always busier when it rained. No one wanted to walk, the tube slowed up and the city slowed down. Judas opened his eyes just as the cab pulled up outside the Yard. He paid the cabbie and ran up the steps in a vain attempt not to get wet. He pushed the front door open and tried to wade through reception, bypassing the front desk. Friends were waiting there for even drunker friends to be released from the cells, people signed papers with trembling post-scuffle hands, and girlfriends lied about how they got last night's black eyes to policemen who wanted to give their boyfriends a dose of their own for a change. The smell of sweat, beer, and bad breath filled the air. They should bottle it, thought Judas. 'Air of the Yard', or 'Yard Blue' – for him, for her, for you if you got caught and banged up. He passed through the security barrier and headed for the stairs. Legions of black-clad constables ran here and there, heading off to interviews and down to the cells, dispensing justice and tea in Styrofoam cups to victims. The Yard was alive. It fairly throbbed with justice. The corridors were awash with the stuff. Judas avoided the lift and some of the Met's finest and took his own private stairs. When he got to the 7th floor, he swiped his key card; the door to his domain gave a little click and opened. He walked down the corridor and stepped into his office.

Williams was making another cup of bad tea. He pressed a mug of the foul brew into Judas' hand and then started organising his desk before staring out of the window like one of those advertising people looking for an idea. Judas liked the way that Williams knew when to talk and when to remain silent. He had built a strong marriage on the back of it. I really must spend more time outside of office hours with him and his family, he thought. Then he sat down and considered The 10. This situation felt familiar. It felt as if he should know about them already. He had an itch in the back of his mind that needed scratching. This gang were a criminal force that held sway over South London. They were into everything, it seemed. They were powerful, and they struck fear into everyone that did business with them. But this lot had a foot in both camps. They were happy in the world of the living, causing mayhem and killing and destroying, and they were very at home in his world too; the magical, the occult and the downright shady part that he lived in most of the time.

That was the bit that was causing him the most anguish. Judas finished his tea and then decided that he and Williams had better catch up with Jack the Ripper.

Moments later Judas swiped his card over the door pad and entered the Museum. The whispering from the artefacts stopped immediately.

'Hello again, how is everyone? Hi-De-Hi, campers!'

Nothing. Silence.

'What about you, Museum? Fancy a chat?' The Museum wasn't up for talking today either, it seemed. The exhibits inside the room were housed in glass boxes six feet high and five feet wide. Dark wooden frames that had been varnished so many times that they'd put on weight held everything together. Inside the cases, weapons of mass murder and bottles of poisons throbbed with the essence of their previous owners. Judas had only to open a case and hold one to relive the crime itself. There were thousands of objects in here, all with their own story and life. It was a hard place to be in, let alone keep watch over. Judas had a thought. It was a toe in the water, a guess, but he just had a feeling that there was something in the way that Michael had spoken about the Museum that had made him curious.

'I spoke to an angel called Michael about you today. He was very, you know, dismissive of you.'

Judas wasn't ready for the reaction, or the noise. The bellow was so loud that it made his head hurt and his ears ring. The cases shook and some of the doors sprang open. Dust filled the air and pictures fell from the walls. Williams was already hiding behind the metal filing cabinet in the corner of the room nearest the door; dust had turned his thick black hair white, and now he looked like he should be attending a performance of the Rocky Horror Picture show. Judas stepped back instinctively and braced himself for the next blast.

'I take it that you know the Archangel Michael then; not a friend of yours, is he?'

Instead of the hurricane of noise and anger that he was preparing himself for again, there was only silence this time; an unnerving silence. The glass doors on the cases started to close softly and carefully, and the brass latches clipped back into place to secure them. The pictures that had fallen to the floor picked themselves up and reattached themselves to the walls, and the dust slowly floated downwards and hid itself in the carpet on the floor. Judas decided not to push his luck and sat down at the table. 'Right then, you're not friends. I won't ask again. I made the last bit up about the dismissive thing, okay? He never said that.'

Judas waited for a reaction, but the room remained silent. After some time had passed, he asked as nicely as possible for the key to the Key Room. It took a while, but eventually the key was produced. Judas had an appointment to keep; he wished that he could just forget it and not turn up, but he needed all the leads he could get if he was going to solve this case before another angel got chopped up in a park somewhere in London. And so he got up, dusted himself down, and stepped into the Key Room with Williams following nervously behind. He picked up the white opera glove in a men's size eight.

After the familiar sounds of the past seeped into the present once again, Jack made his unwelcome appearance.

'Ah, it's the deceiver and his partner, the ever-doughty Williams! Good to hear you again; I'd love to see you of course. Might be fun, you and I; what do you say?'

Judas paced up and down in the small room and tried to stop Jack's words from slipping into his mind. The room felt much smaller than usual when he was talking to Jack. It was as if all of the time that separated the two of them had been compressed and squeezed tightly together inside the room; he could feel the whole of Whitechapel around him: every street, every person, every bad mood and good and fleeting moment, pressing in on him like a damp, dull weight. Underneath the sound was a feeling of dread that made you itch. Judas centred himself and focused on keeping his breathing regular and deep. Stay in the moment, stay calm, and keep thinking clearly, he thought to himself. Jack liked to play tricks; he liked you to have to work for it. Jack liked people to beg and plead for help; to gush and fawn. The best way to handle him was not to give him too much to go on; never let him inside your mind or give him anything that he could use – ever.

'I came across some information this evening about a group that call themselves "The 10". Know anything about them, Jack?'

Judas heard a horse and carriage trundle down a wet, cobbled street and the faint peep-peep of a policeman's whistle somewhere far away in the past, calling for help.

'Oh, The 10! Still around then, still making trouble and trying to gain access to the Grove, are they? Still searching for redemption or whatever it is they're looking for? Nice boys, I always thought; always making lots of lovely noise in the underworld, juicy little cuts of nastiness and snippets of evil. They're very talented, you know.'

Judas' ears pricked up, and he pulled up a chair. 'What's the Grove?' He bit his lip, and almost bit it again, harder, because of his own stupidity. He'd shown far too much interest far too quickly, and now Jack had the upper hand.

Jack laughed his barking little laugh, and Judas imagined him smiling and hugging himself, rocking back and forth; happy that he was in control of the flow of information, happy that he was back in control again, calling the shots and controlling the mood.

'Don't know about the Grove? Never heard of it? Oh, dear me, oh how priceless! The famous Judas, Heaven's Hector, has never heard of the Grove? He's never heard of the one place that all of the nasty, ghastly types want to break into? A lovely place it is, well, a kind of lovely place. Depends on what you're looking for. What's it worth to you, Judas? What do I get in return for the information?'

Judas sat down again and wiped his mouth on the cuff of his shirt. Count to ten, he told himself, give him the time to gloat, let him control the exchange. Jack giggled to himself. It was a nasty, high-pitched, maniacal little sound. You could hear him doing it as he bent over a massacred torso in a dingy little alleyway, knife in hand and smile on lips.

'How do you know about this place?'

Judas looked at the blood on his cuff and then took out his notepad. This was going to be really hard, and he was going to have to make a deal with one of the people he hated most of all. But it was going to be worth it because he'd be able to save lives with the information. He'd done a deal with the Devil a few years ago in Glasgow, the real Devil, Lucifer himself. Hopefully he wouldn't be paying as high a price for this.

Jack giggled again. Silence. More giggling.

'I hear things in here, Judas, inside your prison. Information gets stuck in here; just like me, it can't move on, it just settles. You can pick it up easily if you know where to find it. But as I said, what do I get out of this exchange? What does the Ripper get?'

Before Judas got a chance to answer, something unusual happened. The Museum whispered to him. Soft sounds hugged the walls and words slipped carefully and quietly into his mind. He sat up quickly. The sound of a foghorn in Jack's time floated up from the Thames as the words flowed into Judas. He understood them immediately and realised that the Museum was trying to help.

Judas cleared his throat and felt better.

'You get to go back twenty-four hours Jack; no more than that. The rules are the same as last time. The Museum lets you out and winds back the clock, and you get one of your victims back. Nothing new, no fresh victims. If you try and take a new one then the Museum comes to see you, and just so we're all clear about this, it can do what it wants with you for twenty-four hours. Deal?'

Jack didn't giggle again.

'What kind of deal is that? I offer you some of the best information in here and I get nothing in return. Hardly worth it, Judas, really. I'm sure a man of your experience and means can offer up something a little more illuminating, something more exciting?'

Jack's voice couldn't hide the nervous tension and anxiety inside him. He desperately wanted to get out and kill something. The Museum whispers continued. Jack was going to feel a new sort of pain if he stepped out of line. Judas almost wanted him to so that he could feel the sort of pain that he had visited on his victims. Judas heard heavy curtains parting and polished shoes pacing across a thick rug; swoosh-swoosh they went, the torment and anticipation in equal measure could be felt and heard from centuries away.

Finally, Jack seemed to realise that the deal on the table was the only one he was going to get. 'Okay Judas, you win. I give you the information you desire, and the Museum sends me back. Agreed?'

Judas just cleared his throat. He was waiting for the upper hand to become his upper hand and not Jack's.

'I want to go back to the 31st of August 1888 and dear Mary Ann; she was always my favourite.' Jack tittered again. He couldn't help himself, so Judas just sat still and made him sweat.

The Museum had the power to turn back time. It could re-open a specific moment so that you could see what happened then, how the murderer staged the crime, and sometimes how they got away with it. Judas had used it many times before in order to understand a present-day case better. It looked real, but the people you saw there were just shadows of the people that they used to be, and because they were just shadows, they felt no pain. Judas knew that Jack would live every moment over and over again, the chase, the butchery and the flight. Then he would gloat and preen like a bloody peacock. He loved the fact that he had never been caught by the policemen of his age.

'Okay Jack, you have the floor, tell me everything.'

'Thank you. Are you sure that you don't know more about this gang, Judas? You haven't come across them somewhere else? The 10? They don't sound familiar at all?'

'Get on with it, Jack, I haven't got all day you know. Oh, hang on, yes I have, I've got all the time in the world and then some, Jack, so just give us the information and then you can clear off.'

Before Jack could answer there was a deep, ominous rumble, and the sound of thunder.

Judas looked at Williams and raised his eyebrows. The Museum was listening in.

'The Grove is a mirror place to heaven. It's a place of power, where there are no rules, and no one sits in judgement on anyone else; each man is his own God there. The 10 want to find the gates to the Grove, and they want the key that opens them. Only a couple of entities know where the entrance and the key are, apparently, but the whisper on the streets is that someone down there has been careless. Someone, or something, has let the cat out of the bag, and the whereabouts are known now.'

You could hear the satisfaction in Jack's voice.

Judas was about to say something when the rumble he had heard before started to get louder, and the chair and the table started to vibrate and shudder. Williams moved towards the door, shortening the distance between himself and the nearest escape route. The rumble got louder still, and now even Judas was starting to get nervous; he had never heard or seen the Museum respond like this. This was bad. This was serious. This was get out of town noise.

'Museum!'

Judas shouted as loudly as he could, but the noise carried on. Judas could make out Jack's voice screaming somewhere, crying out for help; somewhere back in time Jack the Ripper was in pain.

After what seemed and felt like a long time, the noise abruptly stopped and the sound of Jack the Ripper and the London he took great pleasure in terrorising was gone. Judas thought he could hear his own heart beating very loudly and very quickly but realised that it was in fact Williams'.

Williams was on the floor in the corner of the room. He was wide-eyed, breathless and not a little scared. Judas felt the same way but was trying hard not to show it. He asked the silence again:

'Museum?'

The room was deathly quiet. If Judas had had a pin, he would have dropped it in order to prove a point to himself, but he hadn't, so he didn't.

He was about to get up and leave when the silence was punctured with the sound of wings beating, and then the Museum spoke.

When he looked back on this moment, he would remember it as the moment when the world turned itself upside down, and then back again. It was one of those 'why didn't I see that before?' sort of moments.

The voice of the Museum said, 'Jack has knowledge that he should not have, so I have decided to make myself known to you, and to deal with Jack before he can tell it to anyone else. He will not roam the streets of his London again until I release him. He is in pain now, Judas, a pain that he will not have believed possible or imaginable. You will not hear from him, nor will you be able to summon him for some time. That is the precaution that I must take now. It would be best that you forget him for now. He cannot help you further.

'The Grove that he speaks of exists, Judas; it is a place that was made long ago, created long before this world was even young. You know of him that built it. He was punished for it among other things, and the High Angels built a secret wall around it and cast it off into time. We thought that it was gone and forgotten but somehow someone has found it. It is a mirror to the city of Heaven but there is no ruler there. It is a place without order or rules; anyone who enters it can be its ruler and fill it with whatever they desire. They say that if the walls of the Grove were cast down and the gates opened, it would fill with all the worst of creation. It would become a second Hell and bring about another war. The fact that you now know about it puts you in real danger, Judas.'

'Brilliant news, Museum, thanks for that.'

Judas got up from his chair and walked around the room, absently picking things up from the floor and replacing them.

'So, there's a new gang in town, or rather an old gang, that are killing angels and searching for this alternative Heaven. If they find it then they'll throw open the gates and it will be a stampede followed by a three-way war: Heaven on one side, Hell and this other place on the other. That about right?'

'Yes,' replied the Museum.

'Why are they killing angels then?' Judas already knew the answer, but he wanted it spelled out for him.

'The 10 think that one of the fallen angels knows the location of the Grove; if they kill enough of them, then they'll find out where it is.'

The Museum sounded strange. It sounded wary but excited, as if it knew that it was about to win a bet and win big. Judas closed the last cabinet door and turned the handle. The room was tidy, but his mind was in a state. Everything sounded plausible. The 10 wanted something badly. They were killing the angels because they thought the angels could help them get it. So far, so simple; nothing out of the ordinary there. But there was something niggling at him. It was all too neat. Straightforward things were suspicious; follow the breadcrumbs and find the big bad wolf, easy. But this seemed too easy. And what was getting to the Museum; why the sudden transparency? First Michael shows up, then there was the slave market, the bloody wings sent to the Yard… why? Judas sat back down again. Williams had finally parted company with the floor and pulled up a chair. He looked shaken.

'There is one who can help you, Judas. Michael is abroad, is he not?'

It seemed the Museum had become talkative.

He sat up quickly.

'Yes, he is. Just showed up last night as it happens; how do you know?'

There was a soft rumble.

'Judas, I am trying to be of assistance to you. Within these walls I am powerful; I am here as custodian of the Museum. I am not "the Museum" as you put it, merely a servant that also acts as a doorkeeper and key holder. Just because I am here all the time does not mean that I cannot hear or see what goes on outside of this building.

'Michael is abroad. I have felt it. Speak to him of the Grove and see how he reacts to the news. I think you will learn something.

"I must leave you now; the exhibits grow restless and angry when one of their own is punished. Jack is hurting, but that does not stop his constant whispering and wheedling. He will find a way to get his revenge given the time.'

This time there was no tell-tale gust of wind or rumble to signal the Museum's departure, just a long sigh that stretched out into the silence and then was gone. The meeting was over.

17 RAY THE SNITCH

Williams couldn't get out of the Museum quickly enough. The big fella could move fast when he wanted to, it seemed. Judas followed him down the corridor at a more sedate pace. Why was the Museum so keen for him to speak to Michael? Watch his reaction and see what happens, it had said. It all sounded a bit theatrical, and Judas didn't like being manoeuvred. He was the one that usually did the manoeuvring. It wasn't a nice feeling and it irked him. When he got back to the office Williams was standing over the kettle in the far corner of the office with a tea mug in each hand. He was holding them tightly as if they were about to be taken from him, and he'd forgotten to flick the switch.

'It's going to take a long time to boil like that, Williams.'

He looked shaken, thought Judas. It took a second for Williams to realise that the switch should be a welcoming yellow colour and not a dead orange. If you were in a muddle or you needed time to think, just make some tea. Easy. The sound of the filament inside cracking and the soft rumble of the water boiling always stopped time. No matter what was going on in the world, the sound always stopped you in your tracks; not for long, but it always made you think twice. Judas sat down and watched his partner closely. Williams hadn't spent any real time in the Museum lately, and it was obvious that he wasn't used to its little ways. He'd accompanied Judas many times and always sat in the background taking notes when Judas questioned one of the exhibits, but this time it was different. The Museum itself had never talked back, and never thrown the furniture around, let alone give one of the inmates a roughing up. Judas liked Williams but he had seen this look before on the faces of some of his old partners, just before they offered up their resignations. He hoped that this wasn't the beginning of the end for their working relationship.

They sat together and drank their tea in silence. Every now and again Williams would stir; he brushed a lock of hair out of his eyes or checked a button on his shirt to make sure that it was still doing its job. Then he pretended to analyse a report or two, flicking the top cover over and gazing intently at the first page, not really reading it but forcing his eyes to do something. Go on, say something, let it out, thought Judas. Williams slurped at his tea and wiped his mouth with the back of his sleeve and blew gently down at the surface of the mug. The steam floated up and disappeared into the map of Greater London on the wall somewhere over Fulham. Judas imagined it as his courage, floating away and leaving him.

'Why don't you take the rest of the day off? Go home, see the kids. I'll see about contacting Michael and then I'll call you and we can work out what we're doing.'

Williams looked up from his tea.

'I'm alright, really. Just took me off guard, that did. Have you spoken to it before, like that I mean? It seemed bigger than the room, it filled it up; there was noise all around us, everywhere, inside the room and inside my head all at the same time.

'Jack was genuinely frightened of it, too. Did you hear him screaming inside the wind? It sounded like he was being ripped apart and then pushed back together again.'

Judas got up and took Williams' coat from the hook behind the door.

'Here, go home.'

Williams took it reluctantly, slipped it on and walked out. Judas watched him walk down the corridor and disappear through the swinging doors at the end. He closed the office door and sat down. It had been a long couple of days. Maybe he needed some sleep, too.

The phone rang and brought him back to the present with a jolt. Why did phones always do that? Why couldn't the ringer start low and increase in volume until it was at a nice friendly, come-and-pick-me-up tone? Someone was going to make a fortune if a phone could recognise a hangover and alter the ring volume accordingly. Judas looked down at it, cleared his mind and then lifted the receiver.

'Front desk here, Sir. All of the power on the two floors below your "office" has gone, Sir. Any idea when we'll be getting it back?'

The front desk sergeant was an old policeman called Henshaw. He'd been with the force since he could hold his dad's razor. He'd been a beat copper and drove one of the first Panda cars, a career policeman, a community first sort of chap, well-liked and experienced, which in this day and age was rare. He was a good man, and one of the only officers left that knew about the Black Museum and the 'special' detectives that worked there. Some of the wags spread rumours about him; the one doing the rounds at the moment was that he had a tattoo of Dixon of Dock Green on his bottom. The only funny thing about that particular rumour was that it was probably true. He most likely had a tattoo of 'The Sweeney', too. One arm a lifelike image of John Thaw and the other a near lookalike of Dennis Waterman.

'I'm really sorry about this, Henshaw. It will sort itself out shortly; everything will be back to normal in a jiffy, or less. Sorry.'

Judas replaced the handset, but just before it cut off the call he heard Henshaw's reply, 'Back to normal? Up there? Don't make me laugh!'

Judas smiled and imagined Henshaw regaling his wife with stories of the odd goings-on at the Yard, and the things he'd seen. If only you'd seen what I'd seen Henshaw, then you'd have a story to tell.

It was no good waiting around the Yard, so Judas decided to head off and get something to eat. He decided on something meaty and heavy, and there was only one place to go for that: the Gay Hussar on Frith Street in Soho. He wandered across town; he avoided the tourists on Oxford Street by heading down Great Marlborough street and then performed a zigzag through the happy media wonderland around Poland and Wardour Streets. Everywhere he turned there were creative and pretentious advertising people, production company producers and their runners. This was the land of the middle-class arty clone, all of whom were dressed in their uniforms. Everyone was wearing the most expensive trainers known to man, and the most expensive Japanese denim jeans in the world, jostling and walking fast to their soap powder television advert voice-over recordings. They didn't talk, but waffled and jabbered into their tablets, hefting their ironic linen shopping bags around, filled to the brim with contracts and call-sheets. Whoever said that the idiots would rise and take over the world was right, thought Judas as he cut across Wardour Street and took a short cut down St Margaret's Place on to Dean Street. He walked a short distance up the road, skirting the southern edge of Soho Square before entering Frith Street from the top end.

An army of Big Issue sellers were adjusting their bright red tabards and preparing themselves to venture forth and do battle for the small change of London's workforce. He rummaged through his pockets, found a new fiver, and handed it over to purchase the roughly printed magazine that he hoped would help the homeless a little bit. The restaurant was situated on the left; a wooden sign ran across its frontage, with big gold leaf letters that announced that this was indeed the Gay Hussar. If you wanted heavy Hungarian food, it was the only place to get the real stuff. You didn't arrange any appointments in the afternoon if you were tying one on in the Hussar; the food alone would put you in a warm, fluffy coma for a few hours, it was that heavy. Judas had tasted the real stuff many years ago, in a castle that no one could ever find, in a valley where time itself was having a breather. The castle's owner was a very ancient and intelligent man with odd tastes and some rather fabulous ideas on recycling. Blood recycling. Judas had been told to visit the castle and introduce himself to the owner, to mark his card, as it were. He'd let the man live on certain conditions: he was not allowed to leave the valley, and he was not to give shelter or allow passage through his lands to anyone or anything that would do the local population harm. He was also informed that he could only feed on the inmates from the gulag in the mountains nearby, and only then if they had done something particularly heinous. As far as Judas knew, that bargain had been kept – so far. The Gay Hussar's menu had meat in it, and on it. There were greasy fingerprints from the previous diner smudged all over it. If you were hungry while waiting for your order you could always lick the menu, thought Judas. Even the walls were meat coloured. Judas took a seat at the back, with a clear view of the door. Some habits were impossible to forget.

The waiter, a short, cubic man with dark cavalry whiskers and a ruddy complexion, ambled over.

'A friend coming?' he asked as he pointed at the vacant chair opposite Judas.

'Just me today, thank you,' Judas replied.

Judas took the menu that the waiter waved at him like a heavy fan and pretended to scan it. He already knew what he wanted, but just wanted to pretend that he was interested in hearing what the special was. The waiter duly regurgitated what the chef had felt was suitably off-piste today like a hairy robot from Eastern Europe. Would he still be here post-Brexit, mused Judas.

The goulash he ordered arrived with a bottle of heady red wine. He polished both off and sat there, letting his food go down and his mind settle. A tiny bead of sweat rolled down his forehead, and he felt its partner heading for the base of his spine. Something had set the back part of his brain working. Something was hiding behind one of the dark clouds in the storm of his thoughts. He knew it was there, but every time he got close to it an annoying gust sent it scurrying away. He nibbled at some thick, crusty bread and stirred his coffee absently. It would come, give it time; the word would trigger the memory and set the machine that was his brain working and the idea would pop out eventually. The key was not to force it, to think of anything other than work, and it would surface. He watched the waiter pinballing between the tables. He clearly had a routine: watch the customer arrive, approach, wave at a table, and then wait for precisely two minutes. Any longer and they'd think the service was awful, any quicker and he'd be being pushy. He was a master. After the two minutes he'd amble over and ask if a friend would be joining. Then he'd hand over the menu and ambush them with the specials list, before retiring until summoned with a nod of the head or a lowering of the menu.

I know what The 10 want, and I know why they are killing the angels; that bit's clear, there's a why and there's a what for. But who is calling the shots here, and how do I get to him and stop him, or them? thought Judas. A lightbulb inside his mind started to flicker and then glow brightly. They're killing angels, so what I need is an angel that owes me a favour. Judas called the waiter over and asked for the bill. The meal was good value as usual, and the time spent away from the Yard had helped.

Judas paid, grabbed his coat and then headed for Charing Cross road and the number 19 bus to Upper Street. Ray was his angel snitch, and he lived near the Angel Islington. Judas had saved Ray ten years earlier, and Ray felt that he was very much in his debt. Judas had tried many times to tell Ray that he didn't owe him anything, that he had just been doing his job, but Ray just waved his words away. Angels lived by an ancient code, and if a human helped them in any way they were bound to the human for as long as that human lived. Angels live a very long time, and humans don't, so it's not so bad for the angel, really; to the humans it was for ever, but to an angel it was just the time it took to wash your hair.

Ray had been beaten up badly and was about to be burned at the stake by the Shadwell Purists. The Purists were a gang of shaven-headed right-wing zealots that saw the newly arrived angels as illegal immigrants and wanted all of them dead. There had already been some nasty murders and the angels were threatening to take up arms to defend themselves. The Black Museum got the gig of course, and Judas had showed up in the nick of time with Tompkins, an old partner, saving Ray from being toasted on a bonfire. Ray had become his contact with the East End angels from then on. He was good at being a snitch, and he always kept his word, so Judas had kept an eye out for him, and Ray kept an ear out for Judas.

As the number 19 bus weaved up the road past King's Cross, Judas wondered why Ray had chosen Angel Islington as a place to live. The bus pulled into the stop opposite the tube station, and Judas stepped off. Halfway up Upper Street, there was an antiques market. Ray had a flat in the building above it. Angels never lived in basements, and they didn't like the tube for obvious reasons. Judas climbed the stairs at the back of the market and then rapped on the door to the flat. After a few seconds of silence, he remembered that Ray was laid-back, but also a bit paranoid, so he stood back in order that Ray could see him through the security glass of the door. Moments later he heard the first of three security chains being drawn, and then the barrel of a Banham lock turning; there was no mistaking the sound of a Banham if you were a Policeman. The door inched open in slow-motion, it seemed, and then a pale white face appeared in the gap between door and frame.

'Hello, Ray.' Judas smiled his best 'I know I'm a Policeman but…' smile, raised his eyebrows, and tried to look as friendly as possible.

The door swung open, and a smiling Ray filled the entrance. He was wearing a t-shirt and jeans and looked to be in rude health. Like all angels he was muscular and had flawless skin. He flapped his wings and folded them snugly against his back, then motioned for Judas to enter.

'Where do you lot get your clothes from?' said Judas.

Ray smiled and wandered down the corridor, leaving Judas to lock up, which took longer than expected.

Ray's flat was also his lock-up. Inside it sat everything he owned, and everything he had to trade. Needless to say, it was filled from floor to ceiling with boxes of all shapes and sizes. Ray dealt in things of a magical nature. He collected artefacts and objects d'art of a dubious nature: books that made you disappear, furniture that talked and sang, and pictures that whispered and faded. His speciality was finding owners for things that shouldn't be owned. Ray easily navigated the small spaces left between the stacks of boxes and sat down in his favourite chair by the window.

'Looking for this, Judas?' Ray pointed at a large, black leather-bound book on the table. Even though he had only just seen it for the first time there was something familiar about it. He seemed drawn to it. But Judas was here on other business and put it out of his mind.

'Ray, you owe me a favour. I'm calling it in.'

Ray looked nervous. His wings gave a twitch. Angels have the same fight or flight instinct that humans have. If they feel threatened you get a little tremor of feathers, then it's either an expensive repair bill to replace all of your windows because they've flown straight through them and made their escape, or you get a limb ripped off and it's a big bill from your health care provider instead.

'What exactly is it that you want me to do, Judas?" Ray was softly spoken. It had taken him a while to speak again at all after the Second Fall, and his words came slowly, like rain in a desert.

'The code is the code, Judas. Ask me what you will and I will do as you ask.'

Judas nodded, and smiled, then moved over to the table, lifted the book up and looked at it closely. Ray got up and started to pace around the room behind him.

'I bought it from a man in a pub up in Camden, in the tunnels under the canals, at a bar where the Low Tribes drink. Wanted a fair bit for it but took less in order to get it off his hands. There's something not quite right about it. Being an angel, I took it. Felt normal to me – at first. Then, there was this sound. Just at the edge of normal. You can hear it, like a tone in the dark, pulsing and reaching out.'

Judas put the book down and stepped back from the table. When an angel tells you something's odd then you give it two wide-berths.

Ray moved over to the window and motioned for Judas to follow. He pointed down through the dirty glass at a man in a long coat carrying another 'bag for life' with a witty marketing slogan on it. The man was tall; heavy, even. He had grey hair combed severely back from a broad forehead and wore dark-rimmed spectacles in a Funeral in Berlin sort of style. Ray and Judas watched him for a few minutes; he never moved, and he kept his eyes trained on the entrance to the market as if were he to blink or look away, the whole place would disappear.

'He's like that day after day,' said Ray. 'I wouldn't be bothered in the slightest, if it weren't for the fact that he's been asking around about a book in German that was bought from a chap in Camden. Everyone in the market knows not to mention me but he never leaves that spot. It's as if he can sense the book.'

Judas made a mental note of the man and then turned back to the room. The book wasn't important right now. Angel killers were important right now.

'Tea?'

Ray had already padded into the kitchen and was running the hot tap prior to filling the kettle. Judas followed and lounged against the kitchen doorframe. The kitchen was spotless and tastefully decorated with glazed pottery in hues of orange and red and the latest shiny stuff from Italy to do the cooking, baking, chilling, freezing and baffling.

'Ray, are you still on that dating site? The mixed one, that pairs angels with humans?'

Ray stirred the teapot and nodded. 'Not as much as I used to be but yes, I still have a profile on there.'

He poured two cups of tea, no mugs here, added the milk and sugar and offered one to Judas. With tea in hand, they returned to the lounge and sat down by the window again.

'Ray, I need you to activate your status and say that you're looking for some human company, then look for anyone that wants to meet out in the open in South London, the Commons, the green spaces, places like that. Then call me if you get any bites.'

Ray drank his tea slowly; his mind was processing the request.

'Does this have anything with the disappearances, Judas? Because if you want me to put my head in a noose, then you tell me exactly who's hanging the rope from the tree, or I don't go.'

Judas sat down and tilted his head back on the sofa. The ceiling was covered in paintings. There was everything there from pastoral scenes of old England, to pop art, to Russian Constructivism. Why did he put them on the ceiling, thought Judas? He closed his eyes for a second. He could hear the sound of the book again; a low hum that crackled every now and again and made him think of really old radios that couldn't pick up the right frequency. Somewhere in the back of his mind, something was happening. Ray disturbed his thoughts with a cough and a feather ruffle. Judas opened his eyes again and sat up.

'It is dangerous, it could be very dangerous, in fact it's probably the most dangerous thing I've ever asked you to do, but before you say no I want you to know that I do also have an insurance policy that should keep even you happy. The

Archangel Michael will be there to protect you and me, I hope.'

Ray looked up sharply. 'The Michael? The big, bad Michael that likes to pull things apart and then put them back together the wrong way? The "I hate people, little angels, beasts and all other not-perfect creatures" Michael?'

Judas took a mouthful of tea. It tasted good, and the look on Ray's face was even better. With Michael on board and riding shotgun he knew he had his decoy angel.

'Yes, that Michael. He's changed a bit since your last sight of him I expect. He only hates most things these days, not everything.'

18 THE WR⦿NG ANGEL

Michael was so far away at that moment that it was impossible for their words to reach him and make his ears. He was at the heart of the City of Heaven in the Great Hall, the place where the angels went to receive their orders. He'd flown there as soon as he'd heard Jack the Ripper tell Judas that a group of dark souls calling themselves 'The 10' had learned about the secret Grove and were desperately close to finding a way inside. 'He' needed to know this, and that was why Michael was standing in the far corner of the hall, waiting to be summoned by one of the heralds so that he could make his report and learn what his next course of action was going to be. There were many other angels waiting silently ahead of him, and in the Great Hall all were equal, so the wait was going to be longer than he hoped, and that worried him. The other thing that was concerning him right now was what Judas and the other angel were planning in his absence. If things played out in the way that Michael saw them playing out, then it would soon be time for the other angel's release. Surely, he'd served his sentence, he thought, as the line of angels in front of him grew shorter.

The City of Heaven sat at the centre of a vast sea of stars. The gravitational pull of each of the stars caused this sea of light and rock to ripple and crack. Small suns that had just been born orbited the city and showered their light down on its rooftops and streets, so that shadows formed and something approximating night fell with regularity. It was a remarkable place, and on first sight it looked like a drawing board for a million civilisations. The City of Heaven had high towers that sat on the shoulders of domed halls, and great libraries with a thousand doors on each side. Buildings built for giants rubbed shoulders with long, low terraces of structures for creatures no bigger than the average Jack Russell terrier. It should've been a mess but somehow the anarchy of it all was pleasant on the eye. All of these places were once full of life, and the city hummed with the songs and sounds of the creatures that lived there, but now it was far too quiet and there were more echoes than beings alive here. The First Fall of the Morningstar, and then the Second Fall, had trimmed the population drastically, and as Michael looked down onto those lonely streets, he felt something like guilt, because he had been responsible for a lot of the trimming. Many angels that he knew and respected had stood in the ranks of the opposition, sheltering, and protecting the half-angel children they had created with their human lovers. He would never forget the look on their faces: fear, mixed with anger and despair. The law had been broken; the one that decreed no half-breed could live in both the City of Heaven and on earth. So, they had to die. That was the price that they had to pay. Not one of the angels was prepared to give up a single child, and so a lot of blood was shed.

The line got shorter and shorter, and then it was his turn; the power of the one true light had fallen on him once again, and he flexed his wings to receive the full force of it. He spoke at length about what had transpired below and the role that Judas had played in those events. He even spoke about the other angel, and of the Grove, and of the possibility of another great war. Of how he feared the collapse of order and the rise of those to set the darkness free and give it power. Then he knelt and breathed in his master's words. 'His' reply was short and over in a flash that was quicker and brighter than a fork of lightning in a darkened room. First, there was an empty space inside your mind, then it was suddenly filled, and afterwards it was as if you had always had those thoughts there. Then the light reduced in its intensity, the sound of the words faded, and Michael nodded in agreement. He understood what he had to do. That was all. There was nothing else. Just understand, and just do.

Michael walked from the Great Hall. He passed some of the others on his way to the edge of the platform, but he didn't have time to stop and talk. They knew his moods and when he did not return any of their greetings, they flexed their wings and leapt into the darkness to complete their own tasks and errands. Michael watched one or two of them flying out across the sea of stars, their silver and grey wings catching the light, creating slices of mirrors as they turned the light away and then disappeared into the blackness of space.

Before setting off from the tower at the centre of the Great Hall he looked down on to the city once again. It was sadly quiet, and each time he returned it felt more open and even emptier. He took his time and collected his thoughts. He'd told Judas that this was the greatest city ever made. It was still magnificent, but it was in decline. Down there, shining brightly was the earth. It was a small place, but it was filled with magic and life, and it throbbed with energy and noise and could be wondrous – in the right hands. Michael looked down on it and wondered why somebody or something was bent on destroying it. What motivated these little specks of humanity to tear down all that had been created for them? There was a plan for Earth, and it must be carried out, blindly, quickly and to the letter. Those were his orders, and because he was his master's vengeance they would be completed. Blood and fear on swift wings cometh. Michael unfurled his great wings, patted the scabbard of his great sword, looked back at the Great Hall and the light that shone from within, then leapt into the cold space between the worlds he was sworn to protect.

Judas was leaping into a cold, dark space too, the cold, dark space between a sheet and a duvet on his bed in his flat.

The crisp sting of the cold material made him tense his shoulders and roll into a ball, then he did what most single men do and sprinted with his feet rubbing against the cotton to warm it up. Friction from running feet was better than a hot water bottle. Soon the bed and the duvet were warm and welcoming, and he rolled onto his side and closed his eyes. He needed to sleep more often these days. It had been the enemy for him in the beginning; he hadn't been able to close his eyes without seeing the crown on that dirty, sweaty brow and the blood that sat on the tips of its thorns like tiny rubies. No other dream came to him in the beginning save that one. It wasn't just a reminder – it was a punishment. Thankfully that dream no longer came and he was able to sleep.

Ray was sleeping too – but not in a bed like Judas. Angels were able to interlock their wings and create a platform of feathers, and then sit back into it to rest. When they slept outdoors, they liked to sleep in trees, and when you saw them perched up there it was just like someone had rolled a great snowball up and placed it ever so gently on a branch. Huge and white, and glowing softly. They snuffled and snored just like the humans and had good dreams and nightmares too, but tonight Ray was far away, dreaming deep down inside the paintings that he loved so dearly; even the sound of the book couldn't bother him. On Ray's bedside table the screen of his mobile phone blinked intermittently like a small blue eye in need of some screen wipes. He had lots of messages and requests starting to fill up his inbox from interested parties who would like to engage in some human on angel action. The following morning, after a shower and his second pot of coffee, Ray started to vet the requests on his mobile, and it didn't take him long to find the young man he was looking for. Everything that Judas told him to look out for stood out in the description under the man's photograph. It was in a different order, of course; clumsy and heavy-handed, but it was as clear as day that it hadn't been written by someone looking for temporary love. He sent a message, arranging to meet. Ray put his mobile down on the kitchen table and looked out of his favourite window, scanning the people coming and going below. He didn't have to look for long to find what he was most afraid of. There he was again, the man in the long coat with the grey hair and the fixed gaze. Ray dialled Judas' number, telling him the good news about the meeting in Clapham, and the bad news about the book lover across the street.

All the time he was talking, he watched the man closely, absolutely sure that he hadn't blinked once. Then, after speaking to Judas, he sent an over-the-top, camp and slightly silly reply to the smiling knife that was the man on the dating App's avatar, accompanied by some risqué emoticons, setting a date and a time to meet with him. The man across the street was still motionless, eyelids and eyeballs included, so Ray decided that enough was enough, and hid the book away, before tidying up the flat. It was good therapy for him. When it was done, he sat down to think about the days ahead. He knew that he had to get rid of the book, the appearance of the grey-haired watcher made that very clear, and that he may need to disappear soon as well. Get some fresh air, fly somewhere new for a change. And, if the man from Clapham who wanted to spend the evening with him was the one behind the disappearances of the other angels, then he'd get the surprise of his life when he saw Michael come flying out of the night with sword in hand. He'd realise that he'd got the wrong angel and it would hurt. It would also put Ray right up there in full view of whoever else was involved, and Ray would rather that that didn't happen, so he needed a plan of his own.

19 THE DEAD OF THE NIGHT

James turned the sign on the front door of the Shoals to the 'Open' position, giving one of the tables at the front of the restaurant a very professional and very accurate flick with a tea-towel, and removing a crumb of forgotten batter. The fryers had all heated up nicely and neat rows of fish wearing crisp golden overcoats were lying down, waiting to be eaten. James heard that some of the others were up early too, speaking to their underworld contacts and private bankers in the back rooms, moving money around and planning shipments from Turkey and Montenegro of arms and drugs. The drugs brought everyone that used them misery and the guns brought the pushers power to order more and more misery for the users to enjoy. The stylishly designed retro-tinkle bell over the door pinged, followed by a metallic rattle, and he nodded at the first customer of the day. At the same time his mobile phone gave a little joyless beep and a smile started to form on his face as he read the message. John would be pleased. He'd be sharpening his knife again, not that he needed to, but he did it all the same. They had a date with a fresh angel to look forward to tomorrow night. Friday night. This time James hoped that the angel would give up the information that John wanted so badly, so that they could finally move to the next stage of whatever plan John was following.

Judas was miles away, deep in thought, when Williams came in to the office that Thursday morning. Judas had slept well and eaten breakfast – a minor miracle in itself – and taken the call from Ray; now he had only to make a plan that would bring these angel slayings to an end and find out exactly who these other idiots were. Williams performed his usual ritual; coat on the hanger, newspaper on the filing cabinet, quick look at his reflection, and then the ugly grimace as he adjusted the waistband of his straining trousers. Jane had obviously fed him well again last night, or he'd stopped jogging – again.

'So, what did you find out about the angel wings and the killings then, Judas?' Williams was always chirpy and happy first thing in the morning. It was bloody annoying.

'Sit down and turn the smile down a bit, you're blinding me with fluoride.

"We've got a trap to set for someone or something on Clapham Common. My snitch is going to be our bait. I'm hoping that The 10 will try and snatch him to get the information they need about this mysterious Grove, and then we can snatch them instead. It's going to get bloody I reckon, so I've asked Thornton and some of his well-dressed warriors to help us out. We also have some extra muscle on top of that, as Michael will be with us too. Hopefully that will tip the balance in our favour. I reckon it would be a good idea for you to forego your usual hero routine and wear a stab vest tonight; there are plenty at the front desk so you can pick one up before we leave.'

Williams sat bolt upright at the mention of Michael.

'A real Archangel! You really are bringing out the big guns then; must be worried. A first order angel down here and on the team – that'll be something to see.'

Williams was on point like a gun dog that had just seen a bush twitch; his eyebrows had jumped halfway up his forehead as if they'd been electrocuted, and his shirt buttons were straining as he puffed up with excitement. Judas just smiled; everybody in London was comfortable with the angels that lived among them now, but mention an Archangel and everyone started acting like a reality TV star had moved in next door. Judas was happy to see Williams' excitement and it made him smile, but he thought it only fair to warn him about the angel he was about to meet for the first time.

'Look, Williams, he's bigger, stronger and more dangerous than any other angel you will have met before, and he's mean with it. Carries a huge sword and reacts badly to anyone who takes the Lord's name in vain. He's not really what you'd call a people person and he's not particularly fond of your kind either. I think he once referred to the race of men and women as a bit of a side-show.'

Now it was Williams' turn to smile. 'You always refer to us as "your lot", Judas and yet you're one of us aren't you? You walk, talk, shave, eat and use the old throne room to do your business, don't you? I've been in there after you and I know that you do, by the way. And you joined this famous institution to defend men and women against all things nasty. If you don't think that you belong, then why do you do it? Why put yourself through all of the pain and the aggravation? You may be old, crusty and immortal but you're flesh and blood, too. No wings on you, my friend. I'd say that you're more human than any of us, really.'

Williams did his little 'I've got one over on you' nod of the head and started going through the reports in the night book. It was good to see that his mood had improved from yesterday. One day, once this is all over, I'm going to have to fill Williams in on a little bit of my history, thought Judas.

'Anything interesting in there?'

Williams quickly scanned last night's report that had been sent up from the front desk, humming a lovely tune very badly as he read through it.

'We got the forensic report back from the lab on the wings we received the other day. Not much in there apart from the fact they found traces of what looks like common flour, the baking sort of flour, in with the wings. The rest of the report waffles on about trauma and evidence of a massive knife blade through the bone at the wing joint. The shape of the blade is unusual, and so is the configuration of the teeth on the blade; one side is razor-sharp, and the other is jagged like a saw. They're having difficulty dating the metal, they say. Really nasty weapon, apparently. They do think that there are similarities between our blade and the one used in the recent murder of a local businessman, and there is also a silver tab with a file number on it. The computer has matched the details of the knife to a couple of attacks that we were interested in last year. I'll dig that out in a second. There wasn't much left of the wings themselves, but some of the bone survived the pulping. Not much else on that, really. They do say that the feathers were removed completely before the tendons, and what was left of the flesh was minced.'

Judas sat up quickly. 'If they removed the feathers first then they had a reason for that; angel feathers are used to make a lot of things: potions, charms and spells, mostly. So, before we go out later to take a look at the Common and decide on where we're going to tether young Ray, I want you to head down to the Witches in Balham and see if they know anything about anyone trying to sell angel wing feathers. Don't let them flog you anything though, Williams, I had a tough time getting them to remove that spell they put on you last time.'

Williams looked up and was about to answer when he went as white as a sheet. His hand came up slowly from the desk and his mouth opened. Judas heard the great flapping sound and the thrumming of the air around them and knew what Williams was looking at without having to turn around.

'There's an angel at the window isn't there? A really big one, with a sword and an angry look on its face?'

Williams nodded and then regained enough composure to stand up.

Judas casually got up and opened both of the huge windows he'd had installed for situations just like this one; even when fully opened, Michael still had to squeeze to get through them. Normal-sized angels slipped in without any difficulty, but Michael was far from normal. Michael stood at the centre of the room and flexed his wings, causing the piles of neatly arranged paper on both desks to flutter and fall off onto the floor. Michael thought about apologising and just pretended not to notice instead.

'Oh, thank you, Michael, why don't you make yourself at home. It only took me a couple of years to get all of that organised. No, seriously, why don't you fly around a bit and redecorate for me?'

Michael cocked his head. He wasn't used to irony.

'I have been to the Great Hall in the City of Heaven, Judas, to report on the situation here in London. We have a job to do, or rather you have a job to do, and I am to assist you wherever and whenever I can. The Grove is to remain locked, and its whereabouts are to be safeguarded. Anyone concerned with finding and opening it is to be killed, and the people responsible for the angel murders are to be punished. They may have fallen, but they are still angels.'

'Just like that,' said Judas.

'Yes, Judas. Just like that.'

'Well, we'd better get ourselves down to Clapham then, and get started.'

Judas grabbed his mobile, found Ray's number and hit call. Seconds later, Ray answered, and Judas told him to get ready because his babysitter was on the way to pick him up. Judas then pointed to where Ray lived on the big map of Greater London on the wall. Michael took one look at it and then squeezed out of the window; he flew off with his wings fully open, heading for Islington.

Judas and Williams put on their coats and headed down to the car park. They took the stairs so as not to be seen. Williams was so excited at having seen Michael he spent all the time texting his wife to let her know. He was so distracted that he left the building without going to the front desk first to pick up his stab vest.

At the back of the Yard was a big car park. Real-estate developers had been eyeing it with lust and envy for the last twenty years. They could imagine tall apartment blocks packed to the rafters with tiny apartments that they could market as a city living oasis and make millions from the Russians that did their washing there. But it was not for sale, and never would be, because there were things under that car park that only a very few people knew about, and that secret was staying top secret. Apart from Judas and the serving Prime Minister, only a few people knew what happened down there. Judas and Williams strode purposely across it and got into the Mondeo parked against the wall near the ramp. Seconds later, Williams was terrifying traffic again. He was even worse than usual today because he kept stooping forward over the wheel and trying to look up into the sky.

'Eyes on the road please, Williams, let's not have to write any more reports to the carpool this week. Michael's got to go and pick Ray up first, and I guarantee that you that they will be there long before us, so just concentrate on your insurance premiums, okay? If you keep staring at him like that, he'll take offence anyway, so keep it to a minimum.'

Williams swerved to avoid another police car coming the other way and settled back into his seat. The roads were getting busy again. It was the golden hour for traffic, the calm before the storm of the rush hour. Even so, London was still heaving, and it took them just under half an hour to travel the meagre distance between town proper and Clapham.

As expected, Michael and Ray were already there, and waiting outside the church. Michael looked angry as usual, while Ray looked absolutely petrified. It was only when you got two angels together that you could see the difference in size and shape. The Archangels were massive – the thoroughbreds. Angels like Ray, on the other hand, were normal, if winged people could be classified as normal, that is. They still stood head and shoulders over the tallest of men, though. Ray was absent-mindedly stretching his wings and fluffing his feathers, trying to look bigger. Michael stood like a statue. He was big enough already. Williams pulled up to the kerb and turned the engine off. Judas got out and walked into the church grounds, and soon they were all nodding as he told them about his plan and what he wanted to happen.

The next hour flew past and the penumbra arrived far too quickly. Night was near, and daylight was running for cover. Judas couldn't help thinking that he'd left something out or missed something. He reached into his pocket for his familiar piece of silver and rubbed it between forefinger and thumb. Across the Common, Ray sat on the ground underneath the tree that Judas had chosen to tether his sacrificial lamb. He was listening to the sighing of the trees above and watching the trains speed past in both directions. Little rectangular pools of light illuminated the interior of the carriages, revealing weary workers trying to avoid eye contact with each other and robotically pressing the next page buttons of their E–readers.

Ray sat still, and watched the world go by. Earlier on that day he had made some calls and set his own little plan in action. Whatever happened, he was getting out of this and disappearing for a bit. A fox ambled across the grass in front of him on its way to an overflowing bin, or an alleyway behind one of Tooting's curry houses for supper. It was within a few feet of him when it stopped, sensing some other living creature nearby. The reflected light from a nearby lamppost turned its eyes into little discs of floating orange as it stared one way and then the other. Ray smiled, and the fox realised that no harm would come from this quarter so trotted off into the night.

The darkness had settled in now, so Judas had to look at Ray through his infra-red binoculars. Seeing Judas using them made Michael snort with contempt.

'We can't all see in the dark, okay. Tell me if he moves, or if anyone approaches him.'

Judas was feeling nervous. Ray had agreed to act as bait for the trap; he knew what The 10 had been doing to his kin, and he was prepared to take the risk. Plus, Michael had laughed at Ray earlier for no reason that Judas could see, and no angel could take that kind of slight. Ray was no hero, but he was not a coward either, and the look on Michael's face had stung him into action. Maybe that was why Michael had done it, thought Judas. A bit of the old angel management, maybe? Judas and Michael were well hidden behind a tree at the far end of the park; far enough away that they didn't risk anyone bumping into them by accident, but not so far that they couldn't react if they needed to. Williams and the Saints had stationed themselves at both railway bridge tunnels, so there would be no escape if Ray was killed or taken – none at all. Judas had warned them all that he needed The 10 alive, or as many of them as possible. There was something going on here that he wasn't quite sure about; something didn't feel right. The 10, whoever or whatever they were, wanted to get into this mysterious Grove to have their wicked way, and do whatever it was that murderers and gangsters dreamed of doing in an underworld Utopia. But something else was gnawing away at him. What was Jack the Ripper so happy about? What was the Museum doing in all of this and what had the book that Ray was hiding have to do with any of this? And why the hell was he thinking about golden paper clips?

It was probably nothing, but that devilish little niggle was still there.

Somewhere off in the dark a twig snapped underfoot, and Michael stirred.

'They are coming; six men are approaching from the far side of the park, and the other four are coming from the pond. Heavily armed. One carries a steel net and there is one big man at the rear marshalling them. I will fly over and position myself in the tree above Ray; when they attack, I will attack. You'd better call your Saints'

Judas was about to tell Michael to hang on a minute and follow the plan, but he knew that Michael was going to do what Michael always did. The 10 were in for a wild night tonight, thought Judas. He pulled his mobile from his pocket and called Thornton – quietly. The Saints were going to be busy, and they were going to have to move fast.

Across the park and under his tree Ray heard the men approaching too, and he stood up. He knew what he had to do. As he steadied himself a leaf floated down from the branch overhead and he heard a sound he knew well; it was the ruffle of feathers and the creak of leather. The sounds reassured him and made him smile, he felt safe – really safe.

20 FACES FROM THE PAST

There was a thunderstorm inside John's head again as he looked out across the empty park. It was rumbling inside him, and he could feel the words pushing at him, and whispering to him. He shook his head to get rid of them and felt dizzy for a second. Where was James? Where was that scheming little weasel? James sidled up to John and took up position at his shoulder. John spat a great white phlegmy gobbet of spittle onto the ground and motioned to James to move in. James smiled nervously and trotted off into the darkness. He would hang back until the angel was in the net and then make sure that the route back to the Shoals was clear. But John thought something felt different tonight. He could sense a presence out there. No matter. Just get the angel, make it talk, then open the box and let the anarchy spill out onto London's streets, and then it's all over. Blood on the streets like nothing ever seen before. It was going to be Biblical. James was the most capable of The 10 but John still didn't trust him. The rest of them were sheep, and their fear of power sickened him. Soon their paths would split. They had travelled a long road together and over the last one-hundred years the bond between them that had first been unbreakable had now been stretched to breaking point. The snap was coming, thought John. Each time the headaches came, he had only to squeeze his eyes tightly together and there in the middle of the waves and waves of shattering light-storms and the dark, rumbling noise would be James and the rest of them, leering back at him. It was inevitable. James would have to go, though, because he was the only one of them that suspected him. Maybe once they had got inside, he could let him go. He could let Jack have him, thought John. That would be the easy way; give him to the Ripper as part payment for his services.

John moved silently over the grass, took up his position at the back of the advancing group, and waited. A silent mist hung over the grass, filtering the light from the passing cars and distorting the shape of the trees that marked the perimeter of the Common. The traffic continued to softly hum all around them. He'd been watching this angel for the past hour, and he was sure that he was the one, the last angel that he was going to need. This one would get him inside, and then he'd find it, and it would all be over. John smiled to himself. Spring the trap and open the door. This time, let it be this time, he thought.

Ray could hear their breathing and smell their body odour and the washing powder they used floating in the air as they approached. The sound they made was hard against the still of the night; they moved in a clumsy, heavy-footed shuffle. One of them was singing quietly and another had eaten garlic recently. Ray would have been scared at any other time, but these men were about to get a rude awakening.

'Hello, are you Ray from Islington?'

One of the men stepped out of the shadows.

'Hello there,' said Ray.

He turned to the man and gave him one of his best 'let's have sex' smiles. The other man was dressed in a leather jacket and looked nothing like his dating app picture. Then again, whose social media picture looked like the real thing, anyway? The man's little eyes were darting about, subconsciously pointing out his friends hidden back there in the dark. He was giving them away before they had a chance to make their move, without knowing it. Men were strong, some of the time – they'd proved it again and again, thought Ray, but this one was one of the shouters from the back row. He was one of the bit-part players, one of the little ones that the big ones send in first. Fight fodder.

'Feel like getting down to it?' said the man, nervously. He stepped closer, and Ray could already read the panic on his face.

'That's why we're here, isn't it?' Ray stepped a little closer. The branch of the tree above him creaked ever so slightly. Not long now. The man reached into his pocket and took out a lighter. This was obviously the signal that would bring his friends to the party. Ray tensed, watched the tiny flame appear in the palm of the man's hand. Then it all began.

The rest of The 10 ran forward. They moved in a fluid, well-rehearsed way. John was a big fan of tactics; everyone needed to know their role and everyone had better do it, or else. John had a pretty effective method of imparting his tactics. A knife in the face is a good way to encourage you to follow the plan. His mantra was not so much 'kill or be killed' as 'kill or get killed by me.' So, the rest of the team reacted well to the signal, and they came running into the clearing between the trees. Paul threw the net they'd brought high into the air over the angel. It shimmered for a fraction, as one of the orange lights from a passing train illuminated it in the air. They had been fisherman back then in the beginning, so throwing nets was something that they could all do well, but something went wrong this time. The net hung in the air and stayed there; it didn't fall, and it certainly didn't pin the angel to the ground as it had done so many times before. James looked up, and so did the others, and then they all wished they hadn't. The biggest angel they had ever seen had dropped from the branches of the tree and was hovering in the air above their heads with the net in one hand and a huge sword in the other. Their trap was not their trap, it would seem, and now was a good time to panic. The big angel flicked its wing in what looked like a pre-arranged signal, and the smaller one took to the air, flying up and into the night.

The bait had flown. The iron hook in the yard would not see any blood tonight.

Judas watched Ray fly away and heard at the same time the rustle of leaves and the shouts of the Saints. Battle was joined, and The 10 were immediately forced back. Blow after blow rained down on them; the Saints were driving them like sheep, into the jaws of the stone bridge over the railway tracks. Thornton and the rest of his men were waiting there. There was no way out, and there would be no mercy.

Judas rushed forward. There was a body on the floor near the base of the tree where Ray had been standing moments earlier. He knew before he saw its face that it was Williams. His head was a mess, and his eyes were wide open in shock. It was the curly black hair and the stout trunk and short legs that told him that his partner had fallen. The blade of a big, curved knife was buried in his chest. Judas checked his stride for a second, and then the anger took him. Some people called it a red mist, but Judas had lost so many partners that his anger was something else altogether. It was cold and detached, and it pulsed inside him. Another partner lost and another widow's tears to be shed. He should have looked out for him better, should have kept him safe.

Judas ran on. Michael was standing in the midst of a mini massacre. Bodies struggled and twitched everywhere, so he knew that Michael had restrained himself, and that they were still alive – just. That was a first for Michael, because the people and creatures he normally fought with ended up in pieces too small for an ant to carry off. He stood with blue energy and fire rippling along the blade of his sword, and he looked even more fearsome in the dark.

His wings carved great arcs in the air; it was like watching a wave crashing against a black shore again and again. Shouts filled the air all around them, and the clang of steel on steel and the sound of a well-timed blow landing with a meaty thud punctuated the night. The fight was raging, and Judas was standing there doing nothing. Get moving, he told himself.

'Michael!' shouted Judas. 'Meet us at the bridge, I'm going to find Thornton.'

Michael acknowledged him with a slight nod of the head, before smashing another of The 10 to the floor with the back of his hand.

Judas ran down to the bridge. The rest of the Saints were there, with one exception. Thornton, their leader, was missing. The rest of the Saints were standing in a tight circle around a group of men that all appeared to be wounded and bleeding heavily. Two in the middle had fared worse than the others and were leaning against each other to remain upright. A strange quiet hung over the Common now. The Saints were never very vocal before or after a battle, but this time there seemed to be something else at work. They would have been two evenly matched forces, but the presence of Michael had tilted the balance in the Saints' favour. The Saints stood absolutely still. One of the wounded 10 started to mumble something.

'John.' He repeated the name under his breath.

Judas stepped closer, and the Saints stood to one side and allowed him to get a closer look at this man.

'Who is John? Where is this John? Is he your leader?'

Judas looked into the puffy, bruised, unrecognisable face and saw immediately that he was nearly unconscious and babbling.

'Who is this John? Is he your leader?'

The wounded man heard his voice from far away and tried to answer, his mouth moving in a slow, chewing sort of way. One of the other men nearby cut him off. 'Be still Thaddeus, John will come.' Judas turned away from the man on the ground and moved towards the man who had just spoken. 'Did you just say Thaddeus? John? You don't mean John the Baptist, do you? And the rest of you are… I don't believe it! This is some sort of sick joke! You can't be them, they died long ago, out in the desert. You, you are the Disciples, aren't you!'

Judas nearly fell over with shock. He looked around the circle of faces and knew them all now. His brothers of old, men he'd loved and then betrayed, standing there, in the flesh, thousands of miles away from the beginning and here in the now. Why hadn't he put two and two together before?

How stupid am I? he thought. The 10 are really the Disciples? You couldn't make this stuff up.

'Look at you all. What the hell happened to you? I thought you were all dead, long ago. Why this, and why now?'

The ring of men stood silently, looking like bleeding statues.

'My old friends from a past I thought I had forgotten have come back to punish me. Is that it? Killing angels and slave pits. Is all this worth it?'

Judas pointed at the blood on their faces.

'You are all a long way from home, brothers.' He had known them all so well back then. What kind of magic or curse had prolonged their lives? he thought, as he read each of their faces again and again.

The answer came quickly to him, of course. He wasn't the only one, was he? God didn't want him walking away, and why should he let them get away scot-free, either?

Simon stood up as straight as he could and looked into Judas' eyes; he had suffered a cruel blow to the arm, and he had to hold it across his chest to stop it from falling off entirely. The look Simon gave him was unexpected. Judas thought that he detected relief and gratitude in those eyes, rather than the anger and hatred he would have expected.

Judas was on the right side now and the Disciples, or The 10, or whatever they called themselves these days, were so far down in the darkness that they did not have a side anymore. Simon breathed out hard and his body convulsed with pain as the air left his lungs. The world felt upside down to him at the moment, but strangely he felt that an ending was close, a way out. John was not here anymore; his despotic and rigid leadership and fanaticism had choked the rest of them to death. It was a walking, living death, of course, but they were all dead inside all the same.

'I need to talk to you, Judas; to help myself by helping you, if you know what I mean. I just need to clear my head. May I walk a bit? I'm not running off, not with this arm.'

Judas nodded, and Simon walked away from the small group and towards the verge that led down to the tracks. He heard the train approaching and wondered what dying would feel like, if he leapt onto the tracks and let the snake-like machine grind him into the gravel. Maybe this time he really would die, so he looked into the night sky for a second, and then as the noise of the train was the loudest it would ever be – he jumped.

There was a rush of air as his body lost its fight with gravity, and a strange feeling of weightlessness came over him, then he felt a massive hand catch him by the wrist. Fortunately, it was the wrist that was attached to the good arm and not the nearly chopped off one, and he was lifted into the air. The train passed on, and he found that he was floating upwards; when he looked up, it was into the eyes of an angel. Michael carried him through the air and set him down on the grass. Angels were supposed to be there when you died, not when you lived, thought Simon before he passed out. The last thing he remembered was the strange dark rings around the angel's eyes, and the dew of the grass on his cheek.

Judas watched Michael set Simon down, and then walked off the bridge to find Thornton and his old friend, and new enemy – John the Baptist.

Down by the tracks at the far end of the bridge a vicious fight was nearing its conclusion. Thornton was battered, bloodied, and tired, but so was the big man that he had chased down here. There had been no quarter given and both men had several wounds that if not tended to quickly would spell the end for them. John was breathing hard. He'd never had a fight like this; the man he was fighting with looked old, but he was as strong as an ox. He stepped forward again, forcing the old man back towards the wall of the tunnel; the trains had been running frequently and each time one approached both men moved to opposite sides of the train tracks, so the train itself formed a temporary barrier between them, and they could gulp down some much-needed air. The respite was well needed – this fight could not go on for much longer. Thornton heard someone calling his name, but he was not going to get distracted; the other man was dangerous, and from the look in his eyes he was also stark, raving mad. The train passed through the fighting ground, and Thornton saw the big man leaning against the tunnel wall, resting and watching. His knife hand was viciously gouged from knuckles to wrist, red blood dripping down the blade of his knife. How much of that was his, and how much of it was the big man's, Thornton wondered. No matter. Better to keep up the pressure, keep the big man there where he could not escape; soon the rest of the Saints would be there, and it would be all over. He heard his name called again, this time closer, much closer, and then he saw Judas drop onto the gravel by the mouth of the tunnel. The big man looked up and saw Judas, and then he went rolling-eyeball crazy.

A new energy had taken hold of the Baptist. He swelled and grew, frothing at the mouth one second, then grabbing at his own head as if there was something in there. He shook and twitched and jumped like a cornered animal. Judas looked calm, the complete opposite; he just circled the big man, softly speaking some language that Thornton had never heard before. Thornton tossed his own knife over to Judas, but Judas ignored it. He left it on the ground and stepped closer to the mad man. What followed was astonishingly brutal, and incredibly fast. The Baptist slashed and punched, thumped and kicked out at Judas. In return, Judas chopped and blocked, and snapped at his enemy. All of his punches landed accurately, as if they were being guided by an invisible hand, and bit by bit, blow-by-blow, the big man weakened, until with one last punch to the throat, Judas knocked him over and out. He seemed even bigger unconscious. Judas thought that he looked like a tranquilised bear. John had changed in every way. He had always been a big man but now it seemed as if he had been enlarged. His head and limbs were larger than they should be, and it made him look like he belonged in the pages of a comic book. But it was unlikely that some distant alien star or magic power lamp had been responsible – John reeked of good old-fashioned earth magic.

Judas used some of his own and uttered an incantation that would hold John; he left him where he'd fallen to help the battered Thornton up the bank, and then they sat in silence together as the Saints tended to their own wounds. Moments later, once the blood had stopped flowing and their heads had cleared, they watched Thornton's troops escort the wounded 10 away. They would take them by the Church Roads and hold them in the tunnels for now. It was the safest and the quickest way. They wouldn't be seen again. Judas watched them all walk across the Common; one second they were there, and then the next they had disappeared into thin air.

Judas looked up into Michael's face and tried to smile.

'Did you know who they were?' he asked the angel.

Michael smiled down at him and shook his head.

'HE does not always tell me everything, Judas. I wish sometimes that he would, but then again it would be too much, even for me. Strange that they should be your old friends, here in this place and in this time. I know what we must do now, though. The Museum is the only place strong enough to hold them until such time as you work out what to do with them. If we take them there, we can ask the "other one" to place them back in different times so that they are separated for now. They will be confined to prison cells in the gaols of the past. They can hurt no one there, and they will be The 10 no longer.

'The big one, John. I think there is something inside him that we cannot allow to escape. The others are as cursed as you are, Judas, and will be safe and no threat, but we must keep them away from John. I know where he must go.'

Judas stood up and straightened his jacket; there was a nasty rip in the arm where John had slashed at him. The wound underneath was disappearing fast, faster than before. The blood had stopped flowing, and the skin had healed itself already.

'The Saints can bring them over to the Museum; they'll be safe with them. I need you to take John over there though. He's out for the count now, but he'll be awake soon. Can you help?'

The angel leaped into the air and was gone. So was the body of John the Baptist. He would be locked up in the Museum before he awoke. The last thing he needed to do now was to go and speak to Williams' widow. This was going to be the hard part of the night. After the killing came the crying.

21 THE SECOND OF THE FALLEN

The following morning Judas woke up to the angry and irritating buzzing of his alarm clock. It had been the first time in a long while that he'd slept all the way through the night. He looked down at his duvet. There wasn't a crease in it. He'd hardly moved all night. The fight with John the Baptist had obviously taken it out of him. He stretched, got out of bed, and took a shower. Looking in the mirror as he dressed, he could see only faint grey smudges where John's blows had landed. There was a nasty one just below his jaw line that could have been bad if it had been an inch or two higher. He dressed and ate breakfast. The television on the wall was alive with colour. Football scores from last night's games scrolled up and down, then black clouds fuelled by the chaos of yet another explosion billowed across the rooftops of buildings in the latest theatre of war. Last night, after Michael had flown off to the Museum with John and the Saints had taken the rest of The 10 off down the Church Roads, he had driven over to see Williams' wife. By the time he got there, the sadness he felt inside that she was no longer his wife, but his widow came crashing down on him like heavy thunder. He'd done his best, but his best was awful as usual, when it came to these situations. He should have been really good at bad news by now. He'd buried enough friends, after all. She had wept and hugged their children as if they were about to be taken from her. He left her sobbing into a pillow with one of the children casting hateful glances at him. He must have looked and sounded like a monster to the little child. He had made his mummy cry and erased his father from his future life.

Afterwards he had driven home in the Mondeo feeling numb and angry. He parked outside his flat and watched moths flying around the streetlamps, sending themselves mad in the process. The faces of Williams' children haunted him for another hour as he sat there, unable to move. Then, realising that time and sleep were disappearing fast, he had got out, locked the car with a beep and gone inside, climbed into bed and fell asleep. That was yesterday. That was the pain of being immortal. Thank you, God!

Judas finished dressing and set off for the Museum. The journey there was short. He checked in at the main desk and took the stairs up to the Museum floor. He didn't bother going to the office. It would have felt quiet and empty without Williams. Best to carry on and get on with things. He swiped his card at the door and entered. He felt it straight away. There was a strange atmosphere in the Museum, stranger than normal in fact. The customary whispers and the shuffling of the walls were gone. It was silent. 'Hopefully not as a grave,' he said to himself. Judas opened the internal door and sat at the giant desk in the centre of the room. He was about to ask for the key to the 'room' when it appeared in front of him.

Judas took it up, placed it in the lock and casually walked inside.

Standing in the middle of the room were two angels. Michael was one and the other, Judas was soon to find out, was the Museum itself. They were both huge, both heavily muscled, and practically identical. The only real difference was the colour of the second angel's wings, which were very grey, and tinged with silver.

'Judas. I would like to introduce you to another one of the Fallen. You know him as the Museum but his proper name, given to him by his true lord, is Malzo. He is one of the first Fallen, a traitor and a renegade once, but now no more than a jailer who is himself locked up.'

Michael's words were diamond-tipped and rounded off with barbs of steel. You could see that they flew straight and true, and that they did more than hurt. They destroyed.

Judas looked from one to the other and then sat down – heavily.

'All this time you've been inside the Museum, I've been talking to you and thinking that you're some sort of well-meaning spirit, and in fact you're one of his lot? Another bloody angel? Great. Nice. Any other little surprises that are in fact not little, but great big, enormous surprises in disguise?

'Come on then, Malzo, or whatever your name is. Chapter and verse, please, spill those beans. Are you a nice angel, or are you like him over there?'

Both angels looked at each other and smiled. Some sort of truce seemed to be in place.

'We are very different in most ways,' said Malzo. Michael sat down on the nearest table and smiled one of his killer smiles.

'Malzo fell with the first wave, many, many years ago. He was a follower, a bit misguided, but not altogether a bad angel. Pride was his greatest weakness, and he was given this position as his penance, by me actually. Before you can escape, you must learn what it is to be in prison, don't you think? And, if you look closely, there, just below the wing, is the wound that he must carry as a mark of shame. A wound that I gave him.'

It was Malzo's turn to smile now. His was colder, as hard as Vulcan's hammer and perfected over a thousand years of confinement. It didn't look as if he had had cause to use it for a long time – but it was good – really good. Michael continued.

'He's been in here, keeping his own counsel, listening to the bile and the poison of the evil ones and keeping all of them in check. That's right isn't it, Malzo? Must have been quite a bore looking after all of the evil that this great city had churned up? Must have been grating? I can't imagine what it must have been like having to listen to creatures like Jack the Ripper mumbling and promising and squealing to be let out. Tiring, I expect.'

Malzo moved around the room with his arms folded across his chest. His great muscles bunched and tightened as he walked around, as if, were he to unfold them, they might act independently and lash out uncontrollably.

Or at least that was how Judas was reading the situation. Here were two of the largest angels in town, like giant lions standing upright on two legs and sizing each other up. There was enough hate in that room to kill a planet. The air was crackling with it. Michael looked calm, bored even. He knew that Malzo was no threat. Judas wondered how Malzo was feeling right now. Apparently, he'd been cooped up in here for over one-thousand years. That was enough to make anything, or anyone, go a little crazy. Malzo stopped pacing and turned to face Michael and Judas, and like all intelligent people he just directed the conversation and Michael's nasty little asides to one side.

'I have placed the one called John somewhere far in the past, deep in the Museum. It's a void really. It is a flat, grey space where nothing good exists. He is bound securely, and he is alone. He cannot move from there save I move him. He is safe for now. You will have to decide where his final resting place will be, though. You must be specific, Judas. You must pick a time in history, and when you have decided where he will be imprisoned, we will go to the room, touch one of the artefacts, and go to that time. From there, we will jump to another time nearby with John and leave him there. Once we return, we will have to destroy the artefact. Michael will see that done. Then John the Baptist will be bound for all time, and the Grove will go undiscovered.'

'I will see the piece destroyed, Judas,' said Michael.

'Well then, I'd better put my thinking cap on, hadn't I?'

'And what of me, Michael?' said Malzo. 'Surely the successful completion of this deed and the time I have served down here is worth a pardon?'

Michael cocked his head to one side but said nothing.

22 STRANGHOLD

Judas clicked the orange switch into the 'on' position and waited as the battered old kettle warmed up. It huffed and puffed a lot, and rattled around on its plastic base, then finally, almost apologetically, it climaxed and switched itself off. He poured the hot water into his blue mug and was in the process of filling up the extra cup – Williams' cup – before he realised and stopped. He poured the hot milky water away down the sink and placed the cup on the draining board. Then, carefully, almost lovingly, he dried it with a tea-towel and put it away in the cupboard over the sink. It was symbolic that he was putting Williams' cup away for good, and it saddened him greatly. He was gone. It was as simple as that. Judas thought back to the face of Williams' boy, full of hate, and shook his head. That little boy would always associate his face with the death of his father. A tall man with a blue suit came and told me that daddy was never coming back. He made mummy cry and all the while he played with that stupid silver coin. And then he just drove away.

Judas sat down and sipped at his bitter-tasting tea. He wondered if the tea that you made reflected the mood you were in. Bitter moments – bitter tea, maybe? He sat down and took out his coin and rubbed at the edges. The 10 were no more. He should definitely stop referring to them as The 10. They were the Disciples. Damn them all for following him here, and damn them all for the death and destruction they had brought with them. John was about to be cast away in time – for ever. Michael was about to fly out of his life, thankfully, and Malzo was going to be freed. What was going to happen to the Museum now that its gate keeper was about to fly off? All these thoughts flooded into his mind like waves on a beach. Judas needed a holiday and looked out of the window and up at the grey skies overhead. Bali? Thailand? Anywhere? Two weeks off, please boss? Of course there would be no answer; there never was. So, back to work then, he thought.

He was just about to sit down and start working out where he could put John when the phone rang. It was Ray. He sounded scared, and he kept repeating himself. 'They've come for it! They've come for it!' And then the line went dead.

Great, that's all I need right now Judas thought, getting up quickly. He was about to tell Williams to bring the car around when he stopped himself. This was going to take longer than he thought. He ran down the stairs and set off for the tube station. At this time of day, it would be quicker travelling under the ground than over it, unless you were an angel of course. Would there soon be an angel flying taxi service? he wondered. Judas played dodgeball with the commuters and the tourists that thronged the pavements and the roads outside the station, and made it to the Tube having only knocked three pedestrians over – a new record for him. After swiping his Met ID card under the nose of one of the station staff they opened the wide gate for him, and he disappeared down the escalator.

Islington was much the same when he emerged from the Tube 20 minutes later. He turned right and nearly collided with an angel holding a sign that said that there was a 'Golf Sale' nearby. He ran down the road and made for the market. As he approached Ray's flat he stopped running and went for the 'I'm just walking up Upper Street and not in fact a police officer on his way to an emergency' look. He needn't have bothered because the man who had been watching Ray's apartment was gone. That wasn't a good sign. Judas ran up the stairs and found Ray's door wide open. That was bad sign number two. He waited. Whoever had put the frighteners on Ray could still be in there, and there was no way he was going to run into a place with no visible exit. He was brave, but he wasn't stupid. Judas could see right down the long hallway to the room beyond. From where he was standing, it looked like the room had been turned over, but he couldn't be sure, because Ray was one of the scruffiest angels he knew. He pushed the door back against the wall gently, just in case someone really thin and dangerous was hiding there. He needn't have worried, because the door clunked against the wall and Judas slipped inside.

The first thing you did on entering a room was listen; there was none of that kicking the door down nonsense and screaming that you were the police. Just open your ears and close your eyes. There was no noise coming from inside, only the ambient hum of the market below. Judas stepped into the lounge. Ray's collection was all over the place. Pictures had been separated from their frames, the rugs and furnishings that had covered the wall had been torn down and now lay in a collection of heaps, and the window was broken; all sure signs that a struggle had taken place. Things had a tendency to fly around when you surprised an angel – they didn't have a lot of control of their wings when they panicked. Judas looked into Ray's bedroom, and then the bathroom. Ray wasn't there, and there were no bloodstains or clumps of feathers with gore attached anywhere. It certainly looked like he'd jumped from the window and escaped. That was the good news. Judas and Ray weren't close, but they had history, and with Williams gone it would have been a pretty sad way to end the week if both had been slain.

Judas didn't have to think too hard about where Ray was headed. He would be safe there. If his maths was correct and the wind was in Ray's favour, he would be somewhere north of Oxford by now, and there wasn't anything that would bring him back to London until he felt it was safe to do so. And if anyone decided to try and follow him up there, then good luck to them, because the Angels of the North were a hard bunch. They were a little crazy, but they were strong. Wings of iron, someone had remarked once, and they weren't far wrong. Judas searched the rest of the flat. There was lots of money lying around and quite a few expensive looking trinkets, so whoever had been here wasn't after cash. Judas closed the smashed window, being careful not to let any of the glass drop to the pavement below. Ray had said that they had come for it, so it had to be the book. The question now, then, was did they have it, or were they still looking? He moved through the flat and towards the front door. There was nothing he could do until Ray contacted him now, so he'd better head back to the station and check on Malzo. The door was open again. He'd been sure to close it when he came in. A quick look at the latch told him that the lock was okay, and it hadn't blown open in the wind because there wasn't any wind. Someone had opened it, and either they had looked in and seen him and decided to come back later, or they were in here now. If it was the latter, then they were going to regret it, because Judas was in a fighting frame of mind. The scrap with John had been touch and go at times, but he'd remembered how to fight, and with Williams gone and now Ray disappeared, he was in the mood. So, whoever it was, they'd better be ready.

Judas closed the door, and locked it.

'You'd better come out now if you're in here, because if I have to come in and get you, you're going to start hurting very quickly, and not stop until I get what I want.'

He moved down the hallway and stepped back into the front room.

'Wer bisst Du?' The voice came from the far side of the room behind the curtain.

'I'm a policeman and you're in the middle of a crime scene so you'd better step away from the window and let me see your face.'

'Wer bisst Du?'

'In English please, my German is really rusty.'

'A policeman? Why are you here?' The voice was calm and heavily accented.

'Step out where I can see you and we can talk about that.' Judas was close now.

'There is no need for violence, all I want is the book. It is my property. It is mine, and it was taken from me. I did not want to harm the angel; he pretended that he had lost the book, and that is not the truth.'

The man who stepped out from behind the curtain was not the man that Judas had seen standing across the road. He looked like he was in his sixties, but he moved with the fluid actions of a much younger man. His clothes were at least three decades too young for him, as well. He spoke with a clipped, well-educated German accent. If you had to call it, you'd say he was some sort of academic – you could almost put money on there being a stick of chalk in his waistcoat pocket and a ticket stub for the latest exhibition at the Tate Modern.

Judas held out his hands, palms facing outwards. He could tell that this man was not a fighter. He was most definitely the grey matter of the operation. But where was the muscle?

'So Talk. Where is my friend, Ray, and why is this book of yours so important to you? Are you responsible for this?' Judas pointed at the heaps of broken furniture and smashed picture frames.

The man shook his head. 'My servants are a bit excitable, and they sometimes act before they think. I'm sorry for the destruction.'

Judas looked him in the eye and had to accept that he was telling the truth. This little chap looked like an ink pen with too much ink in it might be too heavy for him.

'You are not a normal policeman, are you? There is something different about you. Something about you feels old. Who are you, if I may ask?'

It was Judas' turn to shake his head. 'It's a long story that I can tell you another time. Maybe in the cells back at the station, if that suits? Right now, I'm more worried about my friend, the angel who lived here. So, where is he?'

The small man pointed to the only sofa in the room that was standing the right way up and raised his eyebrows. It was a request, sign language for please may I sit down? Judas smiled, and the man took a seat, then lit a cigarette and blew a perfect smoke ring up to the ceiling. It was all very theatrical.

'We could not catch the angel. He leapt out of the window when one of my servants tried to catch him, and unfortunately, he smashed the window instead. We only want what he took. We do not want to harm him, but we will if we cannot come to an agreement over the object.'

Judas sat down opposite the man on a sideboard that had been thrown onto its side. He chose to sit there because he was making sure that he was casually blocking the only way out at the same time. The precaution made the little man smile and he blew another smoke ring into the air. It was obviously either a simple pleasure for him, or it was his way of showing calm. It didn't matter right now. He wasn't going anywhere.

'What exactly is the book? What does it do, and why do you want it back so badly? If you don't feel like giving me chapter and verse right now, we could start with your name?'

The little man just looked up and smiled. Smoke drifted in small white lines from his nostrils and his eyes narrowed like a poker player unsure of what his opponent was holding.

'My name is Stranghold. Hubertus Stranghold. I belong to a group of individuals who would very much like to retain the book. That is all you need to know.'

It was Judas' turn to smile. 'The book. What is it, what does it do and why do you want it so badly?' Stranghold sat bolt upright and started to mutter something under his breath; at the same time, he was gently flexing his fingers and staring intently at Judas.

Judas was about to say that parlour tricks, magic, and things like that didn't work on him, when the front door burst open and two heavy-set men ran in.

'I ask the questions, policeman, not you! Quick, you two! Grab him and bring him along!'

Judas was up and across the room in two bounds, and there were two quick punches and two big thuds as both men went down in a heap. Judas turned around, but Stranghold was gone. Judas rifled through the thugs' pockets; there was absolutely nothing in them, no wallets, no ID and more importantly, no mobile phones. 'Who doesn't have a mobile phone these days?' muttered Judas. He cuffed them to the heaviest piece of furniture and sat down again.

As soon as they woke up, he could ask them a few questions, or their little boss in the charming spats and waistcoat would return and he could ask him a few questions, too. Same difference. Judas sat patiently. He'd learned to wait. When you were immortal it's just something you got used to.

The clock that usually hung on the wall was now lying on the floor. The room had been turned upside down and given a good shake, and the clock had rolled across the floor and was ticking stubbornly by the bathroom door. Judas wandered over and picked it up. It was nearly time for something to eat. He exhaled, long and low; he was tired, it had been a hard few days.

He was thinking of Williams again when there was a loud bang and a flash. He turned quickly and the two thugs had gone, along with the enormous sideboard they'd been handcuffed to.

'That's all I need,' he said under his breath. 'How am I going to explain losing another pair of cuffs?'

There was nothing more he could do so he left Ray's flat and headed home. On the way he called the local nick and gave them the special code he was allowed to use and had two policeman assigned to watch Ray's flat. They were under strict instructions not to engage anyone, just report back if anyone showed up.

Judas opened the door of his flat and stepped inside, locking the door behind him. The flat was tidy and clean; one girlfriend had said that it looked sore because it had been scrubbed so hard. That was back in the day when he had girlfriends, though. He put some music on and sat down on the leather sofa. Only one end of it looked like it had ever been sat on, which wasn't far from being true. The same could be said of the bathroom and the kitchen. Both were spotlessly clean and looked like a single man of considerable wealth lived there. Judas looked around and felt sad. Life was nothing if there was no one to share it with. He'd heard the songs and seen the couples in the park, and he'd even thought of going online to find the special one they were always saying was out there, just waiting for you to swipe left on. He went to bed and dreamed of books and paperclips again.

The morning came around all too quickly, as it always did when he was tired. Someone had been pushing the sun too fast again. He had had one of those sleeps when he got into bed and pulled the duvet up and woke to find himself in exactly the same position. He got up, showered, and dressed, and set off for the Yard. Ray's disappearance was important. He felt it. The book and Stranghold would have to be put to one side for now, though. He had two angels sizing each other up for a no-holds-barred death match, and John the Baptist and the Disciples in dangerous proximity to each other at the Yard. Ray was safe for now. Judas knew that he was up North and under the protection of the angels who lived there.

After a short Tube ride, he reached the Yard. He walked through the main doors and saw that it was Sergeant Wilkes on duty this morning; a racing snake of a man, a keen runner and calorie-counter. He nodded at Judas in that 'I know that you're a sneaky-beaky sort of policeman' way, then went back to processing the long line of last night's unfortunates standing in front of his desk. The office felt even emptier than yesterday. Williams was still here, even though his body wasn't. The coat stand looked thin and skeletal without its familiar brown coat and scarf. Judas reached out for the free paper that Williams normally picked up from the Tube and left on his desk, but it wasn't there of course. He would have to put in yet another call to the Superintendent and ask for another partner. He could just imagine the sound of the sharp intake of breath followed by the silence of disapproval on the other end. Just who was the latest Superintendent? thought Judas. He would put that off until later. He needed to speak to Malzo about John.

He walked down the corridor, swiped his card and entered. Malzo was standing at the far end of the room. He was deep in thought, it seemed, his eyes were closed, and he was looking upwards. Judas watched him for a while. Malzo looked like a statue, with only the occasional flex of a wing spoiling the illusion. He was not asleep, so it was obvious that he was communicating with someone or something. Judas felt odd about watching him and was about to walk out again, when Malzo's eyes opened. His voice was calming and soothing. It wasn't at all like Michael's voice.

'Judas. What is it?'

'I'd like to move John now, please. It's about time we put him somewhere safe.'

'As you like. Have you decided where he should go?'

Malzo walked over to Judas and looked down into his eyes. It was unnerving because you felt that he could see deep down inside you. As if your feelings were being sifted and made good. All the negative parts of your soul were getting a wash and a spin cycle.

'I thought it might be best to take him back to the beginning; to where it all began. If we take him back to the desert, he'll know that his life is meaningless, and that alone will kill his great pride and ultimately him, I think.'

The angel smiled. 'You don't have the heart to kill him after all that he has done, and knowing all that he would have done. Humans are wonderful things. So be it, Judas. Wait here. I will go inside now and return later. Travelling through the ages can be tricky. The way there will take longer than the return. We shall speak later. I have to speak to Michael and then, if I am granted leave, we shall part. It seems that my time as guardian and gate keeper has nearly come to an end.'

Malzo smiled and crossed the room towards the door. He was about to reach for the doorknob but stopped. He stood there motionless for a second and then turned to Judas. 'Do you hear the voices of the ones locked up in here? Do you listen to their stories?'

Judas got the impression that Malzo was about to say something else, but for some reason he stopped himself. He cocked his head to one side as if he were listening or searching for something, then he smiled, opened the door and walked through and into the inner part of the Black Museum. As the door opened and closed, Judas saw Michael for a brief second sitting on the table at the far end of the room, smiling to himself as if he and he alone knew the best joke in town.

Judas wondered what Malzo had meant. It was a strange question. Of course he heard them. More importantly, thought Judas, just how long would Malzo actually be? Angels travelled fast when they wanted to. He sat down and looked around. The walls were covered with files on shelves; boxes of witness statements, paper clippings and picture frames with old photographs. Gruesome weapons and clothing from the murdered and the butchered hung from hangers in glass cases, and every single one of them was talking, all at the same time. The door turned and Michael walked in with a strange little smile on his face.

'Malzo has gone to transport John to his prison. What do you want to do with Simon the Zealot and the rest of the Disciples? They are locked up below in your cells. Without John they are rudderless, souls lost in the wind of a time that they should never have lived through. They have all lived too long.

'If you want my advice then you should kill them now; it would be a mercy. You and I can do it, and Malzo of course. We are the only things on this earth right at this moment who can take their lives from them.'

Michael padded over to the door and opened it. Judas saw him open one of the corridor windows and savour the breeze that flowed over his muscular wings.

'Yeah, let's kill them. Do you want to wring their necks like chickens, or shall I do it?'

Michael turned around and looked back at him. There was a surprised look on his face. He spoke to Judas slowly, as if he were a child.

'It is your job to bring evil to justice down here, Judas. I can help you if you ask me to, but that role is yours, you know that. They are just men whose time has come to an end. Bringing vengeance to those that deserve it is not an easy thing to do, Judas. We have been chosen; you can either look on it with pride or look on it as penance – I choose pride, Judas.'

Judas looked at the fierce angel and shook his head. John was the leader of the Disciples. He'd been the strongest and the bravest, but something had happened to rot him from the inside out. Without him the rest might return to the good ways that they had once lived by. They had not all started badly. They deserved a second chance.

'No. I'm going to set them free.'

'As they say, Judas, that is your call.' Michael looked at Judas and for a split-second Judas thought that he saw pity there. But this was Michael after all, and the look disappeared and was replaced with his usual look of mild contempt.

Judas was about to say something witty, but Michael cut him off.

'Judas, watch Malzo for me. He has been down here a long time. He was a powerful member of the host long ago, and a worthy foe, but I feel something different growing inside him now. If all goes well with me then you will only see him once more and then he will leave. I feel that his time is done – one way or the other.'

Michael was there one second and gone the next. The only evidence of his passing was a great big feather on the floor underneath the open window. Judas picked it up and smiled. A heavy feather? Well, it had to be, didn't it?

23 THE BLACK TRUTH

Judas put the feather in his pocket, or half of it at least. Walking back to the office he caught his reflection in the window; it had to be 50cm in length, and the top half was sticking out so that he looked like a schoolteacher from a Dickens novel. He was still thinking of the feather as he approached the door to his office.

The door was ajar. That was the first thing that started to make his scar itch. The post was never delivered to this floor, it was always collected by Williams. There was that feeling again, sadness. The second thing was the brown package on his desk. It was rectangular, thick, well-padded, and it had been made secure with lots of brown twine. Who wrapped packages like that anymore? thought Judas as he pushed the door open. He made sure to look behind the door again. It was getting to be a habit, this looking behind doors. He was used to looking over his shoulder regularly, but the door thing was new. Looking around the office for anything else unusual, Judas found that the latch to one of the windows had been forced from the outside. So it looked like whoever had delivered the parcel this morning had either come in through the window and left by the door, or come in through the station and then jumped out of the window.

He looked down from the window and there was no tell-tale red smudge and chalk outline on the ground below, so it was obviously delivered by hand with a wing attached to it. Angel post. He closed the window and made a mental note to find out whom he had to speak to about repairing the latch, then sat down behind his desk.

He knew it was the book before he even opened the package. Ray had obviously arranged with a friend to drop it off before he packed his bag and flew off to the safety of the North. Or he'd wanted to deliver it himself to be absolutely sure that it was in safe hands, before something had scared him, and he'd taken off. So, putting two and two together and getting five, Judas was pretty sure that Stranghold and his disappearing henchmen would be coming to see him soon. Judas ripped off the paper and saved the twine; it was an old fishermans' habit, you should never cut string. Untie it and then splice it again but never cut it – ever. The paper slipped away from the front cover like a silk sheet falling off a bed.

The leather gave off a strange smell. It didn't smell of libraries or other books. That was odd. Old, valuable books like this one obviously were normally kept in the company of other equally special or dangerous tomes. The binding looked very strong, and the spine looked very creased, so it had been well-thumbed over time. There were some symbols that he recognised on the top. The Black Sun he knew from past experience, and there were plenty of old angelic sigils around the borders; add to that a few oddities like what appeared to be an ornate paperclip and a sun with a keyhole at its centre, and the book was chock-a-block full of dark magic and other nasty things.

He flicked through the first few pages, scanning the pieces that he could read, and adding a post-it note to the parts that looked like someone had used an etch-a-sketch to write, but he would need a lot more time than he thought he had right now to get a feel for the contents. His scar itched again, and he took out his silver coin to help him think. Everything was coming to a head. The pieces weren't falling into place as he'd hoped they would, but somewhere in the back of his mind a picture was beginning to form. Unfortunately, it was a Jackson Pollock. He slammed the heavy leather cover shut and put it under his arm, heading straight for the Museum. Once there, he placed it in the giant steel safe at the back of the room. He closed the heavy door and spun the locking wheel. Some of the artefacts started giggling. Trust me to have all of the safe-crackers and safe-blowers placed near the only safe in the department, he thought. Laugh all you want, you're dead and this safe is in the only police department that specialises in the occult, so I doubt anyone is going to be creeping in here to try and open it. The giggling stopped and some choice curses and oaths were whispered. Their amusement and comments had made him think twice, though, so he moved the glass case that was full of executioners' masks over to the safe and asked them all to keep an eye on it. The masks saw everything that went on in the Museum; they were cursed to see the end of all things, and they made for a fantastic security camera system.

Then he went back to his office, made another cup of awful tea, and surfed the internet for ideas for holidays that he would never take.

As he dunked his biscuit, he thought about what Michael had said.

It was a warning – obviously. Or was it something else? He put his feet up on the desk and looked at the ceiling. The hands on the clock on the wall marched around and his tea grew a milky white hat and went cold. Never mind, he thought, plenty of teabags in the sea.

The phone rang at 3pm precisely. He knew that because he had been following the second hand around the dial for what seemed like ages. He answered the phone and then took the lift down to the cells. These were situated at the back of the building. The drainage pipes for the sanitation system ran downwards and joined just above them, so there was always a hum of number twos hanging around. Below these cells were the special holding blocks for high-profile prisoners. Simon the Zealot was in number five. He'd lucked out because his was the only cell with a ventilation grate, so he got the full blast of the flush odours.

Judas asked the duty officer to open his door. No matter what prison you go to or find yourself in, the sound of the key in the lock is always the same. Like hope with a jackboot on its neck. Simon was sitting on the end of the stone plinth that jutted out from the cell wall; it was what those in the trade refer to as a 'bastard of a bed'. He sat with his hands in his lap, his legs crossed, and a big smile on his face. He looked happy. Judas knew instantly that the smile wasn't for him, or because Judas was paying him a social visit, but because John had been taken away. The relief on his face was evident. He leaned back against the wall and raised his eyebrows.

'So then, Judas, here we are again. I was going to say that it was nice to see you again after all these years but I'm not going to lie. How does it come to pass that our old friend Judas becomes a policeman and keeper of the keys to the one place that John the Baptist wants to get into? I'd call that fate, wouldn't you? The man in the sky must be laughing all over his all-knowing face. Just look at you, all replete and shiny. And in charge of this!'

Simon waved a well-manicured hand in the air like someone practising a magic trick for the first time.

Judas walked into the cell and gave the duty officer the nod that said, 'close the door and turn the key'. The sound of the iron bolts dropping into their well-worn grooves made Simon's smile even broader.

'I've got John upstairs in the Museum, Simon; it's the safest place to keep him for now. He's quite mad, isn't he? There was always a little bit of crazy inside that big head of his. I could see it and I'm sure you could too. Nothing slithers past you, does it, Simon? Nothing passes without the Zealot's notice.

'John and the rest of you won't be seeing the sky for a long while, if ever, unless of course you decide to do the right thing and help me. You're all mixed up in something bigger than slavery, murder, corruption and whatever else it is that you lot have got good at doing for the last few hundred years. I don't think you know how big it is, but if you tell me everything about what John has had you doing here in London, then I'll try and keep you apart.'

Simon uncrossed his legs and took a turn around his new estate, all three metres of it. He tried to look as if he didn't have a care in the world, which made Judas angry and a little annoyed at the same time.

'We were taking him somewhere else to keep him safe, but I had a thought on my way down here: would it be okay if he was your cell buddy for five minutes or so? I'm sure you'll have lots to catch up on, and the way he was talking – well, not exactly talking actually – more frothing at the mouth with all of his tattoos twisting and changing all over his body and spasms of rage, really; you know how he gets…

'It would only be for five minutes, or however long it would take him to decide that you were responsible for his capture.'

Judas performed his own theatrical wave and Simon got the message, sitting down and composing himself.

'You're not going to take him anywhere that isn't ridiculously difficult to get out of, Judas. You wouldn't risk moving that mountain of madness with all of these mortals about, and unless I'm mistaken you can't magic him here either; that would cause a stir, and it would only be possible if he was willing. I don't think you'll risk bringing him here. Not here. Not here.'

The smile was good but the repetition at the end of the sentence gave him away. Simon was no fool, and he knew that his currency was knowledge. He spent it like a miser with a big bill from the Inland Revenue looming.

'You're right Simon. He's not going anywhere where he can do any more harm, and I'm not going to risk moving him about where he can kill any more innocents. If you help me, you'll never have to see him or hear of him again. I promise that. I intend to set you free. One of my colleagues thinks that you'd be better off dead, but I have enough blood on my hands and I think that you could still try and save yourself. I can't undo what I've done, and my sentence has no term affixed, but if I can you save you then why shouldn't I? Why not try and do some good for a change? You're free. So, as I'm doing you a favour, why don't you do me one and tell me what you were all doing: the angels, the slavers and the Grove?' Judas watched Simon's face carefully. He was expecting to have to work really hard to get Simon to talk, but in the end, he was spared. Simon wanted to talk – and talk he did.

'A long time ago, John started to hear voices. He was in Germany I think, and he was contacted by a source. That's all we ever knew; there was no name and we never got to meet him. John came back with this blood lust for killing angels and every now and again he'd mutter something about allied revenge. Then one night he called a meeting. We'd set up our base in a restaurant in Clapham; it was a good front for our criminal activities – no one ever thinks of raiding a chip shop unless they have a thing for Cod. It does turn a tidy profit though and dealing with the general public isn't as bad as you think.

'So, we were all sitting there thinking that we were on the move again. Some of us thought we were going to the States; a couple of the boys were saying that it was going to be Russia, like the wild west. But no, we weren't going anywhere. John had heard from this secret contact of his that there was a secret place, a second heaven he called it; a place with everything that we ever wanted. All we had to do was kill a few angels and this contact of his would give us the directions and V.I.P. passes. I don't need to tell you that we all thought it stank to high you-know-where and back again, but John was in one of his nicer moods. "Of course," he said. "We've done some bad things."

'I nearly fell off my chair when he said that Judas, "some bad things"? Blimey, Interpol was on our payroll at one time so you get an idea of how many bad things we'd done. Anyway, John was pouring the wine and slapping backs and whispering sweet nothings into everyone's ears all night.

'In the beginning, we'd all been staunch and good. We'd taken from the rich and given to the poor. But then we started taking from the rich and keeping it. John would say that it was all part of the wider plan, that we had to have the money to do his good work, and none of argued with him because we were weak. Then John just drifted away from reality and turned us all into thieves and murderers, and worse.'

Simon shifted on the bed and tried to make himself more comfortable. Judas felt like telling him that it was impossible, but Simon was in mid-flow, and he didn't want to give him any reason to stop spilling the beans.

'Go on,' said Judas.

'Well, we got stuck into turf-wars with the Romans, had it out with the Greeks and the Macedonians, rampaged all the way through Europe, killing and robbing as we went. We made a fortune in property and built our little empire up, then stashed it all away. It's still in some banks in Rome and some in Switzerland, I think. We all hoped that we'd get to see some of it soon.'

Judas raised an eyebrow and smiled at Simon.

'Keep going, Simon, there are fewer gaps that need filling now, but I need more.'

Simon stretched, and then started talking again.

'I want something in return first, not just for me but for all of us. We can help you, help you right now with information about John and this source of his. But think about it: we could also help you in the future. Put it this way: we all want to get back on track, do some good. What do you say?'

Judas wasn't expecting this, but he knew a good offer when he heard one. At this rate he was going to get everything he needed in order to deal with John, and he was also going to gain a network of informers and contacts with an awful lot of money and an undeniable urge to help him. What was not to like?

'I could sit here and pretend that I'm not interested, but I won't. I do need some help in the here and now, and if you pledge to help me with John then I will let you all go. I'll expect to be able to call on you whenever I need you, and for you to drop everything and do what I need you to do, however odd or dangerous it may seem. If you think that's going to work and you and the boys are happy working with me again then we have a deal.

'But first, before we start shaking each other by the hand and organising dinner dates, I need to know everything you know about the Grove.'

Simon sat forward and looked deep into Judas' eyes.

'You're the world record holder in deceit and deception, Judas, you're the most famous turncoat that ever existed. We'll need some proof that you mean what you say, and you'll do what you promise.'

Judas stood up. The smell of the cell was beginning to get up his nose, and he needed some fresh air. Simon was good at waiting. He had taken a backseat with John for so long that he could fall into line very quickly, but there was something about him. He was like a hungry terrier when he got going. They didn't call him the Zealot for nothing.

'Okay. You can walk out of here now, this morning, if you want to. I'm not going to stop you; we can do this on trust. I can't give you any more than that right now.'

Simon smiled his best smile, and sat upright, putting his back to the wall.

'Okay, Judas. John doesn't want to find this special place, this "Grove". I don't think he's really after that. It's a smokescreen.'

Judas stopped pacing. He stared hard at Simon, and he got that horrible old feeling right down the middle of his God scar. That itchy, cold, 'something evil this way comes' feeling. Everything was going way too smoothly.

'Say that again.'

'You heard me, Judas. John the Baptist isn't looking for a way out by getting into the "Grove" place. He likes it right here in London right now. He loves the violence he's spreading, and he loves the pain. He's got it in for the city itself! Revenge. Sheer bloody revenge! As soon as those headaches started, we knew that he hadn't come back alone and that something weird was happening to him. As soon as our Lufthansa flight had landed and he'd smashed a couple of bottles of Johnny Walker that he'd picked up at the duty-free back at the Shoals, we knew we were all in trouble. So John starts having these moments of madness, and we all start getting shoved along towards some mystical doorway to happiness and redemption. It's the only thing that each and every one of us really wants, isn't it? To get back into his good books, atone for letting Jesus down so badly? I mean, "The Grove", some place that only the angels really know about, a mirror to heaven where we can all do what we want and erase our pasts? I didn't buy it, and neither did the lads. The truth is, we're all just scared silly of John. He's properly mad and he didn't get that big just by eating his greens, did he? There is something evil growing inside him, Judas, something very nasty.'

Judas loosened his tie. He knew it was coming. Just let Simon talk for a bit longer.

'During one of the headaches he started rambling on about the Black Museum. It was a gaol for lots of bad spirits and evil forces. All of London's worst criminals and its darkest secrets, all cooped up inside a magical prison with an angel as the turnkey. Just imagine if you unlocked the door and let that lot out. What would happen then? There would be mayhem and carnage, the likes of which this dear old city had never seen before. The spectres and spirits of serial killers from past and present, drifting through the dark streets at night, hand in hand, plague and black magic swilling along the gutters, and words whispered into the ears of the weakest, pushing them to copy their deeds. It would be like a phantom Fifth Column destroying London from within. And there'd be nothing the police, Judas and anyone who stood shoulder to shoulder with them could do about it. Imagine the terror and the bloodshed. You'd be fighting a war.

'All John had to do is get you involved and investigating the angel slayings, then offer himself up as bait. He knew you'd catch him, then where would you take him? Here, of course. Now he's inside your station and your Museum and you know how manipulative and convincing he can be. He'll make a deal with anyone. There must be a few hundred of your inmates up there who would love to help him out.'

Judas knew that Simon was being honest and telling him the truth; he had more than enough to lose. Looking at it from his side of the cell, John's plan seemed like a well thought out one. It just didn't feel like John's plan. It was definitely someone else's, and that person had put a lot of thought into it.

'Simon, I'm going to let you and the rest of the Disciples go. Right now. Get away from here and stay away. If you decide to re-join John, or disappear, or come after me when you think the dust has settled, I'll do worse than kill you. I'll have you locked up inside the Museum. You won't ever see the light of day again, and I promise you that all the rest of your days will be long and unhappy. Deal?'

Simon nodded, then rose and stood by the door, waiting for freedom and a life without John in it.

'Deal. You let us go, you kill John, and we work for you when you need us to. The old gang back together again, Judas. How wonderful.'

'I can be contacted here at any time, Simon. Leave a number at the desk for me on your way out or have one delivered, make sure that I get it, and that I know how to get hold of you. Don't forget to do that, Simon.'

Judas had the remaining cell doors opened, and the rest of the Disciples emerged from the stygian gloom of their cells and the odours of hell that leaked from the Station's waste pipes. He nodded at Simon and ran as fast as he could for the stairs and the Museum. There was a cuckoo in the nest.

24 A MIND FULL OF STRING

Malzo was flying high over the 'Fields of Time', deep inside the Black Museum. They were flat and jet-black and shot through with slivers of silver. Fragments of colour and sound kept erupting from the surface like little fireworks and rockets. He was excited and happy because he was on his way to pick up the prisoner John the Baptist, and, if Michael had spoken well of him, he may have earned his own freedom. He looked down at the ever-changing landscape below and made out his destination just on the horizon.

A slice of time that was Victorian England emerged from the gloom. This is where he had hidden John. The basic geography of the City of London was well known, but Malzo had spent enough time inside the Museum to know that the city's outskirts were a shifting mass of streets that heaved and turned in on themselves, and unless you knew exactly where to go you could be lost for all time within them. Nobody would find him there. He circled downwards, but even before he set foot on the streets of Old London he knew, or rather he felt, that something was wrong. John was not there. But somebody else was. It was a tall figure, dressed in a long dark cloak. He wore his customary top hat and carried his

Gladstone bag in his right hand, as always. It was Jack the Ripper, and he was wearing his largest smile.

Malzo folded his great wings back and waited for the spectre to explain itself.

'You don't need to be a genius to work this one out, angel. You thought that you had hidden him here, and he was safe. How very stupid of you. I have shown him the way out, or rather – the way across the fields of time. He should be in the seventies by now I should think. He moves fast for a big man, doesn't he?'

Jack twirled his cane and ran one white-gloved finger along the edge of his freshly shaved chin. There was no twinkle in his eyes, because his eyes were dead, but there was something akin to joy in his voice. Malzo looked at him and thought of snapping his neck. He had to get the Baptist and take him to Judas, and then possibly he would gain his freedom.

'You are false, Ripper. You cannot change, it seems. I should have hidden him far away from you, but you would have still found a way to set him free, wouldn't you? What did he promise you, Ripper?'

Jack the Ripper set his bag down and took his tall black hat off. His head was a blur and featureless. Over the decades so many people had been accused of his crimes that his face was all of theirs now. It was a blur of noses, mouths and eyes that were constantly shifting under a mass of hair that was all colours and none. Never quite holding still for long enough to be a real face.

'He promised me that Judas would die. Not at John's hand, but at mine, here in my time, where I control the moment and where I am Lord of my own pleasures, and the horrors of the night. His body will heal, but his mind will die a million times over – trust me.'

Malzo's wings twitched. There was someone else close by. He whirled around, but he was too late. John was not travelling across the time fields at all; that was the first part of Jack's deception. He had been here all the time, of course, waiting patiently until his attention had been solely on the Ripper. Malzo felt his huge hands grip his wings and pull downwards. Before he could throw him off, he felt a sharp pain running down his side, and he knew that Jack was not going to stand idly by while one of his jailers was at his mercy. He felt slash after slash, and all the while John's great weight was pushing down on him.

Malzo roared and attacked. Jack was the easiest to deal with, and one straight punch lifted him off the ground, sending him spiralling down the street. Eddies of mist spiralled in the air as his body flew to the ground. He would not be getting up again for a while. John was a tougher opponent, though. Malzo flapped his muscular wings and bent over quickly into a tuck that caught John unaware. A backwards kick landed squarely in John's groin, and the satisfying rush of air from his stomach sounded like a knife being removed from a car tyre.

The next few minutes passed in a blur. John was a shrewd fighter, and he was also insane, which gave a man inhuman strength. But Malzo was one of the First Fallen; the battle in the heavens had raged on for days, and he was not about to lose another.

John was bruised and bloody again. As the fight wore on he slowed down quickly, and Malzo knew that it was only a matter of time before he would be flying back with his prize securely bound.

'Cut him now, Jack!' shouted John. It was the oldest trick in the book, and Malzo was not going to fall for it. He calmly threw another series of punches and flapped his great wings, forcing John back and back. John was tiring, and his guard was slipping. The last punch was the most accurate and John took it full on the chin. He went down and stayed down; a trickle of blood dribbled from the corner of his mouth while his eyes rolled up into his head. It was only then that Malzo turned to see if Jack had come back for some more. He hadn't. Jack was nowhere to be seen. He had escaped into the alleyways and the side-streets he knew better than any other. Malzo bent over and picked John up and flew up into the silvery sky above Victorian England. An intense pool of light on the far horizon indicated the entrance to the Museum. As he flew onwards, he thought of nothing else but the cold, crisp expanse of the heavens and the never dying light that bathed all angel kind in its warmth. He thought of home. He would be free.

The opening ahead got brighter and brighter and wider and wider. He was nearly there. He folded his wings and started to glide towards the centre. He was feeling hopeful, like this light could be the light at the end of the tunnel of his servitude. But his thoughts should have been in the here and now rather than elsewhere. Just as he was about to bring his legs up and forward to land, he felt the coldness of the blade against his side just below his right wing. Malzo would not be going home after all; he had failed. And instead of bringing John to trial and execution, he had in fact brought danger, death, and destruction.

25 BLADES AND WINGS

Judas was waiting anxiously in the room of the keys.

The tables in front of him were covered in thousands of objects and artefacts. Each of them had a uniform circle of space around them, as though they did not like each other, and wanted to keep their distance. How many times had he picked one up and spoken to the spirit or entity attached to it? How many times had the musings of a 17th century murderer helped him to solve a 21st century crime? Each one of the current inmates had paid their dues many times over. The clock on the wall was moving as if it had cramp. The hour hand was dead.

He was pacing up and down, rubbing at his silver coin as if he meant to rub it out of existence, when he thought he heard a scream, followed by a crash, somewhere nearby. He stopped moving and rubbing and cocked his head towards the direction of the noise, but all he heard was silence. As he listened, a bead of sweat ran down the centre of his back and made a cold pinprick at the base of his spine. All he could think of as he ran up the stairs three at a time from the cells below just now was what Simon had said about John's master plan.

He'd fallen for it, all right. He'd been tricked into escorting the Baptist into the Museum, and had brought the flame to the powder keg. He'd been conned by John the Baptist and whoever was conning him, too. The Black Museum was a vast prison; he'd been looking after it for a long time now and knew it inside and out. He knew that it contained all of London's evil and if the doors to it were opened then London's streets would run with blood, and he couldn't allow that to happen. Not just because he was a policeman, but also because it was the right thing to do. In the back of his mind, he wanted forgiveness above all things, sure he did, but now there was something else; he had actually started to like doing what he was doing and in the here and now he knew that he was making a difference to the lives of millions. He looked down at the nearest table and at the objects on it. At a rough count there must be at least two hundred of them on this table alone, and if they were all set free then a lot of people were going to die, and not well. Could he hide them? Should he set a guard on them?

He was thinking about it when the walls started to shake around him. The objects on the tables started to moan and growl – every single one of them. It was the first time that all of them had spoken at once and the noise was deafening. It was like a giant concert full of high-pitched whispering and snarling.

'Not good,' said Judas, popping his silver coin away in his jacket pocket and looking for the best weapon he could lay hands on quickly.

The walls vibrated and there was a muted banging that seemed to be coming from somewhere far away. Then it stopped, suddenly. There was a blinding flash, and Malzo appeared in the centre of the room. For a split-second Judas saw the time fields spreading away to the horizon behind him. Malzo was carrying something large in his arms, it looked like a mound of black and grey rags bound up in a shawl coloured blood red. Then the angel gave a piercing cry. It was a loud, savage bellow, and the shape in his arms suddenly came to life and jumped into the centre of the room. It was John the Baptist, and he was carrying a large, nasty looking surgical blade. Judas didn't need to think too hard about where he had got that particular knife. Jack the Ripper – of course. Malzo staggered backwards and then felt under his wing. He pulled his hand back and it was covered in black, thick blood. John backed up against the wall and looked at Judas.

'I know where to stick an angel, Judas. I've been practising and learning how. He's not going to last long, then it's your turn. I'm going to put your immortality to the test. Right after you touch each and every one of those pretty looking things on the table and set them all free.'

John's head twitched uncontrollably, and he squeezed his eyes tightly shut. He mumbled to himself and seemed to be having a conversation with the air around him. Judas reached for the metal wastepaper bin. It was the only thing he could reach that he could use.

'Hearing voices again, John? Simon told me that someone was pulling your strings again, it seems that you're still doing everyone's bidding but your own. He's downstairs with the rest of the boys and they're having a party because you're on your way to the gallows, my friend.'

John's eyes opened widely, as if he'd just put a wet knife into a plug socket, and he gasped for air.

It was obvious that Malzo had fought him once already, and that the angel had hurt him badly. Blood was oozing from a number of wounds, and Judas wouldn't have been surprised to find that a lot of his bones were broken, too.

The angel had moved across the room whilst they had spoken and put some distance between himself and John's wicked-looking knife. It was the first time that Judas had seen one of the big angels backing off from anything, or anyone. Malzo had other things on his mind, it seemed. The angel reached behind him and pulled out one of his own long, grey feathers. He held it tightly to his chest and closed his eyes. The light in the room seemed to dull for a second, and Judas thought he heard a voice answering from far away. He couldn't tell what the voice was saying, and then it cut off suddenly.

Malzo just smiled and then opened his eyes. Judas thought that he had never seen a more frightening thing in his life.

'I hope that you can still run, Baptist, and that your friend the Ripper can be counted on to stand with you, because your time is coming to an end. Your race is run, and whatever plans you had are now finished. The Archangel Michael is coming for you, and he is vengeance. He is my vengeance, and his wrath will be terrible to behold.'

John just smiled his crazy smile and pink, bloody froth and spittle started to foam around his white teeth.

'He can't count on me, angel, but the plan will still work.'

Jack's oily voice slipped into the room like a cold breeze, and then the man himself stepped into the room. He was wearing his cape and carrying his Gladstone bag of course, and in the other hand was a cane. He looked impeccable and altogether evil. John smiled and tossed him back his knife. 'Thanks for the loan of that, it worked a treat on the winged one. Went all the way in.'

John closed his eyes again and leant up against the wall to catch his breath.

Jack the Ripper placed his leather bag down on the floor and stared at Judas. There was a cold hatred in those eyes. The pupils were the deepest blue, and the whites around them were bright and full of longing.

Judas weighed up the situation as quickly as he could. He was faced with two powerful enemies. John was wounded but he was still very capable, and Jack had obviously picked up a few tricks along the way. He was 'a universe bringing a big-bang in trouble' as Williams was oft to retort. He did have something in his favour though, because he knew that Malzo had called for back-up. Hopefully Michael was in a bad mood and flying fast.

Judas could see that John was swinging the lead, and not suffering as bad as he was making out. Judas had his hands really, really full. He needed to stall for time.

'So, what's it all about then, Jack? I've heard all about John's plan, but what's yours? He's the key to your escape pod, right?

'He doesn't know it yet, but you're on your own, like you always have been, and once the walls come tumbling down, you'll stick a knife in his back just like all the rest. Where are you heading, Ripper?'

Jack watched Malzo slump to the floor and smiled.

'He's wasting time, John. He's the best liar in the world. Ignore him.'

Jack took out another of his long surgical knives and tested the sharpness of the blade by shaving the hairs from his forearm in a smooth downwards motion. He performed it gracefully and Judas wondered if the girls he had butchered in those dank Whitechapel alleyways had thought the same just before he snuffed out the candles of their young lives prematurely.

'The voice in your head, John, the one that tells you what to do: does it need Jack?'

Jack blinked for the first time since he had entered the room. Judas was getting somewhere, and giving Michael more time to get back.

'John, the voice in your head, whose is it? What does it want you to do? Is Jack supposed to be helping you? Because he's not, and you're going to find that out very soon. Will the voice be happy that you're dancing to someone else's tune?'

Jack looked at John. They were standing very close to each other. So far, so good. Jack had a knife and John was injured. Jack started to whisper something to John. Judas couldn't tell whether or not he was trying to reassure John, hoodwink him or just get close enough to plant all six inches of cold steel into him. He didn't really care. All he wanted was for their attention to be on each other. When Malzo had first appeared with John in his arms, Judas had been forced to the side of the room. Then Jack had appeared suddenly, materialising right between him and the nearest table and blocking his nearest escape. He had been edging slowly towards the table as they had all been talking, and as soon as he was able, he was going to grab the first object on the table and disappear.

John opened his eyes and nodded. Whatever Jack was saying was making some sense. Judas had to act now, or it would be too late.

He leapt across the room. Jack whirled around, and the knife in his hand came up in a flash. John pushed himself off the wall with incredible speed, but both of them were too late. Judas grabbed a crude leather eye mask from the table, and the room of keys in the Black Museum disappeared.

26 TURPIN'S GIBBET

He was safe – for now. He was still clutching the mask that he had snatched from the table tightly in his hand, and that meant that no one was else was coming through from the Museum side to this exact moment in time. If Jack or John wanted to find him, then they would have to go the long way around. They'd have to ask a lot of questions of a lot of artefacts, then travel across the time fields to get to him. But Jack had had a lot of time playing around in here, and that made Judas nervous. He looked at the crudely made black leather mask in his hand again. He was in Knavesmire, in York, and the date was 1739. It was raining that fine, grey rain that looked light but landed heavy, and soaked you to the skin quicker than you could say 'your money or your life!'

It was getting dark, too, but thankfully there was a lot of time between him and Scotland Yard – for now.

Judas patted the granite milestone on the side of the road and started walking down the muddy track that masqueraded as a road. The Romans had been gone a long time, and it looked as if they'd taken their roads with them. The trees of the forest all around swayed drunkenly with the wind while the leaves flashed their silver undersides and made the branches look as if they were flickering.

He could see the city of York on the horizon under a muddy, bruised sky. It was the nearest smudge of civilisation.

Just ahead of him on the road and to the right was a set of skeletal gallows and swinging from them was the body of the legendary highwayman, Dick Turpin.

The Museum was a prison, a particularly cruel prison, and it locked the punished up in the places that they loved the most; it was solitary confinement in a place that kept reminding them of what they had had, and what they had lost. They were cursed to live on in the places where they had spread their terror completely alone. Isolated and forgotten. This was Knavesmire, and it was the prison cell that had been made especially for Dick Turpin.

Judas stepped off the road and sat down on the steps at the bottom of the gallows. He needed a few minutes to think about the situation. What were they doing to Malzo? Where the heaven was Michael? What was Ray doing with this book? And who was the dapper gent with the powerful magical fingers?

'Evening, Dick,' said Judas to the cadaver swinging gently in the breeze above him.

A ragged, throaty, staccato laugh came from the body.

'Evening, Judas. Long time, no see.'

'You don't mind if I sit here for a bit do you, Dick?' Judas looked up at the hanging man and gave it one of his best smiles.

'Absolutely not, be glad of the company. What's happening?'

Judas smiled again.

'I'm on the run.'

Dick Turpin started to laugh again, and it started to rain.

'I know just how you feel, Squire. The thunder of hooves, and the Willow-the-wisp of torches through the branches of the trees in the dark of night... oh yes, stirs the blood, doesn't it! Me and Bess could always outrun them though, couldn't we girl?'

Judas watched as a huge black horse ambled out from under the canopy of a large tree nearby, and nuzzled at the hem of Dick's weather-beaten coat.

'I don't suppose you have an apple anywhere on your person do you, Judas?'

'Afraid not, Dick, sorry. I had to move quickly, and I didn't have time to get you anything. Next time. If there is one of those.'

Judas sheltered underneath the gallows until the shower passed. Dick talked non-stop, because he didn't get many visitors. At the beginning it just sounded like babble, but the longer Judas listened, the more sense it seemed to make. The rain shower passed away over the fields towards York, and

Judas left the shelter of the gallows, sitting on the wooden rail at the bottom of the post that Dick was hanging from. Dick kept talking, sometimes to Judas and sometimes to himself. Judas felt like interrupting, but he was about to ask Dick a favour, and it seemed like the best thing to do, so he let him talk on. Then, after what seemed like a long time, Dick just stopped his rambling and focused his attention elsewhere.

'He's coming for you, Judas. He's got half of the time fields up and looking for you. Very nasty is our Jack, and he's got someone with him, a big chap with a knife. The noises in the time fields nearby are getting louder. I'd get off if I was you.'

Judas stood up and scanned the trees for movement.

'Dick, are you sure that Jack has another man with him?'

The noose gave a little creak as Dick's head lolled from side to side. He was listening.

'Will you do something for me if I help you, Judas?'

Judas nodded.

'Will you come and pass the time of day with me every now and then?'

Judas nodded again.

'Definitely has another man with him, then. Giant of a fellow, wearing black, looks mean.'

Judas jumped from the platform and set off for the road.

'Thanks for the warning, Dick. I'll come and talk to you more often, I promise. Not a Judas promise – a real promise.'

Judas ran off. The noose creaked again and then fell silent. Black Bess did not run, though, and stayed by her master's side. That was true loyalty, and he would definitely bring her some apples next time, thought Judas.

He made his way back to the granite milestone on the road and took out the mask that had brought him here.

'You'd better be there, Michael!' He gripped the mask in his right hand, whispered the return spell and started walking into a shower of silver light.

Malzo was sitting against the far wall. The bottom half of one of his wings was stained crimson. His eyes were open, and he was trying very hard to smile. Standing over him was Michael. Judas breathed a sigh of relief and walked across the room. Michael had one hand on the pommel of his sword, and he was wearing that killer look on his face.

'They are both inside the Museum searching for me. Jack has worked out some way to cross the time fields, which is a worry, but I believe that they are in York now, talking to a hanged man.'

Michael held out his hand. 'Give me the key, and I will go and put an end to this stupidity.'

Judas replaced the mask on the table. 'Michael, I think we should get Malzo away from here first. He doesn't look like he could help out much, and the last thing we need is to be constantly hiding him from Jack and John. He's done his duty; we should let him go.'

Michael looked down at Malzo. He smiled. It was a rare show of emotion, and for a second Judas almost felt something like respect for him, but it passed quickly, and Michael casually bent over and picked Malzo up as if he were a sleeping child.

'I will be gone for only a short time, Judas. I will take him to the Halls of Heaven where he can be properly looked after, and then I shall return, and together we shall end this.'

As Michael was walking to the window, Malzo stirred in his arms and turned his head to Judas.

'Goodbye, Judas. You are a good custodian, and I hope that your time will come to an end soon, too. Be well. Good luck.'

Michael smiled at him once again. Perhaps there was forgiveness in store for Malzo up there. Perhaps you could pay your dues? Judas watched Michael open the window, and with one gigantic leap he was gone. The floor that the Museum rested on creaked and shook. Its gate keeper and night-watchman were gone now, and there was a tangible feeling of emptiness and vulnerability in the air.

Judas collected all of the keys apart from one and placed them carefully inside numbered green felt bags; he was about to hide them away where no one would dream of finding them. The remaining key was a small leather glove. It looked like it had belonged to a child who had seen hard times. He picked it up. Judas heard the scraping of a wooden chair on cobblestones and a curtain being dragged quickly across a brass curtain rail.

'Charles Peace at your service, Judas, what can I steal for you today, Sir?'

Judas smiled. 'Charles, I need something hidden today my friend, not stolen. I'm coming through.'

Judas closed his eyes and opened them again in the year 1875; he was in a small, smelly little room that overlooked a dirty street in Camden Town, London. The legendary housebreaker and safe-cracker Charles Peace was sitting on the end of his bed counting some money.

'I'm usually in the finding and taking valuables business, Judas, not the taking and hiding. What's the story?'

Charles Peace was a small man. It helped in his profession; he was a cat-burglar, and a very good one. Some said he was the best of all time, and that even Raffles the gentleman thief admired him.

'This is a big job, Charles. I need these hidden away where no one can find them. It's only a short gig, a matter of hours, and then I'll call you through and you give them back to me. Keep them near, and I'm the only one who you return them to, okay? I don't care who finds you or shows up, just me, okay?'

Charles Peace stood up and took the bags.

'The best place for these is in my glory hole, Judas old chap. The Peelers have turned this place over many a time and never found it. Now you look away for me; just turn your back a moment, and I'll put them away.'

Judas heard a faint scratching and then the sound of something dragging and then a clunk as if a piece of metal had been drawn down.

'Right you are, Sir – all done.'

Judas turned around, and the room was exactly the same as it had been before. The bags were gone, of course, and he couldn't for the life of him work out where they had gone. That was a good thing.

'So what's in it for me then, Sir?'

Judas smiled. 'You have a think about what you want, and when you hand the bags over I'll sort it out. Goodbye for now, Charles, keep them safe, and tell no one.'

Judas took out the glove and closed it in his hand once more, and seconds later he was back in the Key Room. Judas walked out and closed the heavy door behind him. The door closed with a reassuring thud. Judas looked at his watch and willed the second hand to move faster. He needed Michael.

He moved over to the window and watched the sun set over London. At least no more angels were going to be killed, and The 10 were out of action for good. Judas thought about Simon and the rest of the Disciples. He hadn't recognised any of them at first. Had so much time passed that they had become strangers? In the beginning they'd been close. The curse of time had destroyed that. Maybe in the future they would be friends again? Maybe pigs would fly.

Judas stopped daydreaming, because all of a sudden his scar was aching like crazy. He looked at the safe, but nothing was happening there, so he walked through to the outer room. That was empty, too. He left the Museum and headed back to his office. The door was still locked, but he knew that something or someone was inside before he entered. It was no good standing in the corridor though, because there were lots of secrets inside that office that he didn't want anyone knowing about, or prying eyes poring over. He turned the key in the lock and gently edged it open. There was a figure inside standing over his desk.

'Evening, Judas,' said the ghost of Williams.

Judas closed the door behind him and locked it.

'Williams. It's lovely to see you of course, but I do have to ask, what the hell are you doing here? I buried you a few days ago.'

The ghost of Williams walked across the room and sat down at his usual chair.

Judas had seen many spirits, ghosts and phantoms in his time, and it always amused him when they tried to carry on as usual, even though they were dead. Williams sat back, as he always did, and crossed his legs, as he always did. The only thing he didn't do was make a cup of tea for his superior, but Judas felt good to see him there even if it was bloody selfish.

Williams kept touching his arms and his legs; it was obvious that they felt odd to him and that he was having trouble coming to terms with still being here, and not inside a casket. But then, who wouldn't?

'I've been sent back, Skipper. Someone wants me to help you out. I can't leave the Museum and wander about outside, but I can keep an eye on things in here for you. It seems that the position was vacated recently by a big winged chap, and now the role is vacant yours truly has decided to take it.'

Judas sat down on the end of the table and looked down at Williams.

'It will be just like quite recent times then, so get the brews on.'

Williams smiled and raised both hands palm upwards as if to say, 'I'd love to, you know, but unfortunately I can't.' Judas looked at Williams and shook his head. He hadn't had time to miss him or mourn him, and here he was, back again with that silly smile and unassuming manner.

You couldn't say that Williams looked well – he was dead, after all – but there was something about him now that wasn't there before. It was completely at odds with the situation. He was a ghost, and he was a wisp of his former self, but he looked more solid now, if a ghost can look solid, that is. He looked calmer, too, as if he knew everything was going to be alright already, thought Judas. Williams got up and walked around the office. Most people expected ghosts to float everywhere. They imagined them to be white translucent shapes with just enough human features to remind you of the living person they once were – but ghosts weren't like that. They were much more real than you'd expect, a bit blurred around the edges of course, but basically the same. They were invisible to anyone they didn't want to see them, which could come in handy – especially in the Black Museum police force.

Williams stopped suddenly and waved his hand at Judas.

'Someone is trying to get into the Key Room inside the Museum.'

Judas was about to race down the corridor when he had a better idea.

'Go and have a look for me, will you? If it's a smart chap in a black cape and a huge hairy man with a knife, hang back and watch what they do, and tell me what they say to each other.'

Williams walked through the door and disappeared into the walls of the Museum.

Judas opened the window and looked up at the sky, longingly. He was prepared to take them both on if he had to, but if Michael was by his side there would almost certainly be a safer and more positive outcome.

Williams came back a few minutes later.

'No Jack and no John I'm afraid, Judas. There's a small, dapper gentleman in a killer suit standing over the key table, waving his hands around and speaking what sounds like

German with a twist. There's a floating ball of light over the table, and it keeps squeaking. He's getting a bit angry with it, if you ask me.'

'Stranghold! What the hell is he doing here? Right, follow me.'

Judas swung the door open and marched down the hall, with Williams closely behind him. He swiped his security key and pushed the door open.

Stranghold was standing in front of the table.

'Hello there, Herr Stranghold. Where are my cuffs? I've had a devil of a time explaining how I lost them.'

Stranghold stopped muttering to himself, and the ball of light faded, then smoothly floated into the pocket of his jacket. Stranghold calmly turned away from the table and looked at Judas.

'Where is the book that the little angel gave you? There's no point in denying it, I have chased that book for hundreds of years and I know it almost as well as my tailor. Hand it over, and I will perhaps let you live.'

'Look, Herr Stranghold, now is not a good time for me. I'm expecting company, some good and some bad, so if we could do this another year that would be good.'

Stranghold smiled his tight, humourless smile, and waved his hand around in front of his face. He was obviously casting some sort of spell, but that sort of magic didn't work inside the Museum as it did outside. Stranghold waited for a few seconds before trying another variation. Again, nothing happened. 'I know it's in here somewhere, Policeman, I can sense it.'

'My name is Inspector Judas Iscariot and I look after this place, and I also head up the Occult Division here at the Yard. If you can't see my associate Sgt Williams, he's over there. He's dead. Recently dead, now a ghost. You've probably seen many of them, being a magician. Say hello, Williams.'

Williams materialised in front of Stranghold.

'Hello, Herr Stranghold, pleased to meet you.'

Stranghold nodded his head in acknowledgement, and instinctively raised his hand for Williams to shake; it was Williams' turn to smile and shake his head.

'Ghosts are useful you know, Judas Iscariot. They can channel things for you, point them out to you, if you know the right spell, of course.'

Judas laughed. 'Williams doesn't know anything. As I said, he was dead yesterday.'

'Sag mal! Now!'

Stranghold waved his hand in front of Williams' face. It did not have the intended effect because the only thing that it forced Williams to do was to start laughing.

'You've got really short arms for a man.' Williams continued to laugh, casually stepping away from Stranghold and leaning up against the wall.

Judas knew what was coming next. Stranghold had obviously worked out that his magic was diluted and weakened inside these four walls. Judas didn't want to prolong the engagement, because he was expecting Jack and John any second now. He wanted Stranghold gone, and he wasn't going to attempt to stop him.

The small man clicked his heels and bowed his head smartly. He was a cool customer, and he knew that the field of battle was not to his advantage, so he conjured up the same bright flare of light that got him inside this place and disappeared.

Williams detached himself from the wall and walked over to the glass case containing the garrottes at the far end of the room. He bent down, moved a few dusty old boxes to one side and opened the door of the safe.

'How did you know the combination?' Judas reached out for the book.

'It was the same as the last one. You should change it occasionally.'

The book felt heavy in his hands.

'Can you do something with this? It's not the least of my worries right now, but it's not a priority, either. I don't mind where you take it but make sure it's safe. I seem to be spending all of my time hiding things today. Can you hide on the astral plane?'

Williams raised an eyebrow. 'Very funny. People always think that ghosts live on some astral plane somewhere, but it would be bloody crowded if we did. Leave it with me, though; I'll make it invisible and tuck it away in there.'

He pointed to the inner door to the Museum, then casually walked through the wall and was gone again.

Judas left the Museum and went back to his office. He'd have to make his own tea again. Fortunately, he'd only have to make one cup.

He pushed the door to his office open and sat down. 'What have you got me into, Ray?' he said to an empty room.

There was a rush of air that shook the windowpanes and a shadow sped past the window.

Seconds later the mighty figure of Michael appeared outside. Judas opened the windows and the Archangel squeezed inside.

27 INT⦿ THE SM⦿KE

Michael looked even angrier than usual, if that were possible.

'Malzo is safe, now. His wound was far graver than it looked, but he will fly once again, given time. He has been forgiven, and he can now come and go as he pleases. I think that had he not been granted entrance and given a second chance the wound may have claimed his life. Hope is a powerful medicine, Judas. Now, we have bloody work to do. Where can we find this John and his friend, the one that tried to kill an angel of Host?'

Judas rubbed his hands together and jerked his thumb over his shoulder at the door.

'Let's go and find him, shall we?'

Judas opened the door to the Key Room and stood by the empty table at the centre of the room with Michael. He took the small leather glove that he had been carrying and placed it on the table.

'I've put the rest of the keys somewhere safe. This one takes us to the place where they're hidden. We get them and bring them back here, and as soon as they are on this table both ends are open. If Jack the Ripper really has worked out a way to move around in there, he'll know that all the doors between all the times are open, and that should bring him straight to us. Alternatively, we go in there and wait for him to find us, and then we have less mess to clean up.'

Michael just shrugged. Judas knew that it didn't matter where they caught up with John or Jack – the result would be exactly the same.

For the first time since this whole business had started, Judas felt a slight twinge of sympathy for John. He remembered the hammering he had received from Michael in Joppa and wondered just what the big angel had in store. Well, if you live by the sword then you get sliced up by one eventually, he thought.

'We do it inside, then. Come on, let's go.'

Judas picked up the glove and closed his eyes. He heard Charles humming to himself before he saw him. He was sitting on his rickety old chair looking out of the window again. A shaft of grey tinged sunlight played across his face and the steam started to rise from the tin kettle on the small stove behind him. If he hadn't been such a good criminal, you could actually take to Charles Peace. But he was what he was, and that was why he was locked up inside his own prison with only his old memories for company. He had no hope of parole, and his sentence was one year short of eternity. His name was Peace, but he would get none.

He sensed their presence immediately and stopped humming midway through an old show tune.

'Hello again, Judas, brought a friend to see old Charlie, have you?'

The thief turned around, then stood up so quickly that the chair nearly ended up in the fireplace. The look on his face was priceless. Michael had that effect on everyone; a huge angel wearing a massive sword would put the fear into the meanest and strongest of the Museum's inmates.

'Is that... the...?'

Judas gave him the answer to his question before he had finished asking it.

'Yes, this is the Archangel Michael; he is the vengeance of the Lord and the bringer of retribution and justice to all and sundry. Please sit down, Charles, and close your mouth. Unless of course you want to catch all of the flies in here?'

The little man did as he was told. He couldn't take his eyes off Michael though, which was understandable in the circumstances. Charles Peace had seen angels before – but none like this one. The last he'd clapped his eyes on had been painted on the walls of the chapel in Newgate Prison.

Michael looked around the room. Fortunately, Charles Peace had done well in his chosen profession and could afford a large suite. He'd always wanted a large room because of all of the time that he'd spent inside a very small one, where there was a hole in the door and a bucket in the corner. The angel casually went over to the far wall and pushed two bricks backwards. There was a click, and a metal door flapped down to reveal a number of green felt bags.

'Hey! No one knows about that! What's he doing there, Judas, have you been spying on me?'

Judas shook his head.

'He's an angel, Charles; they just know things.'

Michael tied the bags to his belt. They looked tiny in his hands.

Judas poured the freshly boiled water into a cup for Charles, stirred some rank smelling tea leaves into it, and when they had turned the water brown, he offered it to the old thief.

'Has anyone been hanging around here? Seen or felt anyone?'

Charles sipped at his tea and squinted as the steam clouded over his eyes.

'There's been something happening, Judas, something that feels wrong that I can't put my finger on, Sir. Time passes differently here, doesn't it? An hour is a week sometimes, and a minute can stretch on for a year. The streets are always full of people that I can't talk to, that's my prison cell. But you kind of get to know them, their shapes and the sounds they make.

'Just recently there's been another thing moving around on the edge of my vision. Can't quite catch it if you know what I mean; it's there but not there, just on the edge; a black shape, keeps itself at a distance.'

Michael smiled. It was terrifying. 'That sounds like our man, or one of them, maybe. Was it one shape, or two?'

Charles looked confused. 'No, Sir, one big black shape. Looked like it had wings, but no ball of light, no Sir. I would have remembered that.'

Michael looked at Judas. 'It's a cape, Michael. Jack wears a cape. If he's rushing around it could look like wings, especially if he's blurred.'

Michael opened the door and stepped out. Judas followed him. 'Thanks, Charles, we'll see ourselves out.'

Judas and Michael walked down the street. The real Camden Town of that time was a very busy part of London. The canals brought barges down from the North of England and with it trade and lots and lots of people. This Camden, Charles Peace's Camden, was a faded reflection of it. It was dank, dire and cold. People wandered around, or shapes that looked a little bit like people. There was no real colour here, just shades of grey and black against the mud that they walked through. Michael looked unusually bright and white against them.

'Couldn't turn yourself down, could you?' Judas thought he was being funny.

'Couldn't turn your mouth off, could you?' Michael almost laughed at his own wit.

They walked on. They passed groups of people, drunken sailors just back from whaling with money and lust in their pockets. There was the sound of the canals, and the bawdy houses too. They had only been walking for a short time when Michael leapt into the air suddenly, soaring upwards into the rusty, red-coloured sky. Judas watched him until he was only a speck of white, then turned around and headed back to Charles Peace's lodgings.

He was halfway down the street when he felt a rush of air above his head. He crouched down instinctively, but he wasn't fast enough. John thumped him in the stomach, then chopped him on the back of the neck. Judas hit the ground. The mud made it soft. The mud also made it all the way up his nose and the stench of the horse dropping made him want to gag. He instinctively rolled himself into a ball to protect his more delicate areas, but no further blow landed. He looked up and saw John looking down at him. He had a strange, confused look on his face. Then he fell down next to Judas, let out a groan, and passed out. Michael was standing behind him with John's great big hunting knife in his hand.

'He is not dead or broken, Judas, just stunned for now. I think we will get some information from him.'

John was lying so close to Judas that he could hear his breath escaping in short bursts, like a miniature steam locomotive in need of coal and water.

'You left me as bait so that he would attack. Nice move. Let me know next time, will you?'

Michael picked him up.

'I like seeing you get hit.'

Judas cocked his head to one side and then shook it.

'You're not very nice, you know, Michael.'

'You are alive and unharmed, Judas, and we have the Baptist, I thought you'd be happy. Admit it, we are getting the job done; I am starting to see why He set you on your path.'

Judas pointed at the prone figure of John. 'Let's go. We can talk about this back at the Museum. Jack can wait. I think I know where we can catch up with him.'

Michael picked John up and slung him over one shoulder; he smiled at Judas, then spread his great wings and launched himself up into the air. Judas took out the glove and closed his eyes.

Moments later he placed the glove back down on the table in the Museum and loosened his tie. It had been a really, really long few days. He could do with some sleep. Williams floated through the wall.

'There's a nice cup of tea waiting for you in there.'

Judas looked up.

'Learned how to magically turn the kettle on then?'

Williams shrugged.

'Telephone. Canteen. Duty Officer. If you ask nicely, they bring it up in the lift for you and then leave it on the ledge by the window, I even got a couple of digestives on a plate. I thought twice about breaking them up and feeding the pigeons with them, but you haven't been a bad boss so they're on the table. It seems I can lift things and move things about just by imagining the deed. That's why the tea is still fairly warm.'

28 BURIED AT SEA

Judas imagined Charles Peace sitting comfortably in his large room and watching the hustle and the bustle of the world going by outside his window, longing to be able to join it.

The Black Museum worked in funny ways. Maybe Williams would be able to find out more about how it came to be, and why it was created in the first place? That particular chore would have to wait, though, because there were a lot more pressing matters to worry about right now. Seeing Williams move about the office made him smile, but also made him want to jump out of the window. It wasn't his fault that this man had died. He wasn't so churlish as to think that he was responsible, but Death did walk one pace behind him, and it seemed that it always would. So, each new partner was on borrowed time. It made no sense whatsoever to get involved with the opposite sex again, either. Williams looked up from his desk as if he had read Judas' thoughts, smiled his big, awkward smile, then walked through the wall and disappeared.

Judas stirred his tea and nibbled on the digestive. It was nearly fresh. The clock on the wall ticked loudly, and while he was trying to calculate how long Michael would take to get from the time fields to Scotland Yard, a big chunk of biscuit sheared off like a piece of arctic shelf, dropping into his mug. There wasn't a spoon to hand, so he tried to fish it out with a biro, and only succeeded in breaking it up into even smaller pieces. He shook his head. Only an animal would drink tea with soggy biscuits floating around in it.

He walked over to the window and scanned the skies. Angels were going about their business everywhere. He wondered if any of them knew what he'd been going through to try and keep them safe. Not many, if any, he thought, as he drew a sad looking circle in the grime on the windowpane. With any luck Michael would be back soon with the rest of the museum keys and a still unconscious John the Baptist. Between the two of them they should be able to get to the bottom of everything, he hoped.

Williams reappeared suddenly, his washed-out reflection hardly registering on the glass, and looking just like a grey smear, moving fluidly around the office like a sentient cigarette cloud. It startled Judas for a second. They'd have to organise some sort of signal between them to save Judas having more than one heart attack a week. Williams sat down at his desk and gazed up at the map of London on the wall in the office. A mug of tea that he could never drink was steaming away nicely on the jotter pad on the desk beside him.

'I can't leave the Museum, it seems. I can't go back home to check on the family, and I can't come with you when you head off to investigate anything either, which is a bloody shame if you ask me. I could really help. Imagine eavesdropping on any of our underworld chums – we'd have a clean-up rate with more zeros than a lottery winner's cheque. I wish I could go home though, just to watch them and know that they're okay. I'd be heartbroken and really sad if I weren't already dead.'

Judas sat down, taking out his coin and rubbing it between forefinger and thumb. The words weren't coming and all he felt right at that moment was the heavy weight of the guilt giant on his shoulder.

'I haven't had a chance to say thank you and apologise properly, Williams. You've been a good colleague and a good mate – some of the time. I won't go into your shady expenses claims or your sudden bouts of tendonitis that magically appear on the Monday after that football team of yours plays away from home on a Sunday. We'll let those slide – I think you earned them anyway, for working with me in here.

'I've had to tell a few wives that their husbands wouldn't be coming home again over the years, but telling Jane was the hardest yet. She really loved you, and if it's any bonus she really hates me for putting you in harm's way. I'm sorry about this ghost thing, too. I didn't know that you were coming back, either. I'm glad, of course – but I am truly sorry. I hope that you'll forgive me. Would it help if I asked Jane to come here? Make up some story about needing to speak to her about an old case? Then you could see her at least?'

Williams shrugged again, then stood up and pretended to look at the map more closely. If anybody asked him afterwards, or if it came up in some sort of occult quiz, Judas could tell whoever was asking that ghosts did mourn and were capable of tears – lots of them. Williams wiped his eyes and straightened his tie.

'No. I don't think I could see her without trying to speak to her and that would only make things more painful, for both of us. No. Let's start the way we mean to carry on. I have to start getting my bearings, don't I? There's a lot more to this Museum than meets the eye, isn't there?'

Judas felt a great big lump work its way up his throat and stick there. In a funny way he was glad of it, because at least it showed that he cared. It was true that he'd seen dependable Williams as just another body in the office, and not really a partner. He hadn't really prepared himself to like him as a person. Immortality did that to you. It made you as cold as a graveyard bench, and heartless too. It made you blind to the lives and loves of the normal people all around you. He'd have to do something about that.

'You're right. Best to leave that part of your life where it is, for now. Can you let me know when Michael arrives, please? Malzo used to be able to hear the Museum; he said that the walls and the floors had a voice. Maybe you can hear it, too? I'd like to get John dealt with as soon as possible, somewhere safe. You could give that some thought, if you like?'

Williams turned around and shrugged his shoulders in the affirmative.

'Good tea?'

'It was perfect. You didn't make it.'

Williams smiled and walked over to the door. He reached for the handle, then realised the futility of what he was doing. 'I'll have to get used to this really quick, won't I?'

Judas watched him leave, then stood up in front of the map and removed a couple of the blue pins. These were the ones that had marked the first few angel slayings; they could be placed back in the tin, as could those that marked the child snatchings in Clapham. The death of the slave traders at the hands of the Saints in Colliers Wood would keep those nasty little bastards quiet for some time, but it might be worth heading down the Church Roads again and making sure that the pit was out of action permanently. He'd ask Thornton to keep an eye on that. Judas took out a red pencil and traced a straight line from church to church on the map to highlight the invisible Church Roads again. It was time he made some proper records for whoever was lucky enough, or damned enough, to succeed him. He'd have to spend some time walking them, to get used to them again. There was a time when he thought that he knew most of them. He'd only caught Crowley the Imposter because he knew the roads and Crowley didn't. Judas put the red pencil away in his draw and looked at the red spiders' web he'd drawn on the map. If only the real police had access to them, it would make their lives a lot easier. Imagine being able to get across London without anyone seeing or hearing you coming? Half the unsolved crimes on record would get solved, and without any of the collateral casualties.

Williams walked back through the wall he'd left by.

'I think your bodyguard has just arrived.'

Judas ran down the corridor, deftly swiped his entry card, and entered the Museum. Williams was already there. Michael was prowling around the room. John the Baptist was still in heap on the floor. He was conscious, but only just. He kept raising his hand to head as if to ward off a blow. At each movement Michael twitched instinctively.

'He hasn't said much – but he will,' said Michael.

Judas walked over and sat on the edge of the nearest display case. Looking down on this shattered and battered body, he wondered how many times John had been where he was now? Standing over another helpless body, gloating, and watching the blood and the tears seep away into the cold ground. Well, he wasn't going to be doing it ever again, that much was evident from the way he twitched and shuddered.

He was nearly gone, and Judas wasn't going to be shedding any tears over him.

'So then, John, you and Jack the Ripper joined forces in order to unlock the cell doors of the Black Museum and set all of the horrors free to rape, murder and burn London to the ground.

'Who is pulling your strings, John? Who is whispering those sweet nothings in your ear? I'll get Jack and he'll be punished, but you're the one with the answers, I reckon. You don't have long left, so I suggest that you confess, and we'll try to stop whatever it is from happening. A lot of innocent people don't have to get hurt.'

John looked up. His face was swollen and purple. One of his eyes was closed and there was a vivid red mark that started at his jaw line and ran all the way up to his temple. There were purple, wet, glistening patches all over the fabric of his black jumper that oozed and bubbled. He was hurt really bad this time. Michael had taken his frustration out on him for attacking Malzo. John's time on earth was drawing to an end quicker than a moth-eaten rabbit at the dog track. Whatever deal he'd done was unravelling. When angels like Michael wanted to turn your lights off then there was nothing on earth that could stop that from happening. He should have been dead already, so it must have been incredibly strong magic keeping him alive.

John started to mumble in between the gasps and moans. Judas could recognise some of the words, but most were just insane babble and incoherent rambling.

John kept repeating something about the thunderstorms of pain in his head, and white noise that sliced and hacked at his memories deep inside his own mind. He rambled and cursed frequently. Occasionally though, Judas caught something about a secret operation called 'Paper Clip', and the Nazis of old.

'He's fading fast,' said Williams.

Judas looked at Michael. 'We need to know who it was that wanted to destroy the Museum, Michael. We need to know why it was so important. Who, or what, wanted to drown London in blood? We have to know now, because it feels like we're running out of time.'

Michael picked John up from the floor like a rag doll. John groaned and tried to pull away from the big angel, but there was no chance of that happening. He was looking into the eyes of vengeance itself.

'And what about the murder of my kin? What about the angels that died at his hand? Why did they need to die, Baptist?' Michael gave him a shake to help clear his mind.

John flinched at the sound of his voice. Blood started to drip freely onto the lino on the floor. It made a regular tapping sound, as if a sink were overflowing.

'Michael, can you order him to speak? Can you make him talk?'

Michael lifted his arm and placed two white fingers on the forehead of John the Baptist and then blew softly into his face.

'The words will flow quickly, Judas, so pay attention.'

Michael blew a second time and John went as limp as a well-used dish cloth. He twitched twice, then started to talk in clear, plain English.

All of John's life was coming out in sharp bursts. Judas snatched up a pencil and started to write as quickly as he could. Williams just shook his head, walked over and started to jot everything that Michael was saying in very accomplished and particularly impressive shorthand.

'Shorthand, Judas, they gave us classes on it back at the training college. If you'd done the training modules you'd know how to do it, wouldn't you?'

Judas tried to give Williams a pat on the back but stopped just short of actually making contact. He'd never done anything like it when Williams had been alive, and now would be the wrong time to start.

Judas noticed that John's body was still intact. It was not disappearing as the slave trader's body had done on the Church Roads. Nothing was fading away. Michael must have read his mind.

'I'm just taking his words from him, Judas. I have another plan for the physical part of him.'

'Just get me everything inside that big shaggy head, and you can do what you like with the rest of him.'

Williams has already covered the top of the glass cabinets that housed all of the records on London's urban cannibals with notes and was now moving on to the top of the case that housed all of the murder weapons of a magical nature.

There was page after page of markings that looked like barbed wire squeezed between faint grey lines. John kept talking, and Williams kept writing. At one point Williams looked up in disgust. Judas got the impression that Williams would have vomited if he had been able to, but he just kept scribbling away. The only time his hand stopped moving across the page was when he needed more paper. Then John suddenly stopped talking. Judas looked up. John was still alive.

'That is all that he has. There is nothing more to know. May I have him now, Judas?'

Judas looked at Williams. 'Were you able to take much of that in, or did you just bang it down?'

Williams shook his head. 'There was no way anyone could have kept track of that. I just wrote it down without thinking too hard. The little bits I did hear I won't be able to forget, so it's probably for the best. No, we'll be going through that for the foreseeable.'

'Well, if we can't double-check that we've got all the information we need before he shuffles off this mortal coil there's not a great deal we can do is there? He's all yours, Michael. What have you got planned for him?'

Michael put John the Baptist over his shoulder once more and moved out of the room and over to the open window.

He looked back once and then jumped into the air.

Judas watched him fly off into the sky. It was the last time he would ever see John the Baptist alive – hopefully. He only had to find Jack the Ripper now.

Judas closed the window and went to find Williams. They had a lot of deciphering to do.

The sun was setting when Michael started to descend in long banking turns from the steel roof of the darkest clouds that had ever been created. His destination appeared between great banks of sea rain that fell horizontally.

Rockall was two-hundred and seventy miles north of Ireland. It was a bleak place. As its name suggested, it was a rock, and that's all it was. Only the sea birds had any use for it. As Michael approached, they took to the air in fright. He dropped John without care or attention onto the granite outcropping, folding his wings and planting his feet on the stone. Sea spray filled the air all around them. Michael touched John on the shoulder.

'Rise, John. It is the time.'

John stood up as well as he was able to.

Michael's touch had given John just enough life so that he could stand up and be aware of his surroundings. That little sliver of awareness was important, because he had to be able to see and feel the coming despair. He had lost so much blood and broken so many bones during his fights with Judas and Michael that he should be dead, but he was not getting away that easily.

He looked up at Michael, then gazed out into the bleakness of the North Sea. The rolling grey stretched on for ever to a horizon that was fading away in more ways than one. Hope had disappeared from this rock a long time ago, too. It was an executioner's block, far out at sea, for only the darkest of souls.

'Why here then, angel?'

Michael tilted his head to one side. John's question amused him.

'I am not going to lay you to rest out here in the nothingness, John. Your body will sink to the bottom of the ocean, and you shall stay there. You will not be dead in the conventional sense, because your mind will still be alive, and your senses will record the passing of time. In life you were chosen for your leadership, your strength and your faith. But you were weak. You were taken over by something or someone, turned into their puppet, and used for evil deeds. I will hold you under the water, but there will be no rebirth for you, John. This is the end of your journey. Know that I will find whoever it was that turned you, and their fate will be sealed too. Come now, and I will introduce you to despair.'

John closed his eyes and his head fell forwards so that his chin rested on his chest. He didn't struggle or fight when Michael picked him up and carried him to the water's edge and waded in until the water was around his waist. Michael held him there for a second, then looked down into John's eyes.

'We may see each other again, John. I may have to check on you every thousand years or so. This is not a baptism, John, this is not rebirth or resurrection – this is the moment when you pay for your crimes and keep paying for them for ever.'

John wanted to cry but he could only look up at the slate grey sky. He kept his eyes open even when the water flowed over his face and up his nostrils and deep down into his lungs. He should have died then but didn't. Michael dropped the body into the waves and pushed it down even further under the water. John should have died then, but he didn't. Michael climbed back onto the rock and selected a massive, black stone. Then he walked back into the surf and placed the rock on John's chest. John went down into the deep, and still, he did not die. He saw the large faint disc of the sun turn into a pinprick of light as he fell further and further down into the blackness, where no fish swam. The rock pushed him down for a long time, and then he reached the sea bottom, and was welcomed to his resting place with a small and apologetic cloud of displaced mud that billowed around him before settling and going back to sleep. A mile above the body of John the Baptist, drowned but still not dead, the sun dipped under the straightest and sharpest horizon ever and went in search of another hemisphere to wake, leaving only an angel standing on a rock in the middle of the coldest and cruellest sea. The birds started to circle around him on tired wings, calling out to each other.

Michael smiled, unfurled his great wings and flapped them once, then soared up into the black sky. He said no words and left no grave marker because – John the Baptist was not dead. For him, down there in the grey swirling void, it was worse than that.

29 THE LEY LINE EXPRESS

Michael had to fly back to London now, and help Judas make sense of John's confession. It would take Judas an age to get through the notes, so he did not rush. He flew up into the night sky and looked down on the sea and breathed in the clean air. The clouds drifted past, and the lights of civilisation came on far below. He had completed the first part of his task. The Grove was safe. So was the Black Museum – for now. Michael flexed his wings and caught the wind. London wasn't far away.

Judas turned the lights off in his office and started to make his way to the stairwell. It had been a very long few days and he was dead tired. What was the point of having a flat in Zone 2 if you never got to see it or spend any time there? he thought to himself.

Williams appeared and coughed politely. 'I've got somewhere with those notes. It's pretty awful, and fairly frightening, but it can keep until the morning. You need some sleep by the look of you.'

'Thanks, Williams.'

Halfway down the stairs, Judas' stomach started to rumble, and half an hour later he was heating up a meal-for-one in the state-of-the-art microwave that he had used a grand total of ten times.

Back at the office the following morning, he found Williams organising the notes that he'd taken the day before on his desk. There was also a new map on the wall next to the one full of blue pins. Positioned to one side of the new map were neatly arranged red pins that looked ready to attack.

Judas sat down and leaned back in his chair. Its familiar creak made him feel at home. Williams cleared his throat again.

'Before we start going through these, Judas, can you step into the Museum with me? I've made a few changes and I want to make sure you're happy about them before I completely ignore you and do it anyway.'

Williams didn't wait for the reply. He just smiled, turned around, and disappeared through the wall.

Judas shook his head and set off. The dead Williams seemed to have developed a sense of humour and he was definitely growing into the new job. Williams had moved the cabinets with all of the grisly mugshots, weapons and evidence from the outer room further inside the Museum. All that remained was the old desk and the old phone occupying the centre of the room like a quiz-master's chair. There were faded brown rectangles on the walls where the old photographs had been, and not a lot else. It somehow felt right.

'The voices got on my nerves,' said Williams.

'I've been blessed with immortality, and I get a really big build-up of ear wax, so it doesn't affect me.'

Williams pretended to laugh, then walked through the wall and into the Key Room.

Judas followed but had to open the door in the old-fashioned way in order to step inside.

'When you moved everything, what did you do with the "book"?'

Williams disappeared. When he reappeared a few minutes later he was carrying it.

'This thing has been making the rest of the inmates very uneasy and very talkative, Judas. Mumble, mumble, mumble. Lots of whispering and snatches of threats and malice. Some of them even went quiet for a while, which as you know is unheard of. Have you taken a closer look at the front cover?'

Williams handed it over. Judas took it and placed it on the edge of the table. It was a large, heavy book with a thick, well-thumbed leather jacket. The spine was rough to the touch, though. When Judas ran his thumb down it he thought he heard voices. Williams came over and pointed at the bottom of the front cover. There were words and symbols running along it. There were lots of them, and they seemed to be layered over and over each other, so that the top obscured the bottom, making legibility impossible. But as Judas looked more closely, they seemed to separate, depending on which line you were focusing on. If the writing inside was anything like the cover, then there was an awful lot of information stored inside it.

Judas looked up at Williams.

'When you were taking notes last night, you looked up and stopped for a second. It was as if you'd heard something nasty. What was it?'

Williams sat down at the opposite side of the table.

'It was all pretty awful, Judas. Some of it was just plain nasty, and some of it made my stomach turn. There was quite a bit about you, and this place.

'John was very weak and delusional towards the end of his two-fingered interrogation. Whatever it was, or whoever it was that was poisoning him from afar, was doing a very good job. John had been persuaded to kill a lot of people over a long period of time, but the killing of the angels was just a ploy to get you involved. John was being controlled, and he was being told to get your attention. It's all part of some bigger plan, I think, but you're going to have to read the notes yourself.

Judas picked the book up. 'I'm heading back to the office. Let's talk later. I'll have a look at this and then try and go through the notes.

'Can you do me favour? When you take a turn of the new grounds, can you spend a bit of time with Dick Turpin? Have a chat with him and take some apples for Black Bess. He's easy to find.'

Judas left the Key Room and went back to the office. Once there he made another cup of tea to replace the one he'd left to go cold earlier.

The office was quiet, and the desk phone was fast asleep. Judas watched London come to life through the window. Angels flew across the sky like planes with different holding patterns.

Some of them were on their way to work, and some were on their way home. Judas wondered what their lives were like down here. It must be strange for them, even after all these years. Why had they chosen to live down here, amongst the mortals?

Judas sipped at his tea. John was gone, and the case was closed. He hoped it was closed for good, but he knew in his heart of hearts that it wasn't. He was Judas Iscariot, and his life just wasn't like that.

Michael arrived some hours later.

'He is gone, Judas. We will see him no more.'

Judas turned from the window.

'I don't want to know how, or where, just that he's gone for good, okay?'

Michael nodded.

'I have to go now, Judas. We won't see each other for some time. Before I leave, you should know that the people that were controlling John and the people who want the "book" are the same. There are clues in the notes that Williams took. Read them well.

'They wanted to destroy London, Judas. And be under no illusion, they still do. They tried it twice before and failed, but this time they may have found the miracle weapons they need to succeed. Be well, Judas, I will make sure that your deeds are known in the right places.'

Judas watched him climb out of the window and launch into the air. Seconds later he was gone. Judas closed the window and sat down again. Could he hope that Michael was going to speak to God for him, put in a good word, so to speak?

He smiled to himself and was feeling good for the first time in years, closed his eyes, and drifted off to sleep.

All good things must come to an end, though, because all-too-soon he was rudely awakened by the shrill, high-pitched tone of the desk phone. He picked up the receiver and held it to his ear.

'Judas, it's me, Ray. Do you still have that book?'

Ray sounded like he was talking through a sock that he'd placed over his mobile phone, because the signal was very faint. He also sounded very scared.

'I still have it, Ray. It's safe. Where are you?'

Judas heard a strong wind in the background, pushing at the branches of a tree and making it creak.

'Up North. You know where. As far away as possible from little German men and their book-collecting friends.'

Judas waited. Ray was a talker, even when he was petrified.

'They'll know that I sent it to you, and they'll be coming for it. I never came across a more determined little man in all my time.'

Judas shifted the receiver to the other ear, but neither the sound nor the signal improved.

'He's already been here, Ray. But don't worry, because he didn't get it. Magic doesn't work that well inside the Museum, unless it's museum magic, of course. Now Ray, don't say where you are over the phone; I know how to get to you if I need to. Why did you run when you did? And why did you contact me about the book in the first place? You could have handed it over to them and made some easy money. Why hold on to it, and why put yourself in harm's way?'

Judas heard Ray moving about and pictured him standing out in the open somewhere in front of some old stone dwellings in a dense wood that was off-limits to the non-flying kind.

'It's bad, Judas, the whole thing is bad. I got the book from a friend of a friend. He was even more scared than I am. He'd had the book a while, so I can imagine why.

'It talks, Judas. And it changes all the time; always whispering and moaning, never stopping, like it's ill or

293

something and just can't get better. My contact, the guy I got the book from, he said he'd been given it by an old sick angel who came down in the first Fall, way back; said he'd stolen it from one of the lost libraries during the great unrest before the war. You know what that means, don't you?'

Judas shifted uncomfortably in his seat. It was all falling into place now, and he could feel a monster of a headache coming on. His scar was itching like crazy.

'There were these great books, Judas. Books that were full of ancient law and powerful stuff in them – dangerous spells and charms and stuff. They were locked up tight up there in the sky, locked away in libraries that were almost fortresses in their own way. These libraries were hard places to get into, and even harder to get out of.

'The rumour was that some of the older angels, the higher order angels, had been persuaded by someone even more powerful than them to steal some of the books and hide them away down here on earth. Knew they might be useful sometime; you know what I mean?'

Ray stopped talking for a second. Judas heard the click of a lock and the scraping of table legs on a stone floor. It sounded like Ray was barricading himself in.

'Well, this is one of those books, Judas. The old chap that I got it from said that he'd got it from some cranky old scientist who had been on the wrong side during the last big war down here. Apparently, the mad scientist said that some of the chapters in the book had been translated and deciphered. They've been unlocked Judas! That is Godzilla-sized bad!'

'Which war, Ray?'

'The second big one down here, Judas. World War Two, Hitler and the Thousand Year Reich and all that.'

Judas stood up to stretch. 'Listen, Ray, it's safe for now. But what about you? If Herr Stranghold – that's his name by the way – comes back here, I'll sort him out.

'He wasn't able to locate the book properly, but he knows it's here and getting it is going to be a big problem. So I presume that he'll retrace his steps and try and find you again. Are you safe?'

'I'm fine. Some of the big lads here are on my side. If anyone comes looking for me they'll let me know. They're not too happy about strangers, so I'll be okay, Judas; don't worry about me and thanks for looking out for me.

'Look, I wanted to give it to you because you can get rid of it or send it back to the rightful owners. I'm not getting involved with the higher order angels because they're a law unto themselves, and frankly, they give me the creeps. I'm grounded, anyway. They'd kill me if I left the earth and showed up in heaven uninvited, even if I was trying to do something good for change. Do me a favour though, Judas: get rid of that thing, then things should go back to normal.'

Judas put the phone on speaker.

'Ray, sit tight. I'm going to come to you, and we can talk some more. Can you arrange for safe passage and a guide?'

There was a pause, because Ray was not alone and he was busy listening to someone else in the room. After a few minutes he came back on the line.

'Get to the "Iron Angel" tomorrow evening. I'll have someone meet you and bring you over. Thanks, Judas.'

The phone went dead, and Judas turned off the speaker button.

Williams appeared.

'I've got some good news for you. I've found Jack the Ripper. He's feeling a bit sheepish; says that it was all John's fault, he was coerced, that sort of thing. He's back in his own time loop and would like to be friends again.'

Judas shook his head.

'I'll deal with him when I get back. Keep an eye on him for me, though. In fact, keep two eyes on him and spread the word inside the Museum that I want him sent to Coventry. He is totally incommunicado and in solitary. We need to find out how he learned to move around inside the Museum like that, then stop him from ever doing it again.'

Williams looked down at the book on the table.

'Back from where, Judas?'

Judas picked up the book and handed it to Williams.

'Put that in the safest safe we have. I'm off to Newcastle tomorrow to see Ray. I'll be back in a couple of days. Night-night!'

Judas put on his coat and opened the door. He turned to Williams just as he was leaving.

'Oh, and decipher as much of those notes as your stomach can bear for me, please. Be good to make sure we haven't missed anything.'

Williams smiled, but before he disappeared, he gave Judas his 'do you want to tell me about it?' look. He got no answer and floated away to get back to translating the notes and their horrible secrets.

The following morning, Judas packed his overnight bag, and set off to catch a train to Newcastle, and the Angels of the North. He didn't go to any of the normal London terminals because the train that he needed to catch was the Ley Line Express, and that ran from the old Roman Station down by the Thames embankment. The station did not feature on any map of London, and only those who had some training or experience of the occult knew of its existence, so it never got too crowded, and delays were unheard of.

The Express ran along the ancient Ley Lines of Britain. Judas knew most of the staff in the station itself quite well; the porters and the booking clerks and the signalmen all knew him and had worked with him or for him at some point over the last century or two. He was able to buy his ticket and reserve a nice little cabin in next to no time at all. The train pulled away from the platform at exactly 10.30, so he would be in Newcastle just before 14.00.

He'd have most of the day to kill before catching up with Ray, and as he watched London's fringes slip away and merge into the greenery of the countryside, his thoughts turned to Michael. The Archangel was not what he could really call a friend. They'd hated each other even before they'd met, it seemed, at least that was the feeling he got whenever he met the big winged chap. And they'd never seen eye to eye about anything. So why had he protected Judas, and saved him this time around? The conductor gently slid the door to Judas' compartment open and clipped his ticket with some highly polished clippers. He obviously took great pride in his job, which was refreshing to see, thought Judas.

Judas picked up one of the free newspapers from the table. The wider world was in a bit of a pickle again. The front page was crammed with wars, famine, media feuds and celebrity nonsense. There was so much of it that it felt as if the paper could have had forty front pages, such was the hysteria and the doom currently playing out across the globe. Judas got bored of it really quickly and threw it onto the opposite seat. A couple of pages slipped onto the floor of the compartment, and Judas was not going to spend the next few hours looking at an article on mind control, so he carefully retrieved them and placed them back in the right order, stuffing the newspaper into the wastepaper basket in the corner. He'd treated himself to First Class, so the compartment and the carriage were quiet. Which was good. He closed his eyes and slept. It felt as if he'd only just closed them before the conductor was shaking him by the arm. He'd arrived in Newcastle on time. The hours had slipped away into the past, but Judas did not mourn their passing because he felt rejuvenated and fresh.

He left the train and tipped the porter for carrying the incredibly heavy overnight bag he was carrying to the exit. After the journey and a really good sleep, he realised that he was ferociously hungry. He'd fought off para-demons in the sewers underneath London, and traded blows with a drunken gypsy prince, but he hadn't fancied taking on the microwaved bacon butty on the train; there was only so much punishment that the body could take, after all. He walked through the gates of the station and headed for his favourite haunt up here. The Peace and Loaf Jesmond was just how he'd left it the last time. Good food, and staff that greeted you with a smile then left you alone. Which was just how Judas liked it. He ate quickly and quietly, and felt the chasm in his stomach reduce itself into a hairline crack. An angel flew past outside. Judas looked up quickly, but it wasn't Ray. Of course it wasn't. Ray would be hiding somewhere. He'd have gone to ground up a tree somewhere. Judas carried on with his meal, wiping the gravy from his meat pie with a piece of crusty white roll that was soft on the outside and softer on the inside, which made a change from the ones he bought in his local supermarket back in London. He had a coffee without the sacrilegious sprinkling of chocolate powder on the top, then paid the bill and left. It was starting to get dark now. The streetlamps were reacting to the drop in the ambient light and coming to life very slowly. Rain was falling and umbrellas were going up. Judas pulled the collar of his overcoat up and went in search of a taxi.

He didn't have to search far. It was just the same in Newcastle as it was in London, because as soon as it started raining the taxis all came out to play. The drivers must scan the weather reports looking for showers, thought Judas. More people take cabs when the heavens open, because who likes getting wet when you're fully dressed? He knew that he didn't. A brown cab was waiting for a fare by the kerb nearby. The light was on, so he tapped on the window and waited while the electric window slid down inside the car door. A warm fug crept out of the car, and Judas immediately thought of badgers. The driver finished reading the back pages of his newspaper and then stuffed it into the footwell on the passenger side before turning around. He had one of those faces, thought Judas. It looked like he was constantly recovering from the last black eye.

'Where to?' he said in a voice so low that only deaf dogs would have been able to hear him.

Judas smiled his best smile and said, "'Durham Road, please,' in his best 'I'm not from London' voice.

'Gateshead it is. You're off to see the Angel of the North then, Sir? Most people who come up here go and see it; most of them do it during the day though. Fantastic piece of sculpture and engineering that is. Well worth the visit. You know it's twenty metres high? Huge, giant thing it is.'

Judas listened to him and wondered how many times he'd said those words. The journey there was very short, but it didn't stop the driver talking non-stop all the way. He could feel all of the good energy that he'd stockpiled on the way up on the train and during the fantastic meal that he'd eaten slowly leaking out. Thankfully he'd learned to drown out cab drivers and their blarney and wondered if there was an opportunity to copyright an app called Mute the Driver or something witty. He paid the fare and thought about telling the driver that he smelled of old badger but decided against it.

He watched the brown car reverse then pull away into the night, and then took a look at the rust-coloured behemoth that was the Angel of the North. It was bloody impressive, even in the rain and the fading light. Judas had been here many times. The first time he'd been summoned to it he thought it must have been some sort of a joke: 'I'm an angel of the north, so I'll meet you at the Angel of the North.'

But it had proved not to be. The angels felt safe there, for some reason. The sculpture stood on the top of a hill so you couldn't sneak up on anyone there. Maybe that was why they chose it as a meeting place. Judas walked up the hill and sat down on the Angel's giant, rusty foot. He was the only one there.

He looked at his watch. He was on time for a change. Hopefully this contact would be as well.

He didn't have to wait long or get too wet. He heard the angels before he saw them. They were drifting past overhead and taking a good look at him before landing. They were either paranoid, or very good at keeping people alive, or making them dead. After a few minutes of checking the lie of the land, they landed. There were two of them. Both wore long, dark coats over dark trousers. The only flash of colour could be found in the feathers of their wings, which were grey and brown with silver highlights and white wingtips. They approached and just stared at Judas, so he just stared back. These angels were different to the ones he knew in London. They were quiet and aloof. Not particularly friendly, but not threatening either. Judas waited.

'You are the one they call Judas?'

'I am.'

The first angel reached out to Judas and gently placed his palm against his cheek. Judas felt a strange sensation. It was an intense, short burst of heat, before the angel took his hand away.

'Yes, you are.' The angel nodded to his companion and then they both stepped forward and picked him up. It felt like he was in an express elevator without walls or a floor or a roof. They flew high into the sky to avoid the rain. Neither spoke. Judas had to squint, because they were flying quickly now. Their great wings flapped in unison as they carried him away. Judas could see other angels flying around below him. There were a great many of them, and he wondered whether or not it was usual to have so many in the air at any one time, or whether they were here for his security, or maybe someone else's. His winged taxi took him into the darkness of the night sky and away from any light on the ground. Then, as if they had reached an invisible boundary marker in the air, they folded their wings backwards and started to descend. As they got lower, Judas could see a few cottages here and there, but they were heading for one solitary cottage on the edge of a wood in particular. Judas remembered the sound of the creaking tree branches and the sound of the wind from last night's call with Ray and knew that this was where Ray was when he called him. The two angels flew lower and lower; with each beat of their wings they got closer and closer to the cottage. They flew in a wide arc around the wood before landing a short distance from the building. Once they were on the ground they just pointed at it, across the meadow. They were obviously saving up their words for Christmas, because they weren't spending any on him. Both of them watched him start walking towards the cottage, and once they were both happy that he wasn't going to get lost crossing one meadow they leapt into the air and flew off. Judas knew they would be watching him all the way, so he pretended to go the wrong way for a few paces just to take the mick a bit. It was only for a bit of a laugh, but they didn't bite, so he went the right way. These angels didn't have much of a sense of humour, it seemed, and their conversational skills were definitely lacking.

Judas was only a few metres from the cottage when the door opened suddenly and threw a shaft of light across the ground that looked like a big orange envelope. Ray was silhouetted in the doorway. His wings twitched as he looked left and right nervously. Judas just pointed up into the air. Ray looked up and saw the two angels circling overhead. He smiled his lopsided smile and pointed towards the wood nearby. A score of well-armed angels stepped out from the trees. Ray was well protected, it seemed.

30 THE WISDⓋM ⓋF AZRUELA

The inside of the cottage was basic, but very comfortable. It had two small wooden-framed windows, and a fireplace with a fire in the grate that gave off lovely and welcoming warmth. The white walls had been painted with delicate runes and shapes that reminded Judas of something that he couldn't quite put his finger on. Ray had made himself at home there with a few personal touches.

Sitting at the small wooden table in the centre of the room was another angel. If you had only one word to describe him it would be 'dusty'. He had a handsome but lined face, with long black hair that reached down to his waist and wings that were speckled with silver and bronze, and Judas knew that wings that were coloured in this way indicated great age. Angels didn't really show the passage of time on their faces or limbs, so this one had been around a while. He didn't look up as Judas entered. His attention was focused on the small book on the table in front of him. All of his attention was on those small pages. The world was going on all around him, but he was somewhere else entirely. He was in a story.

Ray took a kettle that hung over the fire and poured something hot-looking into a mug, placing it on the table opposite the older angel. He motioned towards a chair, and Judas didn't have to be asked twice. The tea was good; it tasted light and fresh and it revived him, taking the chill off the recent flight through the night and the rain. Ray sat down and smiled.

'Judas, it's good to see you. This is one of my order. He was my mentor and protector, and head librarian here. His name is Azruela. He's going to tell you all about the book.'

The other angel stirred, then calmly closed the little book that he had been reading. He looked into Judas' eyes for a while, the expression on his face exactly the same as the one he'd worn when reading. Judas had heard that some librarians could read people as well as books, and this was an angel that had spent thousands of years with both, so he held his gaze for as long as possible.

After a few minutes had passed the old angel nodded first at Judas, then at Ray, and beckoned them both to follow him. They all left the warmth of the cottage and walked towards the wall of green that was the nearby forest. The same guards that Judas had seen earlier stepped out into the open once again as they approached. They were all carrying weapons, which came as a surprise to him. They were on a war footing, which was not a good sign. A nod of the head from Azruela was enough to make them all stand down; one second they were there, and the next they were gone. Judas, Ray and Azruela passed into the wood.

Under the branches of the trees everything was quiet and still. Someone had turned the volume down, and the lack of sound made Judas feel odd. Only the rustle of the dry leaves underfoot punctuated the silence. As they walked further in, the trees started to look straighter and wider. The branches looked straighter, and ten times longer than they should be.

Judas was trying to work out what was causing this optical illusion when he noticed a glow coming from the heart of the forest up ahead. They stepped into a clearing and he discovered the source of the strange light. There were lots of buildings hidden under and inside the trees. All of them were made from what looked like some sort of dark glass. The moonlight was making the walls glow, and that made them look as if they were vibrating softly. Azruela directed them towards a big building on the opposite side of the clearing. There were more guards outside, but they recognised Azruela immediately and remained motionless. The aged angel walked up the steps and pushed the large doors open, then turned and beckoned for Judas and Ray to follow.

This was the great Northern Library of the angels. There were hundreds of thick wooden shelves that stretched away from them for as far as the eye could see. There must've been millions of books lining them. As Azruela walked on, light started to glow from small circular openings in the ceiling.

'Your moonlight-powered light bulbs must save a fortune in energy bills.'

Azruela turned to him and nodded.

'So you can hear what I'm saying, then? You're not just ignoring me for the sake of it?'

The old angel nodded again.

Judas laughed. 'So which one is it?'

Ray gave him a nudge and shook his head, as if to say 'save the jokes'.

They walked on in silence. Azruela turned first left, then right, and then stopped at a long wooden reading table. He pointed to the chair opposite and walked off in search of a particular book.

Ray took the seat next to Judas and whispered, 'Azruela is one of the original Earth Angels, Judas. He fought in our first war, up there, and wasn't on the winning side, if you know what I mean. He doesn't do a lot of talking now, but when he does it's really worth listening to.'

Azruela came back carrying a huge, dusty tome. The sheer size of it looked like it should be one of the lifting challenges for a strongman competition on television. The fact that he was carrying it like a comic book made Judas sit up. He placed it carefully on the table, passed his hand over the cover, and all the dust disappeared.

'The young angels do not spend as much time in here as they should. That includes you, Ray.' Azruela had a deep, booming voice that definitely did not fit inside his body.

On hearing it, Ray sat up with a start, as if he was back in school and had been caught falling asleep at his desk again.

'I do speak, Judas! I just don't have much to say these days, so I don't. The wisdom of many ages can be very useful, if you know how to use it sparingly.'

Ray smiled nervously and pretended to be even more awake than he was feeling at that moment.

'Also, Judas Iscariot of the Black Museum of Scotland Yard, I can speak into a mind. There may be times ahead when that could be helpful. So I will help you along when I can, if you will allow me to, of course?'

Judas looked intently at the old librarian and weighed his next words carefully.

'Are you saying that I can call on you wherever I am, and you will help me with your knowledge? That would be a powerful and very useful thing to have at my disposal. The answer's yes, of course. I'd be glad of any help, thank you.'

Azruela nodded, looked down at the book on the table, and opened it. He turned a few of the pages over, then pointed down at a single picture in the middle of one of the pages. Judas got up and walked around the table to stand at the angel's shoulder. Halfway down the page was a picture of Adolf Hitler. He was standing in the middle of a large group of men. Judas scanned the faces and found the face of Herr Albertus Stranghold staring right back out at him. If the picture was original, and there was absolutely no reason to doubt its authenticity, then Stranghold was well over one-hundred years old. Possibly more, even.

Azruela was reading his thoughts and nodded in agreement. He turned over the next page and there was the mad man again, this time kneeling before a smaller group of men wearing black robes. Everyone knew that Hitler had searched the known world for knowledge and weapons of an occult nature, and here were some more black and whites in glossy and matt finishes to prove it.

Azruela turned yet another page, and this time Judas was the one to point. Hitler was in the middle of a large room surrounded by marble statues and dark oil paintings. On the floor were strange markings and a chalk circle, and inside this circle were three black books. It looked as if he was worshipping them.

Azruela closed the book and sat down. Judas returned to his seat, and then Azruela spoke for a long time.

'A long time ago when Heaven was but a hamlet, it was decided by some of the angels that we should, and could, intervene in the affairs of man, when there was a definite threat to the earth and its inhabitants, be they human, beast, faerie or otherwise.

'We had the power to get involved and protect you when you could not protect yourselves. We were a police force, if you like, doing a job akin to the one that you do now. We were never many in number, and we have taken or confiscated many powerful objects over the course of time, and hidden them away. Of course there are many still at large out there, in the world of man. Occasionally someone comes forth with the strength or desire to wield one of them, and we must take action to make sure that they are worthy of using one or stopped from doing so – by any means necessary. Some of the objects heal, but unfortunately most do the opposite. So you can see how important our work is. Our great libraries, huge halls and catacombs are home to powerful objects that could destroy all of mankind in the wrong hands. Some of us can hear or feel when something is wrong, and then one of us investigates.

Some time ago this one book was mislaid or stolen; we have not got to the bottom of that yet, and we were unable to locate it. Young Ray here moves in certain circles, and when he heard about something like it he contacted me straight away. Unfortunately, before we could arrange for it to be returned here safely, the magician you identified in the picture with Hitler found Ray instead. Ray did the right thing, for once, and put it in the safest place he could think of at the time, with the safest person he could rely on and trust.'

Judas smiled at Ray. 'Thanks for nothing, Ray.'

Ray smiled back. 'You shouldn't have saved me the first time around, Judas, you know what us angels are like with our life debts.'

Azruela continued. 'This book contains many things, Judas. There are spells and incantations inside that can summon fell beasts and evil spirits. There are clues and directions to the hiding places of other weapons, too. If someone were able to decipher its contents they would be able to unleash an arsenal of weapons that could raze a city and reduce a country to a wasteland in a heartbeat.

'Also inside is a very important list of all of the second world war Black Magicians in hiding today. Most of them are leading uneventful lives, staying under the radar and trying to forget their nefarious pasts. But power can do savage things to the minds of men and women. If they were all called to action again by the book none would have the power to resist it. What you would have is an army of black magicians with access to what Hitler wanted most of all – the 'Miracle Weapons.' These weapons would have ensured his final victory, have no doubt about that. The old Allies and their new partners would be destroyed first, and then the rest of the world would follow suit. That is why we must get the book back here as soon as possible!'

Azruela took a drink of water from a tray on the table. Judas was about to start asking some questions when the angel wiped his mouth and carried on speaking.

'Ray was willing to acquire the book and return it to me, but he has not the strength or ferocity of one of the Archangels. He is helpful and sincere, but he is not a warrior, or so he tells me often. Can I count on you to bring it to me here, Judas?'

Judas got up and stretched his legs with a walk around the table.

'If things are that bad then I'd better get back to London, right now. The book is as safe as possible while it's inside the Museum. I do have a ghost looking after it right now, too. He's new to the job but he learns fast, and I trust him. What's the best way to get it back up here?'

Ray jumped up from the table. His wings were flapping excitedly like a puppy's tail, but all it took to stop them was one withering look from Azruela.

'You will stay here with me, Ray and prepare the library for the book's return. As for you, Judas, we can fly you down to London. It will be cold, but quick, and the angels that will take you there are very fast on the wing. They have never failed in a mission before. They will leave you to get the book, and then fly you back here.'

Judas buttoned his coat up to the neck and held his arms out theatrically.

'Quick and cold it is!'

Half an hour later Judas wished that he'd been sitting in his First-Class carriage on the Ley Line Express, heading back to London in comfort. As it was, he was thousands of feet up in the air, being carried by three very strong and silent angels in a strange leather sack attached to a flying harness through a thunderstorm, with a sprinkle of added lightning on top.

The sack was not uncomfortable, but it did have a flap at the front that allowed the cold and the wind to creep in through, so by the time they began their descent to Scotland Yard, his teeth were chattering, and his hair was full of ice particles. The angels landed on the roof and helped him to stand up, and one of them gave him a leather bottle and encouraged him to drink from it. He was revived after the first mouthful, and tried to keep the bottle but the angel just raised an eyebrow and gave him a wink instead. The largest of the three came forward and gave him his instructions for the return leg of the journey north.

'We will be nearby, Judas. Just come back to the roof and we will see you. Then we'll fly you back to Azruela as quickly as possible.'

Judas wanted to thank them, but they leapt into the air and disappeared into a dark grey cloud overhead before he had the last of the ice out of his hair.

He used his swipe card to open the roof door and walked down the steps that took him to the private stairwell that led down to the 7th floor.

Moments later he was back in the office and starting to feel like he had toes again. He looked at the clock on the wall.

It had taken him a couple of hours to get to Newcastle on the train and he'd travelled the same distance back in under thirty minutes. He was exhausted and felt like he'd done the flying himself. The cold and that leather sack had really taken it out of him.

Judas flicked the switch on the kettle and placed a round tea bag into his mug. He was waiting for the steam to rise from the spout of the kettle when he started to get that uneasy feeling you get when everything is going far too smoothly for its own good. His scar was on constant throb, too, and he felt the need to rub his coin.

31 THE GH☺ST CHILDREN ☺F JERSEY

Williams had not made an appearance yet, and was nowhere to be seen. He was a ghost now, of course, and not being seen went with the territory, but he was different because he was a visible ghost, and Judas could tell that he loved the whole materialising and walking through walls thing. It obviously gave him a little jolt of pleasure to see Judas jump every time he walked into the room. Judas poured the hot water carefully into his mug and watched as the milky water started to turn a lighter shade of brown. He was concentrating on these little clouds of colour in his mug when he felt it. There was a faint pressure in the air all around him, and it was making him sleepy and lethargic. He got angry very quickly and threw his teaspoon down onto the floor. The tinkle it made sounded like it was coming from next door or down the hall; the sound was muted and soft, as if the spoon were made of wood or rubber and not stainless steel at all. Somebody had been in here, and the Museum had gone into self-imposed lock-down. He ran to the window and opened it as wide as it could go without smashing against the wall, welcoming the cold night air in. London's air was not of the highest quality at the best of times, but right now it was as sweet as a spring meadow. The feeling of warmth and pressure receded and then disappeared. He had to get that book and himself back into that overgrown angel satchel and get rid of the thing before anyone got hurt.

The phone on the table buzzed and blinked at him with its angry red eye. Judas picked it up and held it to his ear so quickly that he banged the receiver on his temple. It was Sgt Henshaw from the front desk downstairs, and he had some news that he thought might be of interest to the 7th floor.

A couple of little chaps from some department he'd never heard of had been making a nuisance of themselves and requesting that they be allowed to come up to the 7th floor to wait in the office for DI Iscariot. They'd showed him their warrant cards and everything, but he'd never seen them before, and couldn't place the department they said they were from, so he'd told them to wait there instead. That didn't go down well with the little chap. He was the one that did all the talking and had got a bit vocal apparently; coming it the high hand, sounded a bit foreign too. He was wearing a really nice suit, but his manners needed dressing up a bit.

Judas thanked the desk sergeant and then put the phone down. His scar was itching like mad, and he automatically reached for his silver coin and began to rub at it. Everything in the office seemed to be in the right place. None of the drawers had been forced, and all of the cabinets remained firmly locked.

He did the rounds, checking and waggling the handles of the doors and the windows, but nothing was out of place there, either. Still that odd, unnatural feeling was there, though.

Judas called down to the front desk again and spoke to Sgt Henshaw.

'What time did the odd couple come in, and what time did they leave?'

He could hear Sgt Henshaw lick a stubby finger and then start flicking at the corner of the pages of the report in his incident report book. After a few seconds he found the entry that he was looking for, cleared his throat and gave Judas the bad news down the phone.

'Right, they turned up today at 14.00hrs and then again at 16.00hrs, and then that was it. Nothing. Didn't see or hear a thing from them again. That answer any questions for you, Sir?'

'Plenty thank you, Sgt Henshaw,' said Judas. He put the phone down and loosened his tie. It was so quiet that he could hear himself think for a change. He'd left this morning; they'd been watching him and saw him leave the office. Then, sometime after he'd got on the train, they'd tried to get into the Museum, because they knew that the book was still here.

How did they know that? The answer was simple, of course. He wasn't carrying anything large enough with him, and they almost certainly had some sort of charm or spell or something that sang out whenever the book was nearby. So, once the coast was clear, they came inside and pretended to be police officers, complete with made-up warrant cards no doubt. They tried to get access to the Black Museum but Sgt Henshaw dropped the portcullis on them as per standing orders, and they had to find another way in. Thank heaven for Sgt Henshaw and standing orders.

Judas looked up at the clock on the wall. Both hands had become one and were pointing upwards. It was late. He'd better get the book fast and find out where Williams was as well. He ran down the corridor, swiped the black security card through the vertical lips of the lock and the green light leapt to attention. He heard the door click open and stepped inside. The Museum looked the same – but felt different. All of the cabinets were quiet; not a mumble or a whisper could be heard. There was none of the usual banter and narky comments from any of them. On any other day that would have been a relief, but today, after the journey to Newcastle, the meeting with Ray and the Angels of the North, and what he'd learned about Stranghold and the book, little things like this spelled big trouble.

He could feel it again. People who had their homes burgled got over the loss of their possessions pretty quickly, but it was the thought that someone had been in their home, walking its corridors and maybe even using their toilets, that gave them nightmares. He walked into the Key Room. He flicked the light switch but nothing happened. The only light came from a small lamp at the back of the room that was somehow still getting some current from somewhere. His eyes grew accustomed to the light quickly, and he looked around to make sure that there weren't any uninvited guests in the room with him. All of the keys were there on their respective tables, arranged in neat rows as usual; nothing odd there. He walked past them towards the glass cabinets at the back of the room. He was halfway there when his scar gave a really nasty tug, making his stomach muscles spasm.

Judas knew what he was about to see. He bent down to open the safe but there was no need. The safe had been opened and the book, and everything else inside, was gone. Now Judas started to sweat, and he paced the room, trying to think, and not panic. Either Williams was inside the Museum, trying to hide the book somewhere else, or someone had got inside, taken the book, and perhaps taken care of Williams, too. Judas walked over to the table and placed both hands palms downwards onto it.

'Williams! Where are you? If you are inside the Museum you should be able to hear me. I need you back here as soon as you can. It's really important, so now would be a good time.'

Judas waited for a few minutes, but there was no reply and the good ghost that was Williams didn't appear. Everything was crashing down around his ears. If Malzo had been here the Museum would have been safe. He cursed himself for messing things up, and for not seeing what was right in front of his eyes all along. He shouted for Williams again and again, but there was still no reply. It was no good. Williams was either hiding deep inside the Museum and afraid to come out, or he was gone. And if he was gone, then so was the book. Judas kicked a waste-paper basket across the room in anger at his stupidity, hurting his toe in the process, which was even more stupid, and slightly ridiculous, too. He put it back the right way up, and replaced the used paper cups inside it, then stepped out of the Museum and locked the door.

He ran back to the office and sat down at his desk, trying to stop feeling guilty about everything, and to stop being angry with himself. He needed to think straight for a change; avoid the red herrings and ignore the misdirection. Williams was smart, thought Judas. He would have been able to think of something quickly if he felt under threat. The problem was that if Stranghold had been able to get inside, which he obviously had been able to do, what warning would Williams have had? Practically none. But some chance was better than none, wasn't it? Judas got up and went over to Williams' desk, remembering that he'd cleared it out the day after Williams had died. He'd put the old copies of the Racing Post and the dog-eared football match programmes in a cardboard box and taken it over to his family. So, there was nothing on the desk. It looked unloved and unused, now. 'They' would have gone through it in no time, ripping all of the drawers out and finding nothing.

He looked around the room again. The only thing left in the room that had belonged to Williams was his raincoat, which was still hanging from the hook behind the door. It looked odd though; it was hanging awkwardly. There was something heavy in one of the pockets. Judas snatched it from the peg and reached inside the nearest pocket. Down at the bottom there was something smooth and round, about the size of a cricket ball. Judas took it out, and wanted to cry for joy. It was a green, shiny, Granny Smith apple! It would have made absolutely no sense to anyone else. It was a piece of fruit in the pocket of a raincoat, nothing more and nothing less. Williams had been even smarter than Judas gave him credit for, and it made him smile like a champion idiot. Judas ran back down the corridor holding the apple like it was made of diamond and went inside. There on the second table, right where it should be, was Dick Turpin's mask. And what did Black Bess love most of all? A nice juicy apple, that was what! Judas picked up the mask, and seconds later he was back in familiar territory. Dick was still hanging from his gibbet and talking to the crows, while his trusty steed was nibbling at the grass at the foot of the steps. On the ground Judas could see an apple core or two and his heart leapt at the sight of them.

'Hello Dick, how's it hanging?'

'Almost funny, Judas, almost worth a chuckle or two. I take it that you have come for the notes in my jacket pocket, and the others in my saddlebags over there on Bess.

'I like that new dead partner of yours, Judas. He gave Bess a whole bushel of apples and he sat here with me for a few hours talking about horses and racing them.'

'He's a good man, Dick, and I think I'm going to owe him and you a very big favour in return for what you've done. You may just have saved the world for me.'

Judas carefully removed the notes from Dick's pocket. They were rolled up with an elastic band. He retrieved the other notes from Dick's horse, the mighty Black Bess, and said goodbye, promising to come back when it was all over and shoot the breeze with the brave highwayman. Time was not on his side, so he raced back to his office as quickly as he could and started to read them. Hoping that they would tell him where the book was hidden and where he could find Williams.

The first page was just a series of squiggly lines with the odd recognisable letter or character thrown in here and there. On the second he found more of the same. It was only when he got to page 25 that he found what he was looking for. Written in small, neat lines between John's ramblings were messages for his eyes only, written in Williams' shorthand. He'd written it quickly, but it was all there. He read it three times, just to be sure.

'After you left the Yard to go up north, the little man in the expensive attire broke into the Museum somehow. I was on duty, of course, but even I didn't hear him until it was too late. He opened the safe and he got the book! He kept talking about Jersey – the island, not the piece of clothing – and a miracle weapon. He got really excited, and I heard him say something about London in dust. I don't know what I'm capable of in this new form so I didn't materialise or try to stop him, sorry. I've hitched a ride and stowed away inside the book to go with them. It seems that I can do that, and some other things too. I'm sticking with the book, Judas, and it's not leaving my sight! Thought it best. Come and get me, and get the book back, or this isn't going to end well for anyone!'

That was all that he had been able to write before he'd hidden himself away. Judas rolled the notes back up, securing them with the elastic band again before putting them in his pocket. Williams was a bloody fool, and he was also the bravest partner he had ever served with, so Judas was going to get him back, whatever the cost; hopefully with the book, too. It was either that, or there'd be a new sort of Blitz raining down on London; one that would level the city and kill everyone in it. First London, then New York, Paris and anywhere else they felt like destroying. The enemy had the book, and they were heading off to picturesque Jersey to unearth some miracle super weapons, resurrect an army of World War 2 black magic scientists, and finish off what they started.

Judas put his coat on and went back to the Black Museum of Scotland Yard one more time. When he was inside, he spoke to the emptiness.

'I don't know if you can hear me, but all of the keys in the Key Room are going somewhere safe. So as of this moment, all of you are in lock-down. No visits, and no days out. I'll see you when I get back.'

Judas took the stairs three at a time and stepped out onto the roof of Scotland Yard. The three angels were waiting for him already. He was off to Jersey to find some black books and save the world, with a quick pit-stop in Newcastle along the way.

Other novels by this author:

The Children of the Lightning

The Curious Case of Cat Tabby

Oliver Twisted

The Blind Beak of Bow Street

The Death of the Black Museum

If you've enjoyed this book, please do consider leaving a brief review of it on the Amazon website. Even a few positive words make a huge difference to independent authors like me, so I'd be both delighted and grateful if you were to share your appreciation.

Many thanks, Martin

Printed in Great Britain
by Amazon

26530556R00189